THE PROSPERO CHRONICLES

II

SHARDS

First Paperback Edition: June 2015

For information on subsidiary rights, please contact the publisher at rights@jollyfishpress.com.

For information, write us at Jolly Fish Press, PO Box 1773, Provo, UT 84603-1773, or info@jollyfishpress.com

Printed in the United States of America

THIS TITLE IS ALSO AVAILABLE AS AN EBOOK.

Library of Congress Cataloging-in-Publication Data

Titchenell, F. J. R., 1989– author.
 Shards / F.J.R. Titchenell, Matt Carter.
      pages cm. — (The Prospero chronicles ; II)
 Summary: A precarious treaty exists between the remaining humans like Ben Pastor and Mina Todd, and the shape shifting aliens they call the Splinters, but a new faction seems intent on breaking that treaty by killing off humans who were once Splinter-hunters—and somehow the epicenter of activity in Prospero is the high school that Ben and Mina attend.
 ISBN 978-1-63163-018-7 (pbk. : alk. paper)
 1. Extraterrestrial beings—Juvenile fiction. 2. Shapeshifting—Juvenile fiction. 3. High schools—Juvenile fiction. 4. Friendship—Juvenile fiction. [1. Extraterrestrial beings—Fiction. 2. Shapeshifting—Fiction. 3. High schools—Fiction. 4. Schools—Fiction. 5. Friendship—Fiction. 6. Science fiction. 7. Horror stories.] I. Carter, Matt, 1985– author. II. Title.
 PZ7.T522Sh 2015
 813.6—dc23
 [Fic]

2015004063

10 9 8 7 6 5 4 3 2 1

To Fox & Dana,
Thank you for making us want to believe.

Praises for *Splinters, The Prospero Chronicles I*

"One welcome difference to the archetypal 'final girl' formula of flaxen hair and virginal naïveté is that Mina is tough, possibly insane, definitely brilliant, and has already been terrorized and tormented by the body-snatching Splinters long before the story begins. A snapping, crackling, popping homage to classic horror that alludes to no optimistic resolution—all the more reason for a series."
—*Kirkus Reviews*

"A promising series opener, this will satisfy those readers who like their scary stories to be as clever as they are chilling."
—*Bulletin of the Center for Children's Books*

"There is a lot to like in this ambitious debut. Mina is captivating, and it is fun to watch her change and grow as a character. The book has a massive scope, which leads to some intriguing implications for future installments."
—*Washington Independent Review of Books*

Also by F.J.R. Titchenell and Matt Carter:

Splinters, The Prospero Chronicles I

THE PROSPERO CHRONICLES II

SHARDS

F.J.R. TITCHENELL & MATT CARTER

JOLLY
FISH
PRESS
Provo, Utah

1.

PSYCHOLOGICAL WARFARE

Mina

Marian Kelly died in a one-car accident near her home in Turtle Lake, Montana, on August twentieth, at the age of forty-two.

Marian is predeceased by her parents, Rand and Millicent "Millie" Kelly, and her brother, Christopher.

Marian was born in Prospero, California, and studied Psychology at the University of California, San Francisco. She held black belts in multiple martial arts and was an accomplished member of the Turtle Lake Hunting Club.

I skipped the details of Marian's perfunctory funeral service, put the newspaper clipping back in the plain, unstamped envelope it had arrived in, and filed it out of sight; not that this did anything to clear the smudged print from my vision. Alone, it was unsettling. In a stack of six other recent obituaries of other Splinter hunters, in six other anonymous envelopes with my name stamped on the front, it sent a very clear message.

I'm no stranger to death threats. And at the time of Marian's death, it had been less than a month since the Splinter who poses as my father told me to my face that if Ben or I fought back again, if we even tried to run, the humans would be wiped out of my infested little town of Prospero completely.

I'd fact-checked each obituary as it came in.

Every one of the hunters had died under circumstances that looked very much like suicide. Most of the obituaries didn't say so, exactly, but after the few that did, omissions of the cause of death and euphemisms like "one-car accident" and "chemical overdose" were easy enough to decipher. Sometimes, when the deaths had been a little more bizarre or had occurred on slow news days, there were more details to be found when I looked up the rest of the news sources in the area.

These weren't suicidal people. They weren't quitters. Wondering how someone could possibly have made it appear as if Drake Tymon had slit his wrists and throat alone in an industrial freezer that was later found barricaded from the inside was filling my head quite effectively with distractingly disturbing scenarios.

But the thing bothering me most about the obituaries was the fact that all seven of their subjects were currently loitering around my bedroom.

Sometimes, if I stared directly at them for long enough, they seemed to remember that they were supposed to be dead and vanish accordingly, temporarily. Otherwise I could see them, silently and blankly watching me work, as clearly as I could see my bookshelves, my bed, and the stark beige walls and end tables that, until recently, had held my very large and very useless anti-Splinter amulet collection.

Nightmares are no more new to me than death threats. That's not what these were. A hunter would die and join the rest of the hallucinations in my room the day after the obituary arrived, and then another one would die and join him without fail. If things carried on this way, my room was going to become unmanageably crowded quite soon.

It wasn't even as if I were going to *miss* the hunters. A few of them, like Drake, I'd known pretty well years ago, but I'd stopped assuming they were still alive—never mind still human—long before they'd turned up dead. Others, like Marian, I only knew by reputation in the first place.

Not knowing them well only made it stranger that they were here, after everything I'd lived through and lost without having suffered from any sensory distortions before.

Ready? The text scrolled across my phone's screen after Ben's name.

Almost. I texted back.

I wasn't looking forward to conducting the upcoming meeting for my entire Network, a roomful of people who had nothing in common other than their knowledge of Splinters and their confidence in *my* judgment and clarity of perception. Ben had insisted, though. A lot had changed, and people needed to be brought up to speed.

Billy was gone, lost to the Splinters, if we had ever even had him. Whatever had been passing for my absentminded ally had been using us to breach the peace, such as it was, for no one knew how long.

Ben hadn't even met some of the others yet. Our discovery of portals to other parts of the world in the Splinter Warehouse had put an end to the Effectively Certain Non-Splinters list, or at least had reduced it to a uselessly small number of people. The only people in town I could really be effectively certain of anymore were myself and Haley, since we'd both recently been ripped directly out of replication pods. That wasn't enough to work with, so I'd had to downgrade my entire Network to Extremely Probable Non-Splinters and start training myself to live with that because the alternative was not getting anything done at all.

Ben was still stubbornly under the impression that Haley's presence on the list alone qualified her as a Network member. I disagreed.

Most important, we now knew more terms of the Splinter-Human treaty and exactly how precarious our position was. Two human-on-humanoid Splinter kills by the same human would mean all-out war, and Ben and I each had one strike already. And no matter how careful we were, Billy and any like-minded Splinters would find a way to incite that war sooner or later. We were counting on an unforeseen miracle to make the human side a significant power before then.

As someone who doesn't believe in miracles, this wasn't news I would enjoy delivering, even on my best day.

I finished up some new touches on the map over my desk—the new world map I'd posted under the map of Prospero to track probable Splinter activity at the other portals—and blinked hard, hoping the illusion of the hunters would fade out at the usual time. Their faces were already getting blurry around the edges, right on schedule.

That was something, at least. I was going to be able to function for another day. If my Network, the few humans still invested in finding or building that miracle, found out what was happening to me, it would probably be the end of what hope we had. They would give up on the one thing they all agreed on, my reliability, and maybe they'd be right to do it. I'd probably do the same in their position.

But even if I couldn't *see* a difference between the walls and furniture that constituted my room and the dead people that my brain had decided to superimpose in front of them, at least I still *knew* the difference. I still knew what was rational and what wasn't. Before the first hunter had appeared, the evidence of my senses had been the basis for almost everything I thought and did. It was going to be difficult to get used their new fallibility, just like the fallibility of the ECNS list. As long as the inner workings of my mind were still in order, it was worth at least *trying* to do my job.

At least, that's what I told myself for the thirty-seventh time when I recognized Ben's knock on the front door above.

2.

Ben

My life flashed before my eyes.

More than anything, I regretted how little there was to flash.

"Brakes, brakes, BRAKES!"

In Mina's defense, she did hit the brakes before she could knock over the stop sign, but not before she drove the front right wheel of my mom's SUV up onto the curb. The car jolted to a stop, and, not for the first time since Mina had asked me to show her how to drive, I was glad I was wearing a seatbelt.

After a second's consideration, she said, "Sorry."

"Don't worry about it. You're still learning," I said.

"Not very quickly," she grumbled.

She was having another one of her bad days. She was having them more frequently, days where I could tell she hadn't slept and she was more on edge than usual. It had to be what happened to her in the Warehouse, some kind of post-traumatic stress. I still remembered yanking her from that pod, watching the tendrils that had burrowed beneath her skin, into her mind, trying to make Mina *one of them*, dissolving away in trails of green slime.

Splinters. The word brought up feelings of disgust and hatred. *They* made her this way. *They* broke her. I couldn't fix her, not yet. That was bound to take a lot longer than the nearly-healed gash in her side and the burns on my legs. But at least I could try to make her feel better.

"Yeah, well nobody's perfect. My mom's been driving for more than twenty years and I'm still amazed they haven't taken her license away," I said. "You should've seen us driving up here. She tried to steer the U-Haul into a drive-through and ran down a guy dressed like a chili dog. Squashed him like a bug."

She goggled at me for a moment, then said, "You made that up."

"Replace 'ran down a guy' with 'barely clipped a guy with her side view mirror,' 'squashed him like a bug' with 'ran over part of the sign he was carrying' and 'chili dog' with 'chili cheese dog' and you've got it," I said.

Much as she tried not to, I caught a hint of a smile sneak through.

"Maybe if we want to make it to Kevin's on time and alive and without having to explain to your mother how you allowed an unlicensed driver to damage her SUV, you should drive," she said.

"Fair enough," I said. We got out and switched positions. Though the SUV made a terrible clunk when I reversed it off the curb, it still drove just fine. So neither my mom nor Mina would kill me. Not today.

Not bad.

That just left the rest of Prospero, California, to look out for.

Back when Mom and I were just visiting, that was a stress I thought I could live with. Now that we were effectively imprisoned here for the rest of our lives, surrounded by Splinters, I hoped I could handle it. I was pretty sure I could handle it. Whether or not I actually could was something I'd yet to figure out.

The Splinters' plan for us was working, so far. Shortly after our break-in at the Warehouse, they'd made a job offer to my mother. Nothing too flashy, a clerical position at the town hall, but she jumped at the opportunity as a way of getting out of her rut in San Diego. They even lined up a nice, affordable little house for us that *coincidentally* happened to be right across the street from the Todd family. I'm sure this was Mina's father's way of keeping an eye on me.

We made it to Kevin's place a few minutes after I took over. Compulsively, I looked to the backseat. The bags of binders I'd so meticulously put together were still there. In them was everything we knew about Splinters: all of Mina's notes and lists, the brief history of them we'd been able to put together, and a world map of other possible Splinter cities we had seen linked to the Warehouse. Spread out among the group, at least everyone would know everything.

Mina caught my hesitance. "There's no reason to be nervous. Everyone here already knows of the existence of Splinters. You don't have to win them over."

"I'm not worried about winning them over. I'm worried

about winning *you* over," I said as I began to get out of the car.

"You know I know about Splinters," she said, getting out and helping me gather up bags.

"You know that isn't what I meant," I said.

She said nothing. I took that as a yes.

The meeting was all my idea. Mina's Network was a loose collection of individuals who knew about Splinters and helped her undermine their efforts. Until this point, Mina had kept all of the members on a need-to-know basis, distributing only scant bits of information as she saw fit. When it became clear we were facing the possibility of an all-out war with the Splinters, I argued that it would be a good idea to get everyone as prepared as possible to put up a unified front.

Eventually, I was able to talk her into at least this one get-together so I could meet everyone.

Kevin had made it clear that he was providing his parents' backyard for the meeting strictly as a friend and not as a Network member. His claim of neutrality didn't set the best tone for our purposes, but it was the safest place we had.

We had just started up the walkway to his house when we heard it. A god-awful squeal of metal and gears mixed with what sounded like a machine-gun coughing. An ancient sedan that looked to be held together by rust and duct-tape rounded the corner, followed by a cloud of blue, black, and white that occasionally belched out of the tailpipe. Whoever was driving was doing a rather remarkable job, considering that the driver's compartment was murky with white smoke.

"Ah. They're here," Mina said. The car lurched to a stop within inches of my mom's SUV. Then it jolted forward, tapping the bumper hard enough to rock the vehicle back and forth. I winced as I jogged back to the cars.

A tall boy with shoulder-length black hair and an old army jacket stepped out of the driver's seat, looking first at the van, then at Mina. His red-rimmed eyes and easy smile reminded me uncomfortably of Billy.

"Hey, Mina, hey . . ." he said, snapping his fingers.

"Ben," I said.

"Yeah, Ben, cool. This your car?" the boy asked.

"No, my mom's," I said.

"Oh sh-, oh darn," he said, correcting himself as if I were a child. He looked at my mom's SUV appraisingly. "I think you're fine, really. Barely kissed ya. I know a guy who could buff it out if there's any real—"

"I'll be fine," I muttered. "I don't really think—"

"Wait, you're the Eagle Scout, right?" he asked, that easy smile disappearing astonishingly fast.

"I never made it that far," I corrected. This didn't improve his mood. He looked to Mina.

"How can you trust this guy? You do know that the Scouts in all their forms are the earliest levels of indoctrination into the New World Order's personal strike force? This guy could be—"

The passenger door opened, nearly falling off and letting out a wall of white smoke. A sickly sweet, high-pitched voice called from within. "Oh come on, Greg, that's no way to make friends now, is it?"

Out of the passenger side came what was easily the most patriotic Goth girl I had ever seen. She was fairly tall—though, that might have been her knee-high plat-form boots—wearing a black tank-top cut high enough to show her belly-button ring and a tight black micro-skirt that would have left little to the imagination if she were still sitting. Her skin was even paler than Mina's, probably helped along by a fair amount of white makeup, and her hair was platinum blonde, mostly, though her pigtails had been dyed bright blue and red, much like her lips. She smiled a broad, toothy smile when she saw Mina and me.

"Don'tcha worry 'bout Greg there, Ben," she said, striding over to me and hopping slightly to put a friendly peck on my cheek. "He gets grumpy and super paranoid when he's high. Hard to deal with, but still a big teddy bear, I swear!"

"I prefer the term 'aware,' Jules," Greg clarified as he reached through where there should have been a rear pas-senger window and pulled out a grocery bag of snacks.

Greg Nguyen and Julie Kaplan. Mina had warned me they were a bit eccentric. She almost smiled as she approached them, refraining from rolling her eyes as she too received a red and blue kiss on the cheek.

"Are Billy and Aldo already here?" Julie asked, pulling a stylized, almost antique umbrella from the passenger seat and opening it to shade herself from the sun.

I looked at Mina. "You didn't tell them?"

"Tell us what?" Greg asked.

"I thought that was what this meeting was for," Mina said.

"But this was something pretty important; you could've gotten it out of the way first," I said, irritated.

"Tell us what? Are Billy and Aldo okay?" Julie asked.

I looked to Mina, she looked to me. Neither of us wanted to say it right away.

"Aldo's fine," Mina said.

"Billy's more complicated," I clarified. They both looked confused. "We'll explain it when we get inside."

"I can't believe we're doing this here. This is enemy territory," Greg said as they followed us up the walkway to Kevin's house.

Mina tried to change the topic. "So did you have a good Fourth of July, Julie?"

"Why is this enemy territory?" I asked.

"Yeah!" Julie said brightly, twirling one of her pigtails. "But I'm really looking forward to Halloween. More my colors."

"Kevin's a part of the Prospero machine, his dad's got his fingers *everywhere*," Greg said.

"Black is a much better color," Mina said a bit louder.

"Kevin saved our lives," I said.

"It *is*, but we really gotta do some proper shopping for you one of these days," Julie said.

"And that absolves him how?" Greg asked when we reached the front door.

I wouldn't go so far as to call Kevin Brundle one of my favorite people, but he was a good guy, and Mina believed in him. Hearing Greg trash him put me on the defensive.

Thankfully, seeing this argument about to explode, Julie pressed the doorbell.

"Please be presentable, love?" she pleaded.

"I am presentable," Greg sulked.

"Not now you're not," she said.

He forced an almost cartoonishly wide smile. She nodded her approval.

I looked to Mina. She simply confirmed. "This is normal."

Haley opened the front door seconds later. Seeing her, healthy, mostly happy, and mostly smiling made any bad feelings I had go away. She had had some unsteady days after we brought her out of the Warehouse, rehabilitating her and telling her everything that had happened. She had an even harder time pretending that she remembered everything since her "return," but she was a good actress.

At least we were still friends.

"Hey guys," she said, giving Mina and me warm hugs. Mina resisted only slightly. Looking to the others, Haley kept smiling. "Is this everybody?"

"Yes," Mina said.

"Cool," Haley said. "Aldo's upstairs taking out all the bugs and cameras you guys planted."

"You bugged the Brundle house?" Greg asked with a raised eyebrow. "Nice."

Haley looked at our bags of food. "Please tell me somebody brought meat. Kevin's got the grill going and has about six different kinds of tofu browning as we speak."

"We've got you covered," I said, pointing to the bags Mina carried, showing off some packages of frozen burger patties.

"Thank God," she said. "Get those to Kevin before he decides to put up a fight?"

"Sure," Mina said, leading Greg and Julie to the backyard. I was about to follow when Haley gently grabbed me by the wrist.

"Can I talk to you for a sec?" she asked.

"Sure," I said.

She looked back and forth nervously, clearly wanting to talk but unable to put words to her thoughts. I asked, "Have you been doing all right?"

She tried to laugh it off. "Yeah, sure. Between my mom wondering if I'm bipolar and the others from the theater being pissed at me for dropping out of Alexei Smith's terrible play at the last second *and* not dropping out of the troupe completely just so I can spy on him, I'm just dandy."

"I'm sorry," I said. "You don't have to do that."

"I know I don't have to, but I want to. Mina says he's one of the key Splinters in town, and I want to make him pay for whatever part he had in what happened to me. It's just so hard when I have to make up for the months where my body wasn't mine. I have to constantly fight to remember what memories are mine and what were hers. I have to remember how to walk again. I'm just so angry all the time." she said.

"It's all right to be angry," I said.

"But I never used to be! I was happy. I *liked* being happy, and now I barely remember what it's like to be that way anymore. I don't know if I'd even be able to do this if it weren't for you and Mina," she said.

I made to put my arm around her shoulders. She easily dodged away, then looked up at me, ashamed.

"Oh God, I'm sorry! I'm so sorry!" she said. "It's not you, I swear."

"It's okay," I said, trying not to sound too hurt.

"No, it's not, I don't have any problem touching you . . . I mean, I don't have any problem with you touching me . . ." she paused, laughing angrily as she stomped on the floor. "This isn't coming out right. It's just, you used to do that to *her*, and when you do that, I remember how *she* used to feel when you did that. It made her more excited than anyone should be."

"Okay, note to self: do not put arm around Haley's shoulders," I joked.

She smiled back at me. "Thanks. I mean it's really sweet. Just give me some time to not be weird about it?"

"Of course," I said. "So is there some approved physical act of comfort I can do as a friend?"

"Hugs are okay," she said. In response to this, I wrapped her in a bear hug, lifting her off her feet and spinning her around. She laughed. I laughed. It felt good.

"Better?" I asked.

"A little, thanks," she said as she looked into my eyes fondly.

That moment right there, alone in the foyer of Kevin's house, felt pretty close to perfect.

It might have even ranked perfect had Aldo Kessler not chosen that moment to walk down the stairs next to us, shielding his eyes exaggeratedly with one hand.

"I saw nothing, continue doing whatever it is you were doing," Aldo said as he walked to the backyard, smiling a bit smugly.

Haley and I shared a nervous laugh. I said, "This is going to be interesting."

Though it came with a brief lecture on the horrible conditions of factory farms and the health benefits of vegetarianism, Kevin still gamely cooked the hot dogs and hamburgers we'd brought. It would have been a pretty nice barbeque had we not spent most of the time recounting the story of what had really happened over the summer. It was a long, tiring process, made more difficult by Mina's uncharacteristic reluctance to help tell the story.

I understood she still wasn't wild about full disclosure, but usually, once a decision was made, she was only too ready to take the lead whether she liked it or not.

Not today.

She would pipe in whenever I got something wrong, or if there was some important detail she thought I'd missed, or if I prompted her, but for the most part the story was mine to tell.

"Poor Billy," Julie said after I'd finished. "He was one of the good ones."

"One of the good Splinters," Aldo clarified. "He *was* trying to set us up all along."

"Maybe, but he was still our friend, I think," Julie said.

"If you're really going to split hairs, he was actually just trying to set up Ben and Mina here. The rest of us were pretty clear," Greg replied.

"If his plan had succeeded, Prospero would be Splinter City right now," I said. "He was setting us *all* up."

"According to her Splinter dad," Greg said, pointing at Mina. "Maybe Billy really was helping you all along. Maybe he really helped you defeat some Splinter plot we can't see yet."

"He *was* setting us up," Haley said. "*She* knew it. *She* was being led along, thinking that capturing Ben and Mina meant she was going to help lead in a new era of Splinter dominance over mankind."

"Like they don't have that already?" Greg said, flipping to the page of his binder with the world map of Splinter locations. "Thebes. Rome. Baghdad. Jerusalem. This is some serious Chariots of the Gods shit, man. Like the Eagle Scout said, they've been here from the start, molding us into their own little puppets, just waiting for their moment to take over."

"Doubtful, love," Julie said as she flipped to the same page in her binder. "Look at this distribution. If they wanted to take us over by now, they coulda done that already, easy. The fact that we're not all slaves or Splinters ourselves means they're either incapable of taking us over, or they just don't want to, and goin' by what Haley and Mina've said about bein' taken by their pods, I don't think it's 'cause they're incapable. They're probably just, like, tourists."

"Body-snatching tourists," Greg clarified.

They were odd, but they were observant. I was beginning to see why Mina kept Greg and Julie close.

"Really, though, can we trust this information? Can we trust *you?*" Greg asked, flipping through the pages.

"Hey," I protested.

"Don't feel special, Eagle Scout. I don't trust any free information; it doesn't stay free for long, and it's rarely true," Greg said. "I mean, look at it from our point of view. You guys were here over the summer, we weren't. You could've all been taken over and are just setting us up to be drawn in next to your web of drones."

"Then why aren't we all jumping you now?" Haley asked, irritated.

Greg shook his head, laughing. "Don't ask me to explain how a Splinter's mind works. You should be able to do that better than anyone."

Haley got out of her chair, her fists balled. If Aldo hadn't spoken up, I'm sure things would have gotten ugly fast.

"Throwing around accusations like this isn't going to get us anywhere. Now I'm as much a fan of feeding Greg's paranoia as anyone, but he does have a point. We know all this now. Are we just going to go about the old 'surveillance and sabotage' route as usual? Where do we go with it from here?" Aldo asked.

"High school," Mina said simply.

I looked to her, grateful. This was her show; she had to lead it. She still looked tired, unsteady, but she began to speak firmly. She was in her element.

"Unquestionably, Prospero High School is the most dangerous place in this entire town. Splinters want to lead long, full lives and, as such, take the youngest forms possible. We will be surrounded every moment of every day by potential enemies. But we do have an advantage now that we have never had before. We know there is dissension within the Splinters' ranks. It is possible we will be able to turn this conflict to our favor."

"Any ideas on how to do that yet?" Greg asked.

"Not yet. As soon as I've come up with any ideas, I will keep you . . . informed," Mina said, vaguely. This caught me off guard. We'd discussed a few plans so far on how to pin down the movements and members of the Splinter Council itself so we could get a closer look at their relationship with the dissidents. I didn't know why she was holding back.

"Can I say something?" Kevin asked. Normally one with an opinion on everything, I was surprised he'd been quiet throughout the entire meeting thus far.

"Please," I said.

He stood up and smiled, nervously clapping his hands together once.

"I've no love for the Splinters. In fact, it seems they've done everything possible over the years to destroy my family. They took my brother. They've twice had people think I was a murderer," he said, looking at Haley. "They've done terrible things to this town, to all of us in one way or another. We've got every reason to be angry with them. But let me ask you, is it really necessary that we fight them?"

He raised his hands almost immediately to try and quiet the six voices of argument, my own included, that came up in the wake of his question.

"Please, please, hear me out," he said.

"So says the son of a collaborator," Greg said. For the first time, Julie did not look like she wanted Greg to shut up.

"My father and I have many disagreements in life. The Splinter issue is key among them," Kevin explained. "What

I want you to consider is the scale of this problem. This isn't a Prospero issue. This isn't even just an American issue. This is something that encompasses the *entire planet*. This is not a fight that can be won by a half dozen kids with a few cameras and improvised flamethrowers. This cannot be won through violence. The only way this fight can truly be won is through raising awareness of the problem. Let people know what is going on, people on the outside. Fighting it here, like you're suggesting, is only going to end in sadness and death."

He looked at us, so earnest, so kind. "You're good people. You've got good lives ahead of you. Don't end them here, not like this."

Haley stood to speak against him. "We can't do that. If this were just another of your social justice causes, I would agree with you. But this is different. They're stealing our lives. They took me out of my bed, in the middle of the night. I was hooked into one of their pods for three months. They violated me on every level, and you just want me to back down? No way. That is not going to happen. If you want to be a coward, be my guest. But I am going to fight this, on my own if I have to."

"You won't have to," I said, hoping for Mina to back me up. She didn't, instead looking at Haley as if she were concerned for her. Kevin looked utterly defeated.

The meeting broke up pretty fast after that. I honestly didn't know if we had accomplished anything. Aldo and Haley were with us. Kevin was not, though he still wanted to be our friend. Greg and Julie were believers, but I could also see why she called them Network "casuals."

SHARDS

So, basically, we were right where we started.

Mina and I were the last to leave. We helped clean up, gathering up the two binders that had been left behind, by whom I couldn't tell.

Kevin walked us to my mom's SUV, looking sad, but still holding onto that faint optimistic smile of his.

As Mina loaded things into the back of the SUV, he pulled me off to the side and said, "Be careful, brother. Keep an eye out for them, and keep a level head; you might be the only one who can keep them safe."

"You could, too," I said. "If you were with us."

He shook his head. "I'm sorry, brother, I'm just not up to it."

I wouldn't call him a coward, it wasn't the right word. I did, however, feel sorry for him.

I got in the car with Mina and began to drive us home. I didn't even know where to begin with her.

"Did it go as well as you had hoped?" she asked.

I tried not to laugh. "No, it didn't. I was expecting some help from you," I said.

"You were doing a good job telling the story," she said.

I continued. "I was also expecting some honesty. Why didn't you tell them about the plans?"

"The plans aren't ready. I don't want to say anything unless I am certain it will work," she said.

"We told them we were going to be completely honest with them," I said.

"No, *you* told them that. I'm sorry Ben, I really am, but I don't think I can promise them that. Not yet, maybe not ever," she said.

"What about me?" I asked. "Do I get complete honesty yet?"

She looked at me for a long time with that cold, appraising look she always took on when considering something very grave.

Finally, she said, "I would trust you with the whole truth more than anyone I know."

That didn't answer my question, and she knew it. Still, I knew it was all I was going to get out of her, so I let it pass. A faint trace of a smile crossed her face. It was hard not to smile back when she did that.

"Come on, let's get you an energy drink," I said, transforming that trace of a smile into a full-blown grin. It was enough to let me hope that things were looking up.

3.

THINGS I'LL NEVER SAY

Mina

I'd come to dislike keeping secrets from Ben more than just about anything, short of the Splinters themselves. The secret that was most on my mind, though, other than how little mind I might have left . . . I was sure he'd understand why I couldn't tell him that one.

I hoped he would, anyway.

The Splinter reject before me, the one whose findings my earliest research was based on, was still alive.

At least, he was as of two years ago, when we cut off contact. When I cut off contact. Considering that he trained every one of the dead hunters currently haunting my bedroom, I was pretty sure that if anything had happened to him, I'd have a copy of his obituary, or at least a picture of his body; he'd kept off the grid long enough that even obituaries probably couldn't find him. I'd never been planning to use the signal he gave me in case I ever needed to talk to him again, but luckily, I couldn't forget it either.

I don't forget things.

So with school about to start and the hallucinations as

strong as ever, if not stronger, I had called in to the *San Francisco Chronicle* and taken out the personal ad he'd dictated to me.

Experienced carpenter offers sanding, finishing,
and polishing services to amateur craftsmen.

Sanding away the Splinters. Ha ha.

The other messages I wrote that morning were quite a bit longer and a lot more explicit. They felt more ungainly and exposed in my bag on the way over to Aldo's than incriminating photos or illegal weapons, weighed down with all the heavy, dangerous words that I never use.

Probably the only person who liked being in Aldo's house less than I did was Aldo, and I ran a quick calculation of exactly how many minutes were left before I could reasonably insist that I had to go home for dinner before knocking on the door.

"What?" Aldo's mother answered when she opened it, slightly more irritable than even her standard fashion. I could smell fresh peroxide in her chronically chemical-burned hair. "He's downstairs," she said, forcing a miniscule smile for me.

"Thanks, Mrs. Kessler." I matched the curve of her mouth and hurried past her toward the stairs. She returned to the kitchen table and the hushed conversation with Aldo's father that I'd apparently interrupted.

Both Aldo's parents were skinny and withered-looking, with the tough kind of muscles underneath that other people, people who don't have to account for the possibility of having to fight everyone they meet, probably wouldn't notice.

Aldo had never noticed anything Splintery about them, but whether human or Splinter, they both gave me the strong impression that one legal authority or another was the only thing preventing them from using those tough, skinny muscles to try to snap my neck.

Aldo's house and mine had the same floor plan, and we both called the one room at the bottom of the stairs our own. I don't know if the clutter along the way in Aldo's house of old junk mail and boxes of packaged food and Mrs. Kessler's collection of bath and massage gadgets was better or worse than the empty sterility of my own mother's decorating style. In both places, it was always a relief to get that basement door closed behind me.

"Aldo?" I asked the empty room.

"Just a sec," Aldo called from the adjoining half bathroom. After closer to six and a half seconds, he opened the door and turned a little to his left to strike what was probably supposed to be a jaunty pose. "What do you think?"

I visually scanned him for some new invention, maybe a wrist-mounted, electric dart gun or a near-invisible modified Bluetooth, but found nothing.

"Of what?"

His smile flickered and then stabilized again with an eye roll.

"Of the outfit."

"Oh." I looked again over the black undershirt, the almost unwrinkled blue button-down hanging untucked down to the front pockets of the newly-washed pair of dark, only slightly faded jeans. The hole-free tennis shoes were securely double-knotted.

"No hazards that I can see," I confirmed for him. He kept his unnatural sideways posture, waiting for something more. "You didn't get it dry cleaned, did you? Because you know those chemicals are flammable."

"How does it *look?*" Aldo snapped, dropping the pose.

I thought about the letters in my bag, the dead people in my room, the ad in the paper, the smirk on my mother's face at breakfast that morning when she'd shared the latest town gossip about Sheriff Diaz's fictional alcohol problem. We both knew the only reason he'd been found wandering the streets confused last week was because he'd just been let out of the pod to satisfy the latest draft of the treaty. I thought about how my Network couldn't scatter fast enough after our most recent joke of a meeting.

The tenuous structure of deals and impasses our world had been built on was shaking more violently than it ever had before, and Aldo wanted to know how he *looked*.

"You asked me over for a fashion show?"

"Hey, you only get one first day of high school." There was a hint of attempted irony in his inflection, but whether he was serious or not, I couldn't tell.

"Yeah," I agreed. "You only get one first concussion too. That doesn't make it worth dressing up for."

"Come on!" He punched me on the shoulder with an extra hard thump of frustration. "You're a girl! You're supposed to know these things!"

"I own seven distinct articles of clothing," I reminded him. "I buy them in bulk."

"Okay, fine, but you still have eyes, and you go to high school, so you're the best I've got. If a new guy walked in wearing this on the first day, would it make a good first impression on the average people you keep tabs on all day?"

You don't get to make a first impression, I wanted to tell him. *You don't get to be the new guy. You were the new guy when your parents gave up on homeschooling you when you were eight, dropped you into Prospero Elementary in the middle of the semester, and you announced that you were approximately three-and-a-half times smarter than anyone else in the room, called Patrick Keamy a plebian, and would have ended up in the nurse's office after recess if I hadn't felt like landing myself in the principal's office instead by jumping in and practicing the beginner's arm lock I'd just learned. That's your first impression. You stopped being the new guy when you became the freaky girl's freakier pet mini-freak, and I'm sorry I can't fix that and win you the shallow, pointless respect of a bunch of uninformed humans and Splinters pretending to be uninformed humans by picking out a shirt for you.*

But I didn't say any of that because, before I could start, Aldo grabbed a hairbrush and started re-parting his baby blonde hair on the left instead of the middle, and I saw his ear twitch, that tiny little nervous tic that no other kind of stress, not even being hemmed in by Creature Splinters in the forest at night, could ever draw out of him, the tic that meant that his mother's mood had nothing to do with my visit.

I scanned him automatically for the third time, this time for bruises. For better and worse, Aldo and I both have extremely quick-healing, damage-resistant bodies, whether thanks to blind luck or lifelong conditioning, I'm not sure.

Even more lifelong in his case than mine. At least most of my old scars and clicking, weather-sensitive joints had come courtesy of the Splinters, and not even from the one masquerading as my father.

I searched, but there was still nothing to be seen but that brittle, determined attempt at a cool, carefree smile of the kind that goes with shallow, pointless wardrobe choices.

"You look fine, Aldo."

The smile strengthened.

"Are you sure?" he asked. "Because I've got this one with pinstripes that's supposed to make me look taller. Hang on, I'll get it. You tell me which one works better."

"If I do, can I ask you a favor?"

There must have been something off in my casual tone that more naturally perceptive ears could catch because Aldo reappeared immediately, shirt draped over his arm as if he'd already forgotten it was there, and didn't answer with a joke.

"Name it."

Too late to change my mind, I pulled out the four plain, unstamped envelopes

"It's nothing much," I said. "I'll probably just need you to stash these away somewhere and forget about them. But if you could, just make sure they get to the right people if . . ." *if I get murdered or go completely insane* ". . . if anything happens."

Aldo took the envelopes warily and tried to smile again. "Uh, Mina, is there something you want to tell me?"

"I told you guys already," I said. "We're a lot closer to all-out war than usual. I can't say exactly what's going to happen."

"I can tell you what's going to happen," he said, turning the envelopes over one at a time to read the names on the fronts.

Ben. Mom. Kevin.

"We're going to put up the biggest fight humanity's ever given. Unless the laws of nature suddenly stop applying and you decide to bitch out on us, in which case we're completely screwed."

I tried to smile back, even though this was the last thing in the world I wanted to hear.

"The laws of nature are applying just fine," I assured him.

He turned over the last envelope.

Aldo.

He raised one pale eyebrow at me.

"Just in case," I repeated. "And they're sealed, by the way. As long as I'm able to ask to see that they're still sealed, you'd better still be able to show me."

"Mina!"

"I know my handwriting, and I know what it looks like traced over. And steam's not going to loosen it any. I used real glue."

"Mina, seriously, don't even joke about this."

"I'm not joking," I said, and it took no effort to sound absolutely humorless.

"Uh, okay, rephrasing: Please tell me you *are* joking about this."

His accompanying laugh wobbled even harder than was usual for his half-broken voice, so I eased off the warnings.

"Hey, we're still human so far, aren't we?"

I thought I'd hit pretty close to my target of a reassuring tone, but Aldo apparently disagreed. The tic at the front of his ear was as rapid as ever—if anything, I'd made it worse—and he had a tight look at the inner corners of his eyes that sometimes came with it, the one that, as far as my stunted intuition could tell, looked something like, "Please don't hurt me; it's not my fault." What "it" was, I still didn't have the slightest idea.

I've never known exactly what to say to that look, but I was pretty sure it wasn't "I need you to run the Network if I can't, because they don't trust Ben enough, and no one else has quite the necessary dedication." And it couldn't be anything as transparently false as "everything's going to be all right."

So on a sudden, mad impulse, I just spread my arms.

Aldo stared at me skeptically, expecting some trick or surprise test. I couldn't blame him. I usually avoid non-essential physical contact, even with other humans. I find that too much of it makes it harder to accept, and therefore harder to prepare for, all possible future scenarios involving the other person. I suspect it makes it harder for them to think that way about me too, especially in Aldo's case.

The different kind of risk-taking rush that came from writing those letters and carrying them in public must have left me a little reckless.

Or maybe it was another side effect of my malfunctioning brain.

When he still didn't move to respond, I grabbed him by the collar of the formerly unwrinkled blue shirt and crushed him hard against me.

After another moment of confusion, Aldo locked his arms securely around my middle, the way he used to in elementary school whenever someone bigger than he was looked a little too hard at us, dropping the envelopes and the second shirt around our feet.

He didn't cry. We didn't say anything, certainly none of the dangerously loaded things securely sealed in those envelopes, so we just stood there, I don't know for how long. My usually fine-tuned internal clock chose that moment to black out from some mental power surge and reset to 88:88, refusing to count for me.

I should have been uncomfortably aware of the meager height Aldo had gained in the past six years, how his head now rested just above my breasts, near-nonexistent though they were, how our hips aligned at almost the same level. I should have been worried about the hours this one incident might cause him to waste, pondering useless, impossible scenarios, or about the way he'd very obviously doused himself, in spite of all his good sense, with some kind of sharply sweet-scented aerosol product that I'd probably bought him to use as an accelerant.

Instead, I just counted the slowing twitches of his ear nudging through my black, long-sleeved Costco t-shirt and marveled at Aldo—this one fragile little human, this one tiny ray of human life, human thought, human intelligence that I'd somehow managed to preserve other than myself almost from the very beginning. One tiny, but all-important, perpetually tenuous victory; probably the closest I'd ever come to what it must feel like to hold a baby.

So much for my designs on passing the provisional backup torch.

The terrible awkwardness that I'd had no right to expect to avoid finally settled in, and Aldo tried first to disperse it.

"Not that this isn't nice and all," he rasped into my shirt, exaggerating the pressure I was still applying to his ribcage, "but now you're really starting to scare me. I mean, if it wouldn't be the worst, sickest joke ever made by anyone, I'd ask you who you are and what you've done with Mina Todd."

I let go then and pushed him backward, hard enough to make him trip into the half-open bathroom door and slide, snickering, down the frame.

I collapsed to my knees next to him, choking out paralyzing waves of jagged, uncomfortable laughter at the worst, sickest joke ever not-quite-made by anyone. Our overwrought diaphragms made any innocent traces of reflexive eye-watering entirely understandable.

"Just keep them safe," I repeated with the first bit of steadiness I could drag back into my voice, gathering the envelopes from where they'd scattered on the carpet.

"Of course," Aldo gasped back, taking them and sliding them into one of the many compartments he'd carved out behind his room's baseboard. I picked up the pinstriped shirt and tossed it to him.

"Go on," I said. "I guess I officially owe you some terrible advice."

4.

HOME OF THE POETS

Ben

I've had a lot of first days of school in a lot of different towns, and I was nervous on every one of them. After a while I thought I'd get used to them. I never did. Every time there were the same questions. *Would I make a good impression? Would I make friends? Would this finally be the school that sticks?*

Of course, this time there was also the fact that my school was likely swarming with Splinters to consider.

Mom drove me that first morning. She'd told me she wouldn't always be able to, not with the schedule she had to keep at Town Hall, but she wanted to at least drop me off on my first day. It was one of our few traditions, and it had always been awkward for me, knowing that we would be having another first day at a new school within the next year or two.

Given my imprisonment in Prospero, I at least knew I didn't have to fear leaving anytime soon.

I pulled the folded-up schedule from my back pocket and studied it.

Period 1: AP American History—Blair, 15
Period 2: Wood/Metal Shop—Finn, Vocational Ed. Room
Period 3: Physical Education—Perkins/King, Gym
Period 4: Calculus—Velasquez, 24
Period 5: Biology—Copper, 31
Period 6: Spanish III—Montoya, 03
Period 7: American Lit.—Hansen, 09

Mom was excited that I tested into the AP History program up here, and it took everything I had to hold back my pride. The bigger surprise came when I had first seen who one of my P.E. teachers would be. I knew Haley's mom, my Aunt (but not quite aunt) Christine, did some coaching at the school, but I didn't know she taught P.E. That could be awkward.

Welcome to small town life, Ben.

"Are you excited?" my mom asked.

"Yeah. I think so," I said.

"At least, this time, you'll have some friends going in," she said hopefully.

I remembered how quickly things fell apart after the meeting. "Yeah, that'll be nice."

"That reminds me, I caught Mina's dad yesterday. He said he'd still love to have us over for dinner some night, kind of a welcome to the neighborhood sort of thing. What do you think?"

It took effort not to show anger. Sam Todd, Mina's dad, put up a pretty good human front. Charming, funny, knowledgeable on pretty much every odd topic. He even helped us unpack the truck when we moved in; it was easy to see why my mom liked him. But beneath the surface was a cold, calculating member of the Splinters' inner core. He granted me the kindness (his word, not mine) of letting me leave town so I could help Mom move, but made it very clear that once I got back, I could never leave again.

No, Mom, that would be a terrible idea because if he's inviting us over, he's probably trying to find out more information about us, and since you don't know about the Splinter problem, you're liable to say something offhand that he'll later find a way to use against us.

That's what I wanted to say. What I actually said was, "Could be fun. I just don't know how easy it'll be to get the time together. Mr. Todd runs the hobby shop almost all by himself, and Mrs. Todd's a lawyer and a member of the town council. They pretty much leave Mina alone all the time."

"Oh, I see," she said. "Well, if we can work out the time, that'd be great. Until then, feel free to invite Mina over anytime!"

I smiled. "No problem."

We got to school early, before there were too many cars or students around. She wished me a good first day and drove off, leaving me to get a good look at my new school.

Prospero High School combined the worst architectural trends of the 1950s with what had to be every pastel color the 1980s had to offer. Most of its classrooms were ringed around the outer edges of the school, surrounding a couple of grass-filled inner quads, each with a decorative fountain in the center (only one of which worked). Outside this perimeter to the north end of school was a soccer field, while off to the west side were the gym, football field, and swimming pool. The center of the school was an odd mishmash of zigzagging administrative buildings, the cafeteria, the library, and a massive auditorium. Sticking out of the north edge of the auditorium was a fifty-foot high clock tower. It was, for all intents and purposes, a very ugly school, but for now it was mine.

The sign out front read:

PROSPERO HIGH SCHOOL
HOME OF THE POETS

Under it, instead of a man in a ruff and feathered hat or some other vaguely recognizable visual representation of a poet, there was an emblem featuring half a theatrical tragedy mask, spewing a jet of flame from its mouth to fill the space where its other half should have been.

Something told me that Alexei Smith, the very Splintery drama teacher, had something to do with its design.

I walked across the east quad, trying to follow the poorly-printed map on the opposite side of my schedule to find my locker. Having a locker was kind of a novelty; most schools I attended had phased them out in favor of more metal detectors.

Finding the lockers, on the other hand, was another matter entirely. I was supposed to have locker forty-two, which, according to the map, was supposed to be located along the south end of the science building. However, where there should have been a row of lockers, there was instead a drinking fountain and a bulletin board with a message pinned to it apologizing for the lockers having been moved. If only they'd said *where* they'd been moved to.

"You look lost," a voice said from behind me.

I turned to see it belonged to a pretty girl with long black hair tied back in a ponytail. She wore a tight, white and blue cheerleader's sweater that proudly proclaimed POETTES across the chest. Haley had one just like it.

They both made it look good.

"Yeah, I'm looking for my locker and, well, it's not here," I said with a smile.

She sidled in close and looked at my locker assignment and map. She laughed, rolling her eyes. "Yeah, this school's been under construction off and on for the last five years. They moved these lockers two years ago. I could show you where it should be, if you'd like."

She flashed a pretty, toothy smile that could have come out of a commercial.

"Sure," I said as she led me across the quad.

"I'm Madison, by the way. Madison Holland," she said, holding out a hand.

I shook it. "Ben Pastor."

"I know," she said. "Everybody does."

So it was going to be one of those kinds of schools. I was hoping I'd be past this by now.

"I saw you at Haley's almost-funeral. Let me say, you made quite the impression on most of us girls in the audience," she said.

"Quite the impression?" I asked.

She nodded. "Oh yeah. You should've heard the disappointment when we found out Haley had snatched you up."

"Haley didn't snatch me up. We're just friends," I corrected.

She raised an eyebrow. "Really? Good to know."

It was hard to tell if she was joking or serious. Her smile transformed into a friendly laugh. I joined her.

"I'm not going to blend in very easily, am I?" I asked.

"Doubtful," she said. "You've got the new kid in a small town thing, the handsome mysterious stranger thing, *and* the small-town hero thing working against you. Just be thankful you didn't save someone during the school year; they'd have probably thrown a parade in your honor."

I laughed. She didn't.

"No, I'm serious," she said.

"Oh," I said.

"You have no idea how weird this town is," she said.

I smiled. "I think I'm getting an idea."

Madison finally led me to my locker on the north side of the administration building. More people had shown up, kids looking for lockers, teachers tiredly walking to their classrooms with coffee mugs in hand.

Madison looked over her shoulder as a couple more Poettes wandered in, waving to her. "Listen, I gotta see some people before class starts, but if you need help finding your way again, I'll be around."

I waved as she left to join her friends. They all looked back at me simultaneously and giggled in that way only a group of teenage girls can.

I was getting the impression that Splinters weren't the only thing I'd have to worry about this year.

Thankfully my first few classes were busy enough to make me forget about being Prospero High's new shining toy. My first period AP History class was small. Julie was there, too, dressed more within the school dress code, but still looking like she was ready to attend a clown's funeral. It turned out she was in pretty much every AP or honors class our school had to offer. I gratefully took up her offer to study with me.

My second period class, Wood/Metal Shop, was held in the tiny, cramped Vocational Education room. It smelled of fresh cut wood, and was full of every kind of tool imaginable. Mr. Finn, the teacher, was a stocky, middle-aged man with salt-and-pepper hair and a chin so square it looked like it belonged in a cartoon. Though his hands and wrists were heavily scarred from the craft and he walked with a cane, he proudly showed off the wall of fame behind his desk of various projects he and his past students had put together, including a few abstract sculptures, a beautiful, polished surfboard, and an impressive array of replica medieval weaponry.

"If you can build a birdhouse, you can build anything. It also doesn't hurt if you keep an eye on your fingers at all times. Our school nurse is only a part-timer," he said before going into the fundamentals of safe tool usage. I could tell his would be a fun class.

For third period, I hiked on over to the gym and changed into the gray T-shirt and blue shorts they'd provided for P.E.

Mina and Haley sat in the back row of the retractable bleachers that most of the class milled around on. Haley was trying to talk to Mina, and as usual, Mina did not appear incredibly interested in talking to her. She looked so out of place, so tiny in her large glasses and baggy gym uniform. I ducked between two boys tossing a blue baseball cap back and forth as I climbed the rows of bleachers to meet them.

"Hey, Ben!" Haley said, awkwardly striding down a row of bleachers to give me a hug. Mina just looked at us, unsmiling. I parted from the hug as quickly and diplomatically as I could.

"Hey, guys, how's your first day going?" I asked.

Haley gave a nice, fake smile as she said, "Trying to figure out if I'm more tired of the people asking me how it felt to be a crazy survivor girl hiding in the woods or the people asking if the two of us are together."

"So, pretty standard then?" I asked.

"Pretty standard, yeah," she quickly agreed.

Mina looked less enthusiastic to talk about her day.

"It's a school day. Less unpleasant than most, but the first day usually is," she said. Looking around the class gathered beneath us, she asked, "You're being careful?"

It took me a second to realize what she was talking about. Amazing though it was, for a few hours I'd forgotten about Splinters and remembered what a life without them was like.

"Of course," I said. Mina simply nodded.

I'd have prodded her for more information had a blue baseball cap not landed between us at that exact moment.

"Little help?" a boy called from beneath us. Haley picked up the hat and looked down at the two boys who had been tossing it back and forth. The one with shaggy, dark hair that looked like it belonged underneath that hat looked vaguely familiar, from Haley's (well, Splinter-Haley's) summer acting class. The other, a tall, muscular boy with cold eyes and a narrow smile, I did not recognize. He looked like someone I should steer clear of.

"You know my mom's not gonna let you keep this hat, Robbie," Haley said, amused.

"I'm willing to take my chances," the shaggy-haired boy said as he rubbed a hand across his scalp. "Keeps me glorious mane out of me eyes."

"I thought that was what you had Patrick for," Haley joked. Robbie scowled. The muscle-bound boy I assumed to be Patrick laughed.

"Well, can we at least keep throwing it until she confiscates it?" Robbie asked.

Laughing, Haley tossed it back to them.

After Haley sat back down, Mina leaned forward and said, "Robbie York and Patrick Keamy. Both Probable Splinters."

When Haley and I both shot her confused looks, Mina added, "In case you were wondering."

"I wasn't, but thanks," I said.

"Probable Splinters? Seriously?" Haley asked.

"Of course. Didn't you read the lists? Anyone in the Theatrical Society gets an automatic Probable spot because of Alexei's involvement," Mina explained. "And Patrick because—"

"He's kind of a jerk?" Haley finished.

Though she clearly sought better words to explain him, Mina nodded.

"Humans can be jerks just fine on their own," Haley said. She looked to me, explaining. "He *can* be a bit of a jerk, but if you don't get on his bad side, he can be pretty cool. Throws good parties whenever his parents are out, and that's a lot. If you're ever invited, check it out. Could do a lot for your social standing."

Looking at Mina, she added, "Yours too."

"I don't go to parties," Mina said defensively.

Soon after, Aunt Christine and the other gym teacher came in and asked us to gather on the gym floor. True to what Haley had predicted, the first thing her mom did was tell Robbie to take off his hat. Dejected, he stuffed it in the back of his gym shorts.

They started us off with some basic stretches and calisthenics to get the blood flowing. With that, it was time for the ever-classic high school death sport: dodgeball.

For the fun of it, we were split down the middle, boys versus girls.

"You're not gonna trip up on us here, are ya?" Patrick asked.

"Wasn't planning on it," I said.

He smiled. "Cool. This school's all about losing when it comes to sports. And if we lose to *them*, well I don't think we'd hear the end of it, do you?"

I watched the girls, most of them trying to pump themselves up with Haley, and Mina, standing behind them all, left out, quiet. Everybody would underestimate her.

None of them knew what she was capable of, not like I did.

The whistle blew. Patrick clapped his hands and yelled, "LET'S KICK SOME ASS!"

"Language, Keamy!" Aunt Christine called out.

"Sorry!" Patrick shot back.

The opening volley was messy. The weak, the slow, the disinterested, they all fell quickly. The boys' team gained momentum, catching a few balls to eliminate girls, dodging appropriately. Haley was taken out when Patrick caught a shot she intended to hit him in the stomach. Robbie got hit in the ankle. He fell to the floor screaming, pretending to be riddled with bullets, getting laughs from the entire room.

Eventually, it came down to three of us, me, Patrick and another boy, who was fast but couldn't throw worth a damn, against Mina. Though hardly graceful-looking in her uniform, she was nearly impossible to hit and could throw with deadly accuracy. Most of the girls had started chanting, "*Raingirl! Raingirl!*" It took me a second to realize that they were doing this for Mina. I had no idea why, maybe it was some hippie thing or joke I didn't get, but Haley clearly didn't like it.

Mina looked at us for a long time, gauging her shots. She threw one ball at the fast boy, and he moved to dodge. As soon as he moved, she threw a second ball harder, pegging the boy in the leg. This got groans from our side, but a few scattered cheers from the girls. Most of them clearly didn't like Mina, but they wanted a win.

Just me, Patrick, and Mina. Some of the guys who had been tagged out on our side rolled us free balls.

Mina would probably win, but I wasn't going to make it easy for her. I waved Patrick to me, telling him I had an idea. He listened, smiled, said he'd give it a try. We spread out on opposite sides of the court, each aiming for Mina. I pulled my arm back, made to throw it at her, but fumbled my release. The ball bounced harmlessly towards Mina. It looked perfectly natural. As soon as it crossed onto her side of the court, she adjusted slightly to the side to catch it.

That was his cue. Patrick fired a fast, powerful throw at her. The ball bounced off her hip, hard enough to make her stumble. A whistle blared. We'd won. Patrick pounded me on the back, telling the other celebrating boys that it was my idea. It felt awesome to be welcomed in.

Looking across the court, I saw Mina, collapsed to her knees, looking utterly defeated. It felt like my heart had been ripped out. I just wanted to win, just wanted to have fun. I thought she of all people would understand friendly competition.

I got dressed as quickly as I could, intending to catch Mina on her way to lunch. I wanted to buy her some lunch, or a dessert, or a soda, anything to smooth things over. I waited by the girl's locker room for her to come out, listening as the lunch bell rang. Haley came out after a few minutes.

"Is she still in there?" I asked.

Haley shook her head. "No, she can dress really fast. I don't know where she ran off to, but she did it in a hurry."

As sorry as I felt, I was also annoyed. I thought, as the closest thing to a best friend I had here, that Mina would want to do lunch together. Then again, I was also sure she had her own lunchtime rituals that she would want to take part in. Thinking she'd wait for me was probably presumptuous of me, especially since we hadn't talked about it in advance.

We'd talk about it and I'd apologize to her on the walk home. At least we'd agreed to *that* before school started.

Haley walked me to the cafeteria and invited me to sit at her table. Seeing some familiar faces, like Kevin, Robbie, and Madison, along with an odd assortment of other cheerleaders and some of Kevin's senior friends, all of them welcoming me in, felt pretty good.

If this kept up, I was looking forward to my time at Prospero High.

5.

THE CATALYST AND THE CLASS PRESIDENT

Mina

"There you are!"

When I finally stepped out of the front gates of Prospero High after the first of the seventy-eight school days before winter break, Ben was waiting on the sidewalk out front, looking like he'd been there for a while.

I'd been dreading this pretty severely since my fit in gym, and I still had the strong urge to turn and run the opposite way, but I *had* promised to share the walk with him. If I backed out now, it would only lead to lots of questions.

"Here I am," I agreed. "Did something happen?"

He shouldered the backpack he'd had resting at his feet and fell into step beside me with enough evident agitation that he could have been preparing to tell me about an open Splinter attack on his History classroom. Instead he faltered at the question.

"No, I just . . ." he seemed to be trying to hold on to the urgency of his mood. "I just couldn't find you."

"I told you I was here."

I had. In answer to his unexplained, "Where are you?" text at 12:06, I'd confirmed that I was still safely at the school, as if my tracker couldn't have told him that.

"I knew you hadn't been taken. I didn't know where you were," Ben clarified.

"But you didn't actually need me for anything?"

Ben looked as if this were a surprising and difficult question.

"I . . . no."

I was relieved to hear that this was nothing serious, but the tension at the near corner of his mouth said there was still something wrong.

"Haley showed you around okay?" I asked

Ben had acclimated to plenty of new schools before, always by following the crowds rather than avoiding them the way I needed to. Haley wasn't the soundest Network candidate; I certainly wasn't about to put a flamethrower in her hand and point her toward the woods, but she was human and well-meaning and—considering Ben's long-standing day-to-day survival style and the social circle he was best suited to infiltrate for us—a much better guide than I would be. I'd assumed he'd be fine with her.

"Yeah, I just thought you'd be there."

I had been planning to check on him at least once or twice, just to make sure. That had changed when, for the first time, my hallucinations had failed to fade out at the usual hour.

I'd been prepared for a few extra complications this semester.

On top of my usual beginning-of-semester census,

catching up on who was new, who was returning, who had spent their summers under circumstances with high or low risk of replacement, I'd also had to deal with dodging Haley, who was trying so hard to corner me that I was almost afraid to go into the girls' bathrooms. It was a wonder she'd had any time left to help Ben.

And I'd had to get Aldo settled in. He'd lasted three whole periods in the crowd before asking to share my hiding places.

Those things I could handle, but I honestly didn't know how long I'd last trying to read my syllabi and summon my best impression of normality for the teachers while the whiteboards kept melting whenever I looked at them.

I'd made it through my morning classes without drawing any undue attention. I'd very nearly fallen apart during those last few seconds of dodgeball, when Ben had meant to distract me by dropping the ball and *succeeded* in distracting me by melting into a pool of Splinter matter before my eyes.

Only, obviously, that hadn't happened.

"I have a lot of work to do during the school year," I explained. "Lots more people to keep track of and a lot less time to do it. I don't really get to take downtime when I'm there."

I didn't go on to add that if anything dangerous *did* happen at school, he'd be a lot safer having another Network member nearby to ask for help instead of me.

I also didn't tell him that if the floor suddenly turned to snakes, I didn't really want him to have to see me jumping on the nearest chair, like a child pretending to cross a fume-less lava flow.

And I didn't tell him that I was hoping our mismatched schedules might make such incidents less frequent for me.

Ever since the hallucinations had started, I'd been struggling to come up with any likely cause. My mental faculties had never been strictly normal, always enhanced in some ways and wanting in others, and it was possible that there had been some sort of insanity time bomb inside me all along, triggered recently by the ordinary neurological rewiring of being a teenager. Or it was possible that when the Warehouse pod had read me and found me defective, its probes cutting directly into the tissue of my brain, forcing sixteen years' worth of memories into a few seconds of consciousness, it had left me even more scrambled than it had found me.

"You don't even go to lunch?" he asked.

"I eat in one of the classrooms. It's out of the way, easier to work on stuff there."

But that morning in the gym, watching Ben play opposite me, watching the perfect arcs and angles of his natural human body exploring its impressive normal capacities and the over-bright tint it gave my vision, so different from the labored clarity dodgeball gave me alone, the one possible correlating variable had clicked into place *other* than the aftereffects of the pod.

Ben.

Hadn't I been noticing cognitive changes since before the Warehouse? No hallucinations yet, but there *had* been changes. It had felt healthy, at first. His presence had given me moments of clarity I could only have dreamt of before. It had also caused a few undeniable lapses, including what seemed very much like a precursor to my odd recent episode in Aldo's room. The few minutes Ben and I had spent carrying my medical kit back to Haley, walking with our hands clasped together for no practical reason, had stirred up that same manic, reckless feeling in my chest that was returning more and more often.

"Which classroom?"

I tried not to hesitate visibly before answering, "Room 12. A few other people use it too. Aldo does now."

I stopped myself just short of adding, "You could join us, if you want."

I wasn't about to put a stop to vital Network activity or cut Ben off from regular safety observation, but all these other things we did together, swapping nice but non-essential skills like driving and even frivolous things like gambling had to stop. Even these walks home—as soon as I caught Ben in a better, more credulous mood, I had to find a way out of them.

The idea put a knot in my stomach. If he was the catalyst my latent insanity had been waiting for, reduced contact was my only hope to stall my deterioration long enough for me to come up with a more permanent solution.

"You know, you could join us," Ben offered, as if on cue. He wasn't going to make this easy. "I mean, if you're really making progress on the Splinter problem, by all means, share the wealth, give me a lead and tell me how I can help, but if that's not why you aren't there—"

"It takes a lot of time just to keep the information we have up to date," I explained. "It's not exciting, but it has to be done."

"Haley knows you're avoiding her," Ben said.

"And yet she keeps looking for me."

"She *likes* you, you know. And you really are the best person for her to talk to about what happened. If you'd just give her a chance, I really think you'd—"

"I don't dislike Haley!" I reiterated for the twenty-eighth time. "I'm not sure she's got what it takes, but I don't dislike her."

"I think you're wrong."

"Duly noted."

"I'm just saying," he diverted the conversation slightly from the topic I knew he still hoped I'd change my mind on, "if you gave people a chance in general, you might like it. I don't mean wandering off into the forest alone with a bunch of PSs or anything, but it's pretty easy to be careful in a cafeteria."

"You haven't seen *me* in a cafeteria," I said with more honesty than I'd been able to afford on most topics lately.

In my peripheral vision, I saw him give me a look that I'm sure was meant to be sympathetic.

"I've heard the names," he said softly. "Some of them, anyway. I figured it was just some hippie thing at first."

Raingirl.

Like Rainman, but a girl. One of my better-constructed and, therefore, more enduring and popular nicknames. There are others, most of them less teacher-earshot-safe. They're a minor inconvenience, the least of my worries, but for some reason the reminder bothered me more than usual, coming from Ben. I shrugged my acknowledgement.

"But Haley's friends, at least," he went on, "they're really not so bad. They wouldn't give you any trouble. If they did, she'd shut them down. Or Kevin would, or I would, for what that's worth."

I returned the only answer that seemed to fit—a shrug and a "maybe."

Ben sighed. "Look, if I'm being too paranoid here, just tell me, okay? I can't make you talk to Haley's crowd, and if you're busy, fine, but just tell me you're not avoiding m—"

Ben cut off in mid-accusation, looking intently at something over my shoulder.

We were a few blocks from the school by then, on a nearly vacant side street, and I turned around to look at the only other humanoid figure in eyeshot.

Courtney Haddad had just stumbled around a corner into view and was awkwardly half-running along the sidewalk parallel to us with none of her usual senior-class-president composure. Even from this distance, I could tell her eyes were wide, shocked, and disbelieving, and with every third step, she turned to look behind her. When she noticed us, she paused a moment, debating between hope and further fear, and then continued the way she had been going.

That's when I saw that her left shoe was missing.

Ben and I exchanged a glance, all trifling disagreement instantly set aside. We both knew that look. She had seen something.

"Courtney!" I called across the street.

I shouldn't have been surprised when this only made her

look more frightened and confused. I'd never addressed her directly before.

"Hey, Courtney!" I shouted, and Ben picked up her name and echoed me.

Courtney kept running, and we both took off after her.

"It's okay!" Ben called out.

We had followed her only a block when a darkly-tinted SUV pulled out in front of her on the nearest cross street.

She shrieked, skidded to a stop, and turned back the other way.

Whoever was in that car didn't waste any time pulling level with her. I couldn't make out the face behind the wheel, but I could tell by its angle that it hadn't spared a glance for us.

Ben broke off from me and wandered briskly, though casually, into the street, right into the SUV's path, causing it to brake suddenly and honk, giving Courtney another few strides' lead on it, while I dug through my bag for a weapon—even when weighed down by both my backpack and my shoulder satchel, I felt naked with just what I dared bring to school, not that I thought I'd need it now.

I was fully expecting the driver to give Ben a neighborly wave of apology for nearly hitting him and then drive on past, as if hurrying to pick someone up late from school, pretending until a more opportune moment that whatever we'd just interrupted hadn't happened at all.

Instead the SUV swung hard around Ben as if he were a six-foot-tall spike strip and went for Courtney again, the front passenger door swinging open toward her.

I grabbed a half-finished bottle of green tea from the

side pocket of my backpack (an insipid brand that's mostly corn syrup and hardly any caffeine, which I buy mainly for its packaging), cracked the bottom open against the curb, ran out to meet Ben at the back of the SUV, and buried the glass in its rear tire.

The force of the escaping air shattered what was left of the bottle, slicing me across the palm, thankfully missing all tendons and arteries, and the SUV wobbled badly, even at the six miles per hour it was taking to keep up with Courtney, drifting momentarily out into the middle of street, out of arm's reach of her.

Ben sprinted ahead to join her before it could straighten out, and when it did, when the door came close enough again, he reached in and, with one decisive, jerking motion, dragged something out onto the sidewalk.

Courtney screamed again when the three of us got a good look at the thing that had been reaching for her.

It was definitely a Splinter; nothing else could look so unnatural, but I'd never seen one look quite like that.

Then, in the next five seconds, I saw it twice more when the SUV skidded to a stop and the driver and a second passenger disembarked.

All three of them had to be connected to kidnapped humans in the Warehouse. The structure of their bones and the perfect fit of the muscles over them were too precisely human for a Creature Splinter's best approximation, but any hints of *which* humans they might have replaced were carefully and systematically obscured. They were all uniform in height, a little shorter even than I was. Their skin was a blank, hairless grey, their ears, noses, mouths reduced to the simplest, most nondescript orifices, their oversized eyes made up of nothing but colorless, expressionless pupils.

It took me a moment to realize why they looked so familiar. There were sketches of them all over the Soda Fountain of Youth for the benefit of visiting UFO enthusiasts.

"Go away, Wilhel-mina Todd," the driver hissed at me in its clicking, popping, characterless voice, the Splinter equivalent of a synthesizer, to go with their apparent equivalent of ski masks.

Neither Ben nor I moved from the places we'd assumed on either side of Courtney, cornered against the nearest yard's wrought iron fence.

The Splinter on the ground, the one Ben had dragged from the car, grabbed for Courtney's ankle. She squealed slightly and kicked it hard in the nose with her remaining shoe. There was apparently enough of its human structure left intact to make it recoil in pain.

The response from the others came very quickly.

The driver lunged at me, its simple, equal-length fingers elongating to a slashing claw to make me dodge out of its way. As soon as it passed me, before it could touch her, I grabbed my heaviest, sturdiest 3-hole-punch and clubbed it across the back of the head with my full strength, leaving a small, noticeable dent in the skull.

The one on the ground was recovering, and when it went for her again, it shot a handful of sticky tentacle-fingers out in front, attaching to her wrist, beginning to spread the rest of its small body into a flat sheet, ready to envelope her. She twisted away, pushing against where its thumb should have been, but its new tentacles were too flexible to mind. With the hardest point of her free elbow, she went for its nose again. It was ready this time. Its imitation nerves rerouted, its face split into four, toothy wedges, hissing and spitting at her with twin forked tongues.

To Courtney's credit, if it *had* been human, she would have escaped. It wrapped around her legs, and Ben jabbed at it with the sharpest thing either of us had left, a ballpoint pen, tearing gashes in it that healed faster than he could lengthen them.

When I finally reached the lighter in my satchel's inner pocket, inconveniently hidden to keep me from being accused of something as mundane as smoking at school, I shot a flame at it from my most innocent-looking aerosol can.

Body spray flames are more colorful than effective, but the long streak I burned down its back stunned it enough to loosen its grip and let Courtney kick it into the gutter.

If the face of the other passenger Splinter had been capable of expression, I was pretty sure it would have looked exasperated when it stepped over the disabled bodies of the other two toward Courtney and me. Identical as they looked, this one was definitely their supervisor.

Ben must have looked a little pathetic to it, crouching next to its most misshapen associate holding nothing but a pen. It pushed past him without acknowledgment. As soon as its back was turned to him, Ben signaled me with the slightest flick of his eyes and quirk of his eyebrow, cool and focused and far from helpless. I got the message.

I dropped my weapons, shielded Courtney's body with

mine, and screamed, the loudest, shrillest, most desperate sound my lungs could produce.

The supervisor looked automatically at the houses on either side of us, watching for humans coming to investigate a sound that no longer resembled rambunctious teenagers innocently and happily walking home from school. The instinctive need for physical protection momentarily overridden by the instinctive need to be able to look normal at a moment's notice, the supervisor's form was as solid and humanoid in appearance as its disguise allowed. Ben straightened up behind it, grabbed it by its shoulder and what passed for its chin, and, in an instant too brief to allow for a reaction, cleanly snapped its neck.

I grabbed my things, and Ben gave Courtney's shoulder a rough but encouraging squeeze to shake her from her shock.

"Run," he advised her, and the three of us took off around the nearest corner, back toward the school, back to the densest population we could reach.

"Are they dead?" was Courtney's first breathless question.

"No," I answered. I could already hear the wood-snapping sound of them re-forming, their consciousness recovering from the minor inconvenience of the damage we'd done to their imitations of physical brains.

"What the hell were those things?"

Neither of us tried to answer her just then.

"We're really sorry this happened to you," Ben panted as we ran flat out along the fourth block from the SUV. "We're on your side, and we'll explain everything as soon as we get to a safer area."

He glanced at me, and I had to stall for a moment to consider, digging gauze out of my bag to bind my hand, before confirming or denying.

The situation was unprecedented. The only people I'd ever spoken to about the Splinters (with the exception of Haley) had been selected through careful research, and the only people I'd ever helped save from them (again, with the exception of Haley), had only needed someone to make it impossible to take them inconspicuously, no fighting required.

The boldness of this attack still had me shaken. It was possible it had been staged, that Courtney had already been taken and was playing on our sympathies as the first step of another Network infiltration, but after Dad's very blunt lecturing of Ben and me, it was also perfectly possible that the Splinters simply didn't care what we saw if we were the only ones.

Already I was trying to guess at the repercussions of interfering like this with no long-term plan. Ben and I had responded automatically. The idea of looking the other way hadn't even occurred to me until it was too late, and probably still hadn't occurred to Ben.

We hadn't killed anyone, neither of us had incurred our second strike, so this wasn't a treaty violation, but if I got home and Dad told me (now that we were sort of openly talking about this stuff) that we had to hand Courtney back over or he'd kill one of us or something, I had no idea what I was going to say.

At this point, I decided I couldn't see the harm in talking to her. It wasn't as if the basic Splinters crash course would include any information about us that the Splinters didn't already have, and if she was human, she might be able to tell us if there was something exceptional about her situation. At the very least, it never hurt to spread the knowledge to one more human who was in no position to call us crazy.

I gave Ben a nod as we slipped back into the still-thick afterschool crowd, slowing to a brisk walk. The Soda Fountain of Youth was just ahead, a block down from the school, and when Courtney turned to check behind her again, Ben slipped a protective arm around her in that effortlessly comforting way he had.

"You look like you could use a malt."

6.

Ben

The Soda Fountain of Youth was packed when we got there. We were able to get a table in the back and the attention of one of the part-time waitresses who was filling in until they could find Billy's replacement. It wasn't the ideal place for a debriefing, but it was public, which would prevent any Splinter-related interruptions.

That just left trying to figure out how Courtney Haddad fit into all of this.

Neither Mina nor I knew much about her, aside from reputation. Haley had pointed her out in the lunchroom when showing me the various important people in school. I knew Courtney was an overachiever; senior class president, editor of the school newspaper; counselor's aide, member of about a half dozen clubs. She ran track in the spring, was almost a certain lock for valedictorian, and was still debating between Harvard and Stanford. Haley also said she was cold and not particularly friendly.

I'm sure the three of us must have looked odd together, Mina and me nursing our fountain drinks (a Cherry

TimeWarp for me, an unholy-looking malt for Mina) while Courtney sipped slowly from a mug of black coffee. She listened silently as we told her what had just happened to her.

After a while, her hands stopped shaking.

"So let me get this straight," Courtney said, taking a tentative sip from her mug. "For more than a hundred years, Prospero has been home to a race of shape-shifting monsters from another dimension who regularly kidnap people so they can steal their bodies and live their lives? And those *Splinters* that you rescued me from back there were trying to do that to me?"

"That seems highly probable, yes," Mina said. "Why were you scared?"

Courtney's face flashed anger. "I was being chased."

"Before that," Mina asked. "The Splinters . . . what? Appeared on the road behind you without warning? What happened to your shoe? Where did it *start* for you?"

Courtney looked over her shoulder, nervous. There were some eyes on us, but nothing exceptional. Mostly kids who looked curious as to why the three of us were sitting together. Courtney must have been satisfied that this wasn't a problem, as she began to talk.

"I don't get scared. This wasn't normal," she started defensively.

"It's okay to be afraid. Being afraid means you're still human," I said, trying to comfort her. "I mean, I spent a good chunk of my summer fighting these things, and I still get scared. Mina here, she's been fighting them her whole life, and even she still gets scared."

I motioned toward Mina, hoping for some confirmation. She had lapsed back into that distant, impassive look, like she was fighting a splitting headache. "Sometimes," I clarified.

Courtney sighed, pulling herself together as she recalled what she had seen.

"I was running late. I told Mr. Montresor I would be by to help him with any filing he needed in the counselor's office since he can't keep anything in order, but I was delayed by Robbie asking me incessant questions about getting published in the paper. I told him if he could learn to put two sentences together I might consider his work. I got to Mr. Montresor's office five minutes late," she said, taking a sip from her coffee. She waved for our waitress and got a refill.

"Mr. Montresor wasn't in the front office like he usually is. Nobody was. I could see his personal office door was open a crack. I thought I heard voices inside," she shuddered.

"I couldn't understand what they were saying. I thought maybe it was some students playing a prank, or trying to look at confidential records. I thought about reporting them, but then I thought I would take care of it myself. I *am* the senior class president. Surely that title must command some respect, right?" she said.

"Not really," Mina said blankly. I shot her a harsh glare. She just replied, "What?"

Courtney was undeterred. "So I opened the door, and I saw two of *them* standing there."

She took a breath that was clearly necessary to keep her voice so perfectly businesslike. "I heard the door close behind me, then one on top of the cabinet whispered my name and grabbed my hair. I fought it off."

"How?" Mina asked.

Courtney pulled what looked like a thick pen from her purse, though where there should have been a cap was a white plastic nozzle.

"I maced it. It reacted poorly, screaming, seizing, vomiting. The other two ran at me, so I threw a chair through the window and jumped out. One of them took my shoe when it tried to grab me. I ran, I saw you, and you know everything that happened after that."

We did, not that that helped any. Her story only raised further questions. What were the Splinters doing in the counselor's office? Were they looking for her, or for something in the files? Both maybe?

"Thank you for this information," Mina said. "You have been very helpful."

"That's it?" Courtney said. "You tell me about an alien invasion, you hear what they did to me, and you just send me on my way?"

"Yes," Mina said.

"No!" I said quickly, looking to Mina. "We need her."

"No we don't," Mina said.

I looked to Courtney, explaining. "Sorry, we've got some trust issues."

"I can see that," Courtney said.

I turned my attention to Mina. "Look, she already knows about Splinters, we know they're interested in her, and we need every set of eyes we can get."

"We do, but we can't trust her," Mina said. The way she

would talk about people like they weren't sitting right next to us was really beginning to irritate me.

"Please?" I said simply.

Mina sighed, rooting through her bag and pulling out a cheap, prepaid phone. Flipping it open, she programmed in a quick succession of numbers and slid it across the table to Courtney.

"This phone has numbers for Ben and myself on it. Should you see anything strange, or should you feel threatened, call us," Mina said.

"And we'll keep you in the loop," I added.

"Provisionally," Mina added quickly.

I tried to smooth that over. "Don't get me wrong, we really are glad to help you, and for whatever help you can offer us, but like I said, we've got some trust issues. For now, though, you have to act like nothing's wrong, because if they think you'll be a problem to them, they will be after you whether or not we're protecting you."

She looked at me like I'd just asked her to pull out all of her teeth.

"It's not easy," I said. "But you do get used to it. You have to keep your eyes open, you have to remember that not everybody is who they say they are, and that just by knowing this you might be in constant danger. But you also can't let this run your life. If you let them change how you live your life, then they've won."

"So this is one of those 'living well is the best revenge' situations?" Courtney asked.

"Essentially," I said.

Courtney put her head in her hands. "This isn't going to be easy, is it?"

I smiled, waving for our waitress so I could get another Cherry TimeWarp. "Welcome to the other side of the looking glass, Courtney."

Courtney caught a ride home with some of her friends at the Fountain. She offered us a ride, but we declined, deciding to walk home.

"You could've been a bit nicer to her, you know," I said. "She just wants to know what's going on."

"She could be a plant. We need to screen her more before she can know anything," Mina said, staring off into the distance. She looked distracted, unfocused. It was not a look I was used to seeing on Mina's face.

"Are you all right?" I asked.

"This doesn't make any sense," Mina said.

"What doesn't?" I asked.

"Everything," she said with finality. She looked at me like I should be able to put the pieces together.

"I'm sorry, but I'm gonna need you to throw me a bone here," I said.

"Courtney. If she isn't a plant, then her selection doesn't make any sense," she said.

I shrugged. "Makes perfect sense to me. She's class president, which means she at least holds some token influence at school, she has a finger in almost every extracurricular activity. Honestly, if you're looking to recruit, she seems ideal."

"But that's it, the fact that she makes so much sense is what makes no sense," Mina said. "Splinters select people who better enable them to blend into a crowd. The small-town drama teacher, the hobby shop owner, the mailman, the short-order cook, nobody pays any attention to these people. Julie's analogy of Splinters as tourists is crude, but it doesn't look that far off. They're all over the world, perhaps in every major city of influence the world has seen, and they have not taken over."

"Maybe they're just waiting," I said.

"For what?" she asked.

"I don't know," I said.

She nodded. "My point exactly. And then there was the nature of her attempted abduction. In the cases I have been able to study, every time a person is taken, it's usually by someone they know and trust, or, like Haley, they're taken in the middle of the night. They wouldn't use those blank alien faces to conceal their identities, they wouldn't attack in broad daylight. Nothing about this fits the profile of a typical Splinter abduction. Meaning this was either a faked abduction for our benefit . . ."

As the pieces came together in my head, I finished her sentence. "Or this isn't a typical Splinter abduction."

We still knew next to nothing about the rogue faction of Splinters that Billy and Splinter-Haley had been a part of. We knew they had set us up, attempted to frame us for murder to spur on an invasion of Prospero, and they had mostly failed, but other than these simple facts we were completely in the dark.

"They're recruiting," I said.

"Exactly," Mina said. "We interfered with their first plan to invade Prospero, so they may very well be taking a more subtle approach now. Taking over influential people in town to better facilitate a backup invasion plan. Probably looking up student records for their targets."

I shook my head. "Great, so now we've got Splinters *and* Slivers to worry about."

"Slivers?" Mina asked.

"Well, they're quietly getting under the town's skin, they're even worse than regular Splinters, and the name kind of sounds creepier. *Slivers.* Just say it, it does sound creepy, right?" I said.

"That's a terrible name," she said.

"Hey, I didn't start the whole Splinters thing," I said.

"Neither did I," Mina said, almost smiling. It was good to see a little optimism sneaking through.

"Are we sure Courtney's safe now? If they really aren't playing like regular Splinters, will anything prevent them from taking her again down the line?" I asked, trying to get back on topic.

"I don't know. Again, this is assuming that this isn't all a big charade to blind us to some other plan they have going on," she said.

"Of course," I agreed.

"Still," Mina said, smiling a bit wider. "If she *is* human, her connections and access would make her a valuable asset."

Though her ability to look at people as people could have used some work, I was glad to see her smiling again. I knew it wouldn't last long. I knew she would retreat back into that fog she'd been in ever since we escaped from the Warehouse. For now it felt good to be human with her again.

7.

TOO CLOSE TO IGNORE

Mina

Dad never did mention Courtney to me. I didn't feel like contemplating whether this confirmed that she was an infiltrator or just the target of a faction of Splinters (*Slivers*) that didn't report to Dad. I barely had the energy to think wistfully of the days when there hadn't been as many options to consider.

My cognitive faculties were still deteriorating steadily, and by Tuesday morning of the third week of the semester, I was too busy trying to will my monitor in the computer lab to show me what was *really* on it under all the imaginary, Splintery, sickly-looking centipedes crawling all over it.

Help me.

My neural malfunctions were becoming more vocal as well as more frequent, and this was one of the preferred phrases. *"Help me,"* along with *"freak, loser, dead girl, your fault,"* and a few others, spoken in a rotating set of voices, unintroduced, but always familiar. Identifying them hadn't made them any quieter when I'd tried, so I was doing my best not to look for the face to match the tone, not to

picture Mom or Dad or Ben or The Old Man or . . . (*Shaun*)
. . . whoever else the sound might be imitating.

That's why Robbie had to flick an empty white-out dispenser across the desk at me before I connected him with his hiss of, "Hey, Mina, can you help me out with this?"

No, I almost hissed back. *No, you have no idea how sincerely I can't.*

"Why me?" I complained, keeping my head to my hand as if I were simply exhausted or slightly sick.

"Uh . . . 'cause you're smart?"

I almost hoped I was imagining the imploring, expectant way he was looking at me, the way non-Network members hardly ever did, almost like an equal. I wanted to blink and find in a brief flash of clarity that he hadn't really used my name. I searched for any sign of unreality in the way he followed it up with, "Come on, *please?*"

"With what?" I asked.

"With Excel. It keeps changing all the example phone numbers with extensions into these weird equations."

"Scientific notation," I explained, without needing to be able to read the screen to understand (and without adding that a mathematical expression requires an "equals" sign to be called an equation).

"Yes, that. I can't figure out how to turn it off."

I glanced around, sure that someone else must have had the same problem by now and had somehow solved it, since they weren't complaining, but our mismatched computer lab hadn't had a uniform overhaul in over a decade. Robbie had one of the nicest computers. Everyone else probably had an older, more sensible version of Office.

Or maybe none of them were actually bothering with the half-hearted suggestions that passed for Computer Sciences assignments.

I dragged my chair over to his. At the moment, all his menu options appeared to be written in Arabic, or at least what Arabic looked like in my brain since I don't read Arabic, and clumsily scrawled in glitter pen, but I was pretty sure I remembered the steps.

"Go to 'Formulas,'" I began.

"Oh, sorry, go ahead," Robbie said, scooting back to give me room to use the mouse.

I squashed my silly flutter of panic. "No, you go ahead. You'll remember better that way."

Robbie looked tempted to laugh at my didactic tone, but he took the mouse back and I heard it click. I had to congratulate myself a little. My talent for hiding the symptoms was developing nicely, almost keeping pace with their severity.

"Okay, 'Formulas.' Now what?"

I searched through my memory of Aldo teaching me exactly this function, hoping I'd actually listened to all the information, meaning that it was there in my head somewhere.

"'Calculation,'" I named the first menu button I could picture clearly, hoping it was the right one.

The ceiling was made of occupied spider webs, the teacher's legs and lower torso had turned into a glimmering golden filing cabinet, and Robbie, who had never paid me a shred more attention than school projects required, was sliding his chair closer to mine, very close, his pretty boy actor's face studying mine intently, raptly, almost as if he were excited—excited by formatting a dummy spreadsheet at the same computer with me. Along with that fresh deluge of obvious impossibilities came a crystal clear snippet of the voice I was trying the hardest to tune out.

Do you have any idea how beautiful you are?

"You're not Sh—" I snapped at the voice, cutting off the moment I realized I was speaking out loud.

Robbie startled and rolled his chair backward, raising his hands theatrically off of the mouse and keyboard and smiling defensively. "Not what? Sorry, I swear I'm not trying to screw it up, just show me how to do it."

"You're not—"

I froze for a moment, looking at the monitor that probably hadn't become a vortex of swirling raw Splinter matter, but *was* probably about as far from the right function as it could get. The other students probably weren't stretching out their newly grown, misshapen batwings, but *were* probably staring at us after my outburst. I scrambled through the rest of the tutorial memory for any possible way out.

"You're not sh-showing the dashes in the phone numbers!" I blurted out, cuffing Robbie lightly across the shoulder as if wanting Excel to work without dashes were the dumbest mistake anyone could have made. "Put them in the way you'd really write a phone number and watch!"

Robbie took the mouse. I heard a few clicks and the tap of a few keys, and then he clapped his hands as if this obvious little cheat were the most brilliant bit of programming he'd ever witnessed.

"You're a genius, Mina. Thanks!"

After gym, I reached the entrance of the girls' locker room to find a solid quarter inch of water flowing out into the hall and several caution signs blocking the way. The spray of the overhead sprinklers continued to patter against the water's surface for a moment, then faded to a trickle and died out while I watched.

"Great," someone muttered behind me. "Who's been smoking in here?"

At the light tread of Haley's tennis shoes behind me, I tried to cut ahead, past the signs, into the vast puddle. One of the janitors wheeled a cart right in front of the entrance just then, gathering a tall pile of already grimy-looking towels in her arms and starting to spread them out on the floor.

I tried to turn back to make a break for Room 12 and come back later, but for once, my ability to stay ahead of the crowd proved a disadvantage. A forty-foot-thick wall of irritated girls and curious boys had formed behind me to survey what could be seen of the damage, and not one of them seemed to notice my desire to leave distinctly enough to move slightly to one side or the other. Even Haley had to struggle to get through them toward me, but she had always been better at parting crowds than I was.

My current window of clear perception was closing, shortened, maybe, by the sudden stall of purposeful action. The water was sloshing and rippling in ways the stationary floor and still air couldn't cause, thickening to a Splintery consistency, its quarter-inch-deep bottom dropping away into an unfathomable ocean trench.

Ignoring the janitor's noise of protest—as well as the way

she suddenly morphed into a living version of that bulbous, tentacled statue from the Warehouse—I splashed away into the water anyway, my shoes instantly soaking through, finding the floor that my eyes insisted wasn't there.

"Mina, hold on, please!" Haley splashed after me. "I need to—sorry," she apologized over her shoulder to the janitor that *she* could still see. "I need . . ."

The slapping of the water helped me tune out her latest request for reassurance and explanations I couldn't give.

I was fast, but Haley's legs were longer, and she didn't have to override her own vision to coordinate her movements. I reached my gym locker only two rows ahead of her, not even enough time to get the padlock open before she caught up.

"Mina! Please, don't you think you owe me at least—?"

This time I didn't need any sound, real or imagined, to help me ignore her.

The inside of my locker was drenched, the towel and canvas outer surface of my bag soaked through, but the homemade plastic liner had done its job and kept the books and electronics dry. The only damp thing inside was the plain white envelope that had been sandwiched between two of my textbooks, my name printed on it in plain black letters.

The ocean under my feet instantly settled back to being a quarter inch of plain, clear water. The world was, for a moment, as normal and simple and comprehensible as I'd ever seen it, and the envelope was still solid and opaque in my hand. I turned to Haley before opening it, interrupting some analysis of how much I'd certainly want to talk were I in her position.

"Do you see this?"

Haley stopped and looked at it, annoyed and slightly curious. "It's an envelope. And it's addressed to you." I nodded and slit it open without stopping to respond to her question of, "Am I supposed to know what that means?"

The hunter obituary inside was just like all the others, except for the handwritten scribble in the margin of this one.

Guess who I'm saving for last?

I didn't bother trying to hide it, or arguing with Haley's little gasp as she read over my shoulder. I just shoved the clipping back into the envelope and the envelope into the front pocket of my shorts and started examining the damage to the rest of the locker's contents. The good phone I'd left out in my pants pocket when I changed was soaked through, and I'd given Courtney my last burner.

"What the hell was that?" Haley breathed.

"I need to use your phone," I said.

She narrowed her eyes at me, still waiting for a real answer, but handed it over without argument.

I flipped through it to Ben's number. Whatever was wrong with me, whatever role he might have in it, I could still tell when there was progress to be made, real help to be had.

Room 12. Now.
—Mina

The message sent, I handed the phone back and headed for the other door, away from the janitor who would still be upset with me. There was something defiant in the way Haley followed me, precisely matching every step. I didn't try to stop her.

8.

Ben

Every Thursday was Pizza Day in the Prospero High School cafeteria. Not just the standard cafeteria-grade fare—real pizza brought in from Fulci's, the second-best pizza place in town. They only brought in a limited number of pizzas, which meant there was always a rush to get an early spot in the lunch line.

I ran out of gym class as quickly as I could and made fourth in line.

The only problem with this was that the third person in line was Madison Holland.

She was a nice girl, a smart girl, a very pretty girl. She was also a very pushy girl. She seemed to find me whenever I had any free time at school and oftentimes after, finding me at the Soda Fountain of Youth or posting public messages for me online. I'd talked to Haley about her after the first week. Though she looked a little annoyed when I told her what Madison had been doing, she also looked unsurprised.

She told me that Madison had gone out with a lot of guys in school and gotten rid of them just as quickly, but was otherwise harmless.

Harmless. Right.

"So you got any plans for homecoming?" she asked.

"I was gonna check out the carnival and the game," I said.

She laughed. "You mean the annual Prospero High School Football Team Slaughter?"

I laughed back. I'd heard stories of how legendarily bad Prospero's team was, but since Haley would be cheering, I'd promised I'd go.

"What I meant was, do you have any plans for *after* homecoming?" she asked.

I shrugged. "Go home probably. I've never been much for dances."

She raised an eyebrow. "Well, if you don't want to go to the dance, Patrick's throwing a party. Nothing big, just some good friends, good music, and there'll probably be some beer."

I knew she was holding back in an effort to try to talk me into going. Haley and Kevin were regulars at Patrick's parties and had told me how loud they usually wound up getting.

Still, it could be fun.

We got our pizza and began to walk back to Kevin and Haley's usual table. I couldn't see Haley anywhere yet.

"I'll think about it," I said.

"Do that. You'll have a good time, I guarantee it," she said.

"Do I need to ask Patrick to get an invite?" I asked.

"You got my invitation," she said, playfully punching me in the shoulder.

"That'll be fine?" I asked.

"That's as good as, if not better, than his. Patrick and I used to go out. He lets me do pretty much anything I want because he thinks it'll get him to third base again," she said casually.

I choked. She giggled.

At that moment, my cell phone vibrated. *Thank God.*

"I gotta take this," I said, ready to pick up the message even if it was spam.

Room 12. Now.
—Mina

Room 12 was located in a small cul-de-sac of classrooms that were about as physically far from the crowd in the cafeteria as you could get without leaving school grounds. The windows were covered in a collage of class projects (a variety of civics, economics, and psychology from what I could see), making it nearly impossible to see inside.

I tried the door. It was locked.

I knocked. The door opened maybe an inch. A foot below my line of sight, a curious, nervous eye looked through.

"What's the password?" he growled.

I said, "I'm here to see Mina."

"Not the password." The door slammed shut. Mina hadn't told me anything about a password.

I knocked again. Again, the door opened about an inch. That eye looking through the crack.

"What's the password?" he growled again.

I grabbed the door handle and pulled. The gatekeeper tried to fight, to pull the door shut, but I was much stronger. I pulled the door with all my might, swinging it open and spilling the tiny little nerd out into the hallway. He scrambled on all fours, looking up at me as if I'd just murdered his pet hamster.

"Sorry," I said, offering to help him up.

"You can't do that!" he squealed, scrambling to his feet and into the classroom. "He didn't have the password, he can't be here!"

Unlike most classrooms, this one was set up around a half-dozen round tables instead of desks, with a few comfortable chairs and couches along the walls. Though there were only about fifteen kids in the room, the noise level rivaled the cafeteria's. Most of this came from one particularly raucous table of Magic card players, slamming down their spells theatrically as they cast them and announced at the top of their lungs their superiority. The rest of the noise came from a few boys who ran around the edges of the room, throwing paper airplanes at each other. *Hyperactive.* There were some pockets of peace, like the two senior boys who sat on one of the couches holding hands, or the sophomore girl who sat staring intently at her sketchpad.

If this had been the cafeteria, all eyes would have been on me when I entered. Instead, everyone kept pretty much to their own business. I spotted the table that Mina, Aldo, and an uncomfortable-looking Haley sat at, and started toward them.

"Excuse me?" a calm voice called.

I looked to the teacher's desk at my side. The gatekeeper I'd knocked down stood beside a pretty teacher in her mid-20s. She motioned me to her. The placard on her desk read:

MS. LAURIE CRAVEN.

"He didn't use the password!" the boy protested.

"He doesn't need the password, Cayden, this classroom is open to everyone," she said pleasantly. Cayden looked scandalized and stormed off.

"You're new here, aren't you?" she asked.

"Guilty as charged," I said, laying on the charm extra thick in the hopes of getting to see Mina sooner.

"Well then, since I'm sure you're tired of formal welcomes by now, I will skip that step and get to the point. I open up this classroom for anyone who wants to have their lunch in a safe refuge, free of any conflict or persecution. You do understand the need for there to be a safe zone like this, don't you?" she asked.

"Very much so, ma'am," I said.

"Good," she said. "I don't need to tell you how difficult high school can be under the best of circumstances, and most of the people who come here aren't in the best of circumstances. This room provides them an environment where they can feel free to be themselves for an hour a day. Do you understand?"

Her pleasant smile and tone of voice never wavered, but it was impossible to ignore the faint threat in her words.

"Entirely," I said.

"Very good. Then all I ask is that, while in here, you observe all school rules, leave any conflicts outside, and treat everyone with the respect they deserve. If you can abide by those conditions, you are welcome here anytime you'd like," she said.

"I don't think that'll be a problem, ma'am," I said, meaning every word.

"I don't think so either," she said earnestly, letting me go.

I went to Mina's table.

I grabbed a seat and was met with an odd mix of reactions; Mina looked as focused and grave as ever, Haley looked like I'd just ridden in on a white horse to rescue her from a dragon, and Aldo smiled up at me, laughing at my discomfort in this room.

"Like our little hideaway, Ben?" he asked.

Ducking beneath one of the hyperactives as he leapt by to catch one of the airplanes, I said, "I feel like I just walked into the Mos Eisley Cantina."

He looked over his shoulder nervously. "Don't say that too loud around here; someone's bound to correct you on the cantina's real name, and in a much less friendly way than me."

"Thanks for the safety tip," I said. I looked to Mina. "What's going on?"

"It's nothing *too* out of the ordinary, but it is a useful break we need to take advantage of," Mina started.

"Not *too* out of the ordinary?" Haley repeated. "You don't consider getting a death threat out of the ordinary?"

"Death threats," Mina corrected. "And no, I don't. I get them all the time."

It took a second for all the words to sink in. I let them work their way through my brain, checking out every word, making sure I'd heard each one correctly. Once I realized that I had indeed heard everything correctly, I responded with all the restraint I could.

"WHAT?"

The room fell silent, all eyes on us.

Aldo stood up. "We're all right, just having a bit of a disagreement about who shot first!"

That seemed enough of an explanation to bring the room back to its previous level of activity, even if it did briefly start a chant of "go Team Greedo!" from the Magic table.

"You're getting death threats?" I asked, still trying to wrap my head around what she had said.

"Yes," Mina replied.

"Why didn't you tell me about these?" I asked.

"They never came up," Mina said without any irony.

Ever since the school year had started, I could tell that she had been holding back on me. She was hardly even speaking to me outside of gym and our are-we-still-human check-ins lately, and I still wasn't entirely satisfied that her reasons were scheduling-related. I knew her well enough to understand that what she was saying now at least made sense to *her*. The threats hadn't come up, so she hadn't mentioned them. I knew that getting angry with her would do no good, but it just felt so easy.

Take a breath. Relax. See what you can make out of this.

"What kind of threats?" I asked.

She slid a wet envelope across the table to me. I opened it, pulled out the soggy newspaper clippings. One an obituary of a youth pastor named Bradford Park from a newspaper in Tampa, the other a brief article about how the man, described as perfectly friendly and healthy, had been shot multiple times by the police after he had threatened to set his live-in girlfriend on fire. Probable suicide by cop. The picture that accompanied the article was of a man in his mid-20s, a surfer bum with spiked hair, tattoos and one of the friendliest smiles you could imagine.

That note, written in the margin, *Guess who I'm saving for last?*

It sent a chill up my spine.

"Who's Bradford Park?" I asked.

"I told you once that there were people in Prospero who knew about Splinters, who fought them before me. He was one of them," she said.

"He's not the only one, is he?" I asked.

She shook her head. "All told, eight previous hunters from Prospero have been killed in a series of accidents or unexplained suicides. Given that all of these fatalities have occurred since we rescued Haley from the Warehouse, it is likely that these killings are a retaliatory act."

That made a frightening amount of sense. It also brought up an unsettling question. "From the Splinters or Slivers?"

"I don't know," she said.

"Slivers?" Aldo asked.

"Later," I said.

"So does that mean we're all in danger? That by wanting to fight them we've put ourselves on, like, some sort of death list?" Haley asked.

"I don't know, but I don't think so," Mina said. "All of those who have been killed so far were members of the old organization, Splinter hunters from before the Network."

"Are there any out there still left who we could ask for help?" Haley asked.

"Or warn at least?" Aldo added. "God knows I'd want to know if I was on some kind of 'death list.'"

Haley glared at him. Aldo looked defensive. "What? I liked it! It's a good term!"

Haley's glare softened, her defenses dropping enough for her to playfully stick out her tongue at Aldo.

Mina spoke up. "Most of these people have done everything possible to stay off the grid once they left Prospero. Contacting them can be incredibly difficult."

"We have to try," I said. "Aldo's right, they do need to be warned, at the very least."

"Those arrangements have already been made," Mina said.

Once again, she'd done something without keeping me informed. Sensing my anger, she quickly added, "I apologize for not telling you about any of this sooner, Ben. I didn't say anything about the death threats because I *do* get them all the time. It's the Splinters' way of keeping me on my toes, and if you haven't noticed, I'm still alive. As for the hunters, I kept you in the dark on them because I have to keep everyone in the dark on them. I've made promises to these people, promises long before I ever knew you, to keep their secrets safe. You of all people should understand the importance of a promise."

"Yeah. Yeah, I do," I admitted.

She nodded. "As soon as I knew what was going on for sure, I set about contacting them through the agreed-upon channels. Anonymous contact is a time-consuming process, but it is being made."

That was something, at least.

"You said something about a break? How you got something useful out of the last threat?" I asked.

Her eyes brightened, some. "This one was put in my gym locker, during or very shortly after class. They set off the sprinklers, getting the note wet, and placed it inside with the otherwise dry contents of my backpack. They were here during the brief few minutes that the sprinkler had been set off. Whoever's been making these threats, whoever has been killing the hunters, is likely here, at school."

Now it was my turn to be skeptical. "Are you sure? There's no way anyone else could have gotten in from outside?"

"Not a chance," Aldo said. "There are no exterior windows in either of the locker rooms and the side entrance has been blocked off by stalled construction since last spring—the school's gotten a lot of crap from the fire marshal about that. The only way into the gym would have been through the front doors."

"And we would have seen it," I said. I tried to remember if I'd seen anyone come into the gym while we were playing volleyball.

"And it's probably a boy. Or maybe a teacher," Haley added. With our attention turned to her, she quickly added, "A girl wouldn't have needed a distraction to get in, right? She could just walk right in there, look like she belongs and plant the note, so it's probably gotta be a boy or a teacher, right?"

"Good deduction," Mina said. Haley smiled, proud.

"So they're at school, what does that give us?" I asked.

"They're at school, and they're probably a very recent replacement," Mina said. "I've never received threats quite like this before. These are too creative. Too personal. This is someone new."

"Someone who's traveled to Tampa recently?" I suggested.

Mina shook her head. "They could be using the portals we saw in the Warehouse to perform the executions. The travel wouldn't have to be noticeable."

"So we have someone at school, who was taken recently, probably right after we rescued Haley, who might be wet right now unless they know how to use a towel, and is probably a boy or a teacher. That doesn't narrow it down much," I said.

"Well, there is a way we can narrow it down further," Mina suggested a bit hesitantly.

"What's that?" I asked.

Mina looked first to Haley, then to me.

"I need you to talk to Courtney Haddad."

9

NEW ASSETS AND OTHER NECESSARY EVILS

Mina

He would want me to destroy it.

No number of years could have made me uncertain of that. Never mind that the card contained nothing but a sequence of numbers, uncrackable without prior knowledge of our system of twelve randomly rotating book codes. Never mind that all it translated to was a time and date, a set of unmarked geographic coordinates, and the words "bring the new boy."

The Old Man would consider even that much information a perilous exposure, and he would expect me to burn the card itself as soon as my eyes recorded it.

It wasn't the nest full of fluffy baby birds on the front wishing "Happy Seventeenth Birthday to a Very Special Girl" that made me keep it intact in my bag's inner lining. The prepackaged sentiment was almost as wasted as the crate of my favorite chocolate protein bars currently rotting in the school dumpster with Dad's card still attached, or my mother's fantasy that the replacement smartphone and case of nicely sharp luxury fountain pens she'd bought me would be used for social and academic purposes respectively.

I tried to pretend I was keeping the card because it was a harmless way to annoy The Old Man. He certainly deserved that. The truth was that I didn't trust the recordings of my eyes anymore. I wanted to be able to go back and touch it if I started to doubt that it had ever really been there.

My birthday, the day of the Homecoming carnival, was a pretty good one for me—hardly any hallucinations at all after I left home in the morning and found the card under the seat of my bike. Yet I did end up touching it several times, always with relief and an irritating dose of guilt, as I coordinated the counselor's office surveillance operation.

All Prospero High students are scheduled for a mandatory checkup meeting with the counselor once every two months, more often in some problem cases. If anyone had shown sudden behavioral changes, they would show in the counselor's records. And if students were being replaced by Splinters with particular priorities, like the job of threatening me, rather than simply to blend in and live stolen lives, some behavioral changes were likely to show.

I'd burnt out a few bugs in the counselor's office before with varying levels of success. Courtney volunteered there, even after school sometimes. She had full access, codes and keys for systems we'd never broken into, and now we had her ear, or Ben did.

I knew it was going to be a hard sell, but Ben's a good salesman. It only took him fifteen minutes of that reluctant, excellent charm routine when we found her after school.

"You're sure you two will be okay?" Ben asked three

separate times once she had finally agreed to help, when I told him to go enjoy the carnival.

"We'll be fine. And no one will come looking for me. People will notice if you're not there."

That was true. It was also true that I needed to keep having a good sanity day if we were going to pull this off, and once we had, when it was too late to screw it up, Ben and I were going to have to spend some intensive, probably very uncomfortable time together, thanks to four mono-syllabic words.

Bring the new boy.

Just like that, after all the trouble I'd gone to keeping the secret, Ben now had permission to know about The Old Man, right at the most inconvenient possible time. I wanted to tell him, yes, but I'd missed the window when he might not take it too badly, and if I'd ever felt tactful and charming in my life, it certainly wasn't now.

Aldo and Julie sat within view of the hallway intersections on either side of the counselor's office, "studying." They were both bluetoothed and ready to sound the alarm, and, in Aldo's case, ready to talk us through any unforeseen technical problems.

"I do this under extreme protest," Courtney reminded me yet again when she'd let us into the office and immediately pocketed her spare key, as if it were a beacon of guilt that she could contain with the signal-blocking power of her delicate cashmere sweater.

"Noted. Now, first of all, what files were the Splinters you saw looking at?"

Courtney fished another key out of the counselor's desk, as if it were a tiny venomous snake, and stared at all the drawers it fit, lost, by the look of her, in recollection as well as doubt.

"I'm not sure. Here," she said, opening a drawer and pointing to a ridiculously large section of it. "I think it was here."

"Great," I said. "So, the Slivers might be interested in looking up a junior whose name might or might not begin with A through M."

"Sorry, I wasn't exactly paying attention to the *files* at the time!"

I left her there doing her panic-control deep breathing and started unscrewing the panel over one of the electrical sockets, focusing hard on the feel of my shoes' rubber soles beneath my feet. Aldo had made this process as quick and idiot-proof as possible for me, but the risk of electric shock is one I've always found difficult to measure rationally.

No miraculously useful recollection had struck Courtney by the time I finished planting the new bug, so I straightened up, shook the computer mouse, and cleared my throat.

"Password," I prompted her.

She balked as if we hadn't discussed this.

"You're here," I reminded her. "I'm sure you're very uncomfortable and conflicted. Being difficult about it isn't going to cancel out what you're doing, so you might as well make it as quick and easy and productive as possible."

"I'm *here* because you and your friends claim to be

enemies of the things that tried to kidnap me!" Courtney hissed at me. "Or at least, Ben says so, since apparently I'm not worth your time to talk to yourself!"

"Would you have agreed to help if I'd been the one asking?"

"You never know," said Courtney. "Maybe I would!"

This didn't help her case any.

"Ben gets me better odds than that," I said, and she made a noise of irritation that didn't seem to have anything to do with the solidity of my argument.

"If you'd just tell me what you know and what your plans are, if I could think about the problem without one hand tied behind my back, if I could understand what we're looking for, maybe I could be a little more useful!"

"I know you haven't been studying them long," I said, "but you have to realize how much you sound like one of them right now."

"What do you want me to say? That I prefer being kept in the dark? Are you telling me you wouldn't find *that* suspicious?"

"Ahem," Aldo pronounced dryly over the line. "Not that I don't like a good catfight as much as the next guy, but I feel obligated to remind you that the program will take at least ten minutes to work its magic, depending on the precise specs of the lovely state-budget-provided computer in there, and I'm sure neither of you feel like hanging around for the sheer thrill of it."

I looked pointedly at the computer and then back at Courtney. She took the keyboard.

"Don't watch," she said.

This time I gave the disbelieving stare.

"Tick tock," Aldo reminded us.

"Fine." I turned around and covered my eyes while she logged in.

I plugged in the flash drive and clicked through Aldo's instructions. Courtney and I waited for the spyware to load in a silence that was quite awkward, but not particularly silent with all her sighing. At last, he announced, "I'm in."

We both turned to the computer and watched the cursor moving spastically across the screen by remote access.

"Let's see what we have here."

"Can we go now?" Courtney asked.

"I wouldn't," Julie told us. "Mrs. Whannell's headed your way."

"Is it a problem?" I asked.

"No, I think she's just getting something from her office. You'll be fine if you stay still a moment."

"*I* got a problem for you," Aldo said. "Half the activity on this thing is in Outlook, and it's got an extra password on it."

I stepped aside and gestured for Courtney to take over again. She folded her arms stayed where she was.

"You said you needed to get into the office computer. You never said anything about Mr. Montresor's accounts."

I folded mine too and made myself smile a little, for purely communicative purposes, even though the situation wasn't at all pleasant. "So you do know his password, then."

"I—no!" But she must have realized it was too late for the lie to stick. "And supposing I did, that's not just school security. Mr. Montresor uses that account for personal stuff! That's why it's locked!"

"If there's anything useful here, it'll be in there," I explained as reasonably as I could.

"Think of it as practice," Julie coaxed in our ears. "You're an investigative journalist, aren't you?"

"Yes. Let's say I'm practicing protecting my sources," Courtney countered.

"We don't have time for this," I said. "The next teacher who passes by could be headed here. You have my word, we're not interested in his credit card numbers or porn collection or secret unpublished romance novels or whatever else he has in there that's so 'personal.' This is strictly Splinter related. Are you going to help us or not?"

Courtney's arms stayed folded. "No. He trusted me with that. We're not even supposed to share passwords, but it was the only way I could get any real work done when he's never around!"

I knew already that I was going to regret whatever happened next.

I lie a lot. I spy, I coerce, I trick, I steal when I have to. There are reasons not many people trust me. But I had never betrayed anyone's trust once I'd willingly accepted it. I respect that boundary and other people who recognize it.

And I'd never forced a Network member or another ECNS to do anything. Strongly encouraged, maybe, but not forced. I'd never found it necessary. People were either cut out for membership or they weren't, and those who were appreciated the stakes.

Courtney wasn't a member, and she wasn't an ECNS. Under the old system, I probably never would have selected her, and if I had, there would have been time to help her see how things were, to come to an understanding. This was exactly why I'd dreaded all this business of working with people who couldn't be kept entirely uninformed, but couldn't be trusted either.

"Is Mrs. Whannell still in her office?" I asked, even gladder than I'd expected that Ben wasn't on the line this time. He didn't need to hear this.

"I haven't heard her leave," answered Julie.

I could practically hear Aldo craning his neck. "Yeah, she's still there."

"If I screamed right now, would she hear me?"

"Definitely," said Aldo. Then, "Um . . . what?"

"Mina?" Julie added her apprehension.

"On the count of five, then," I told Courtney, "I'll appease your conscience and turn us in. One."

Courtney's arms stayed folded, but her face tensed with shock and, in spite of her politician's restraint, an easily detectible quantity of panic.

"Nice try," she said with artificial confidence.

"Two."

"You won't get yourself expelled just to spite me!"

If I'd been in a better mood, I might have laughed at her. Perfect students, people who toed the line right down the middle, always imagined such a ridiculously narrow margin of error around it.

"No, I'll get in trouble. I've been in trouble before. You, on the other hand, stand a decent chance of being deposed. Three."

I didn't know if that was true, if the line for student government was that thin. By the look on Courtney's face, she believed it might be.

"Please. I can't."

"Four."

Courtney released her arms, narrowed her eyes, and said, as if it were meant to be the most devastating piece of news ever delivered, "I don't like you, Mina."

I pushed the keyboard a little closer to her.

"That's a big club," I told her. "Do it. Now."

She never took those dark brown, reprehensive, very possibly human eyes off me while she typed a hybrid of Mr. Montresor's three favorite candies right into Aldo's waiting key capture program.

I didn't seek the pointless, artificial comfort of looking away.

10.

HOMECOMING

Ben

I didn't want to think about Splinters.

I didn't want to think about Mina Todd's crusade.

More than anything, I just didn't want to be afraid.

I just wanted to be Ben Pastor, ordinary high school student, for one day of my life.

We only had a half-day of classes, letting out early so we could enjoy the Homecoming carnival on the soccer field. Though I wanted to look out for Mina, she said I'd be more useful enjoying myself.

She didn't need to tell me twice.

Like everything in Prospero, the Homecoming carnival was small but enthusiastic. Most of the faculty participated, either sitting in on the dunking or pie-throwing booths, or supervising activities. Mr. Finn stood by a catapult he had built, wearing a garishly striped jacket and a straw hat like an old carnival barker, promising to launch a pumpkin all the way to the football field.

Nearly every club hosted a fundraising booth, and with allowance money saved up, I made sure to check out almost every one of them. (I was brave, but no way was I going to stop by the drama club's massage booth and listen to Alexei Smith giving his students tips on proper massage techniques.) I won a few cheap trinkets at the dart throw and ring toss booths and gave Kevin a run for his money at the obstacle course, though his years on the soccer team left me in the dust during the final stretch.

I had to buy him a frozen lemonade after that loss—a price I was willing to pay. Hanging out with Kevin was refreshing. He knew about Splinters, but he wouldn't let them rule his life. Though I didn't agree with his decision not to fight them, it was good to be able to spend time with someone I could talk to about them without having it steer every conversation.

After my loss at the obstacle course, I wasn't going to let him take the day unchallenged. Looking for a victory of my own, I led him to the most popular part of the carnival: The Poettes' Wrestling Ring of Doom.

Really, it wasn't so much a ring of doom as it was a section of lawn near the faculty parking lot that had been roped off so kids could wrestle each other in padded sumo suits, but it looked like a lot of fun. Top it off with most of the Poettes themselves standing on the sidelines cheering the fighters along in their warm-weather cheerleading outfits, and it looked like a good time all around.

I had a good thirty pounds of muscle on Kevin, but it didn't make that much of a difference once we were both strapped into the sumo suits. We toddled and hopped toward each other, getting laughs from the audience and particularly loud cheers from Haley and Madison. Kevin pushed me flat on my back once. By the time I was helped back to my feet, I had figured out how these suits worked and knocked Kevin down the next three times. I yelled triumphantly as the student referee declared me winner to the applause of the small audience that had gathered, which probably would have been bigger if this hadn't been when we finally heard the cursing and screams preceding the sound of breaking glass as Mr. Finn's airborne pumpkin destroyed the windshield of a car in the faculty parking lot.

That night, the Prospero Poets went up against their bitter rivals, the Braiwood Tigers, packed bleachers on both sides of the football field. While the Braiwood side was mostly full of students and parents, it seemed like anyone from Prospero who could show up did, with plenty of Prospero pride to go around.

If only Prospero pride were a little less creepy.

The problem came from our school's mascot, the Prospero Poet. From what Haley had told me, the Poet had been chosen sometime in the mid-seventies because the school's previous mascot had been deemed politically incorrect. Apparently, the matter had been put to a popular vote in the school, and the rather vocal minority in the drama club had won out in getting the Poet adopted.

The main problem with the Poet was that it was, well, rather horrifying. The Poet's costume was a giant head, split down the middle with white on one half and cracked gray on the other, representing the comedy and tragedy masks. The cotton fire coming from its mouth, I'm told, was supposed to represent the "breath of inspiration," while its giant ruffed hat came about because someone probably realized that a big ruffed hat made a giant disembodied head with tiny arms and legs sticking out of it less terrifying. While Braiwood's idea of showing off pride in their football team involved dressing in orange and black, Prospero one-upped them by selling cheap plastic comedy and tragedy masks for audience members to wear.

Looking into the sea of blank, staring faces, half of them laughing, half of them crying, all of them cheering and waving Prospero High flags, was as unsettling as anything non-Splinter related Prospero had to offer.

I could have tried to distract myself with the game itself, but true to their reputation, the Prospero Poets were a pretty pitiful team. Kevin and I sat in the third row, not too far from the fifty-yard line. Even his perpetual kindness faltered when it turned into a contest between the two of us trying to crack each other up as we commented on their play.

The Poettes did their best to keep spirits up from the sidelines. During a particularly long time-out, Haley looked up at us and smiled. She lingered on me for a moment, biting her lip slightly and turning a little too quickly to face the field again. It brought a warmth up in my chest that I wasn't sure I could properly define.

Kevin didn't have that problem.

"God, she's beautiful," he said.

"Yeah, she is," I replied.

He sighed sadly. I felt for him. I knew he still loved her, and that he still hoped to salvage something with her. I also knew she still cared for him, just not in the same way. Ever since we'd gotten the real Haley back, she'd made it clear to everyone who would listen that the breakup had had nothing to do with Kevin being less than a good person. Their renewed friendship, awkward as it often was, had helped him regain much of the natural popularity he'd lost while the town had thought him a kidnapper.

"She still doesn't want to give you another chance?" I asked.

He shook his head. "She's made it clear that she would like to remain friends, but a future romantic relationship is out of the question."

"Completely?" I asked.

"Completely," he said. This didn't make me feel good, necessarily, but it didn't make me feel bad either. Yeah, you could say I felt like a terrible friend.

"You know, I'd never been in love before I met Haley. I thought I had bigger things to worry about, but then she came barreling into my life like a freight train, and I was lost. We were good together; I brought the patience, she brought the passion," he said.

"I thought because we thought a lot alike that we wanted to live the same lives. I was wrong. I stand a good, and I mean *real* good shot at getting into Berkeley next year. I told Haley that she could get in, too, if she wanted. She's so damn smart, but she would never admit it. I just knew that if she applied herself—" he said.

"And that didn't go over well," I said.

"It didn't go over at all. She said she didn't know what she wanted to do with her life, that she didn't want to plan that far ahead, that she wanted to live life one day at a time and enjoy herself. It got heated after that. I raised my voice—I'm not proud of that—I said that if she didn't start getting her act together now, she'd stay in this pitiful town forever. She said, 'What if I want to stay here?' I told her she was better than this place. She called me arrogant, and she stormed off. We made up after that, tried to make things work, but the damage had been done. She broke up with me a few days later," he said.

He looked down at her again, waving when she looked over her shoulder at us. She waved a blue pom-pom back.

"I feel lucky that she still wants to be friends with me, after all of this. She's so special. I don't know what I'd do without her in my life. Letting go is hard, ya know?" he asked.

I may not have liked Kevin when we first met, but seeing him in pain made me realize that, like it or not, I considered him a friend now, and if there's one thing I can't stand, it's seeing a friend in pain. I looked down at the field, to the game, to Haley, to Madison.

An idea formed. Maybe not a good one, but I thought it might do Kevin some good.

"I know this probably sounds really random, and feel free to say no, but earlier I got an invitation to a party, and I'd rather not be completely surrounded by strangers. You want to come with me?" I asked.

"Patrick's?" he asked.

I nodded. His smile started to return. "Sounds fun, brother."

The first thing I thought when I entered Patrick Keamy's house was, *Wow, Mina would hate this place.*

There were too many people, the music was too loud, there weren't enough visible exits. Surveillance would have been next to impossible. There was beer and more than enough debauchery to go around.

It was everything a party was supposed to be.

"Ben, Kevin, my boys!" Patrick said enthusiastically as he welcomed us in.

I shook his hand. "Looks like you got half the school in here."

"The better half," Patrick clarified, laughing a deep, throaty laugh that smelled of cheap vodka. "Nah, not as many as I'd like really. Some people still wanna go to the 'official' homecoming dance with their 'kings' and 'queens' and 'adult supervision,' but they're losers. Come on, lemme show you around."

I looked to Kevin for rescue, but he'd already ducked off, called over by some of his friends. I didn't know most of the people there. I could see a few familiar faces hiding in the mix, Robbie and Madison and even Haley. She flashed a smile my way, but seeing Patrick with me, she made no move to join.

"Got some good tunes and dancin' in the backyard, got a pool table and Guitar Hero in the rec room, karaoke goin' in the living room, enough drink to paralyze a herd of elephants. If you can't have fun here, man, you're doing something seriously wrong," he said.

He guided me through the living room, grabbing a couple of plastic cups of beer from a nearby table and handing one to me. While he quickly drank his down, I set mine on a bookcase.

"Your parents are okay with all this?" I asked, trying to draw attention away from not taking my drink.

He laughed. "Yeah. They know this sort of thing's gonna happen, and they'd rather have it happen under their roof instead of under some stranger's. Now *that* is nice."

He took a long, leering glare at Madison. Given how low-cut her top was and how short her skirt was, he had plenty to leer at.

"She's not bad," I said noncommittally.

"'Not bad,' he says," Patrick mocked. "She's a frickin' goddess, my man. Limber, too. She makes you an offer, you take it, because it don't get much better than Madison Holland. Why else do you think she invited you here?"

Patrick must've seen the look on my face because he laughed, loud and braying. "Seriously, Ben, you gotta live a little!"

"I live just fine," I said.

"Awww, come on, nobody ever sees you doin' anything after school. You just sit with the same people during lunch, and I hear you spend most of your free time with Raingirl."

That nickname set me on edge.

He backed off with the smoothness of a used-car sales-man, putting a placating hand on my shoulder. "Nothing wrong with a little charity work, man, especially charity work that could be that cute with a little effort. I'm just saying that, if that's why you're hanging out with her, you're really selling yourself short."

Before I could explain that Mina and I were friends, he wrapped a powerful arm around my shoulder and started guiding me around the party.

"Guys like us," he said, "we're special, and I don't mean the short-bus special. No, we're good old Grade A, all-American special. We're young, strong, good-looking, and smart enough to realize we're all three of these things, am I right?"

"I guess," I admitted.

He slapped me on the back. "Don't guess. *Know.* We are special, and all we have to do is take advantage of it because, you see, since we are smart, guys like you and me know we won't live forever. We know that we're only young, strong, and good-looking for so long, and that if we don't take advantage of these things, we're gonna miss out on some of the best years of our lives. If we hold back, we only hurt ourselves," he said.

"I don't hold myself back," I said, defensive.

"Yeah, you do," he said. "I've had my eye on you. You seem like a good guy, but why be good when you could be great?"

I wanted to think he was a drunken fool, but there was truth in his slurred ramblings. Mina wasn't holding me back, and she was a good friend, most of the time. She needed help fighting the Splinters, and I was more than willing to offer it. The problem was that she expected this to be a lifestyle. She thought that just because she had signed her life over to the cause that the rest of us ought to do the same. I couldn't do that.

I turned back, found the cup of beer I had set on the

bookcase, and drank it down as quickly as I could without vomiting. It was warm and tasted terrible, but I knew the buzz I could feel it bringing on would be nice.

Patrick looked impressed. "Now that is what I'm talkin' about! So, are you ready to start living life to the fullest?" he asked.

"Yeah," I said.

"You ready to seize every opportunity that crosses your path?" he asked more vehemently.

"Yeah!" I said, getting more pumped by the second.

"You ready to get drunk and do stupid shit?" he asked.

"How stupid?" I asked.

"As stupid as you want," he said.

"Hell yeah!" I nearly shouted.

He clapped me on the back even harder. "Then let's get this party started!"

I've been to enough parties to know how to drink without getting truly drunk. I never drink hard liquor, always keep a running tally of how many I've had written on my wrist in pen, and never, ever actually finish a cup of beer. Set down a half-full cup somewhere and pick up a new one and people will think you've drunk just as much as them. They're cheap, dishonest tricks, I know, but they've allowed me to socially drink while still keeping most of my wits about me.

Considering how blurry most of that night was, I imagine that I broke at least one of my rules. It all ran together in a mix of dancing, with Haley, with Madison, with some girls I didn't even know, and of very poorly singing "Take On Me" on the karaoke machine.

At some point, a couple hours in, I stumbled into someone and got a cup of beer spilled all down the front of my shirt. I cursed at my stupidity.

The line to the main bathroom was long. I asked Patrick if there was any other that I could use, and he said I should try one of the upstairs guestrooms. There were fewer people up there, mostly looking for quieter places to talk, to make out, or pass out on one of the chairs. I found a guestroom, but it was dark, and three voices inside yelled at me to shut the door.

I continued down the hall and finally found an unoccupied guestroom with an unoccupied bathroom. I washed my shirt in the sink, getting most of the beer out of it.

The mirror showed me a face I hadn't seen in a long time. Myself smiling. Not worried, not scared, just good old Ben Pastor, with maybe a couple too many drinks in him.

"You're having fun," I said to my reflection, smiling. "You are having fun, right?"

Someone closed and locked the bedroom door behind me. I turned and saw Madison Holland standing by the bed, looking at me and smiling.

"Ben Pastor. I've been looking forward to getting you alone for a while," she purred as she sauntered into the bathroom doorway.

I put my hands on the sink and sighed. We had to have this conversation sooner or later. It looked like it was going to have to be sooner.

"Look, Madison, I'm really flattered by the attention, I really am, and you are a really beautiful girl, but I just have to tell you, I'm really not looking for . . . whatever it is you're looking for right now," I said, firmly.

She didn't respond. She did, however, cock her head violently to the side with the familiar, unsettling sound of splintering wood. Five spindly, spider-like legs burst from her cheeks, pulling her lips aside as she hissed at me.

The bottom half of her face erupted and flew toward me. The spider-like legs latched around my head and pulled themselves tight, pushing what had once been her pretty, red lips against mine as a fleshy, inhuman tongue tried to force itself into my mouth. It was cutting off my air and was so strong I couldn't break it away. It was connected to Madison by a thick, flesh-colored tentacle that throbbed grotesquely, jutting out horribly from where her bottom jaw should have been.

For a brief moment, I thought about how this wasn't exactly how I imagined my first kiss going. I just hoped it wouldn't be my last.

She jerked her neck violently, throwing me to the floor and dragging me out into the bedroom. Almost effortlessly, the tentacle lifted me up from the floor and sat me on the edge of the bed. Cocking her neck again, the tentacle broke off from her head and wrapped around my arms and chest like a snake, the end forming a thick, dagger-like protrusion of bone that the tentacle curled up against my neck, threatening to slit my throat. She cleared enough room so I could breathe through my nose.

She just stood there, casually checking her nails as her bottom jaw and face grew back in. As soon as she looked more or less like herself, she looked back at me gleefully.

"You're a hard guy to corner, you know? I mean, if I wanted you in your house I could've broken in at night so easy, but to pull this off, I have to get you alone in a public place. Do you have any idea how hard that is?" she asked, blowing a stray lock of hair out of her eyes. "No, I don't imagine you would."

I struggled, trying to fight my way free from the tentacle's vice-like grip. As if correcting a naughty dog, she flexed her wrist, forcing the coils to tighten, the dagger of bone pressing threateningly against my throat.

"I'm not supposed to kill you, but if you keep fighting me, I might have to. That'll make some people happy. God knows Jess and Hermes wanted you dead after what you two did to us. Alexei thought that would be too messy, he just said we should bring you into the fold, make you one of us. Trust Sam to come up with another option."

Reaching into her purse, she pulled out her lipstick and began to apply it to her new lips.

"He's authorized me to make you an offer."

Checking a handheld mirror to make sure her lipstick was even, she pursed her lips and leaned over, kissing me on the side of the neck. I could feel her lipstick drying there and felt sick. I struggled, trying to yell, and only getting a monstrous tongue forced into my mouth for my trouble.

"Unless you want me to get to first base with your stomach, I'd really recommend you stop squirming," she said. I relented, for the moment.

"Now, since you're a smart guy, like Patrick said, you must be wondering just what this offer is," she said, tearing a slight rip in her top. "Right now, we're willing to offer you whatever you want. Money? Power? Women? Anything and everything you could want will be yours. All we ask, in exchange, is that you stay away from Mina Todd."

She reached down to her skirt and gave it a good tear, then carefully removed her lacy black thong. She considered it for a moment, then tore it in half, forcing the pieces into one of my jeans pockets. I tried yelling at her through my living gag, wanting to ask her what the hell she was doing.

"Don't worry, this'll all make sense in a minute," she said, adjusting the tattered fabric so it stuck slightly from my pocket.

"Now, where was I? Right. Mina. She's gotten far too efficient since the two of you have started working together, and we can't have that. I know you're probably thinking to yourself that this is crazy, that nothing could get you to leave Mina behind because she's your friend, and you two are fighting the just and right fight," she said as she climbed up on me and straddled my hips. She caressed my neck gently for a moment, and then slashed at the side with her fingernails. I howled in agony against the Splinter beast that held me in place.

"You might be thinking that, but that's only because I haven't gotten to the best part yet. The best part is that if you say no, if you continue this fight with Mina, we will destroy you. We will take from you everything that you love. Your friends will abandon you, adults will think you are scum, and your mother will wonder how she lost her way with you."

I felt a cold stab of rage as she mentioned my mother.

She touched her hand to the tentacle-beast surrounding me, slowly, grotesquely absorbing it back into her arm. I coughed and retched as my mouth was freed, and that horrible, probing tongue withdrew.

Climbing off of me, she walked casually over to the door and turned back to me.

"So what do you think?" she asked perkily.

I coughed heavily, wiping the taste of bile from my lips. "I think that if you're resorting to crap like this you're more scared of us than we thought, and I think you're right. You must be crazy to think I'm going to collaborate with monsters like you."

Madison rolled her eyes dramatically. "Sticks and stones, but I forgive you. You don't know how bad things can get yet, but if you keep going like this, you will."

Her body shuddered and snapped with that crackling, splintering wood sound. Bruises formed on her arms and neck. Tears flowed freely down her puffed up, pink cheeks, trailing mascara and eyeliner. A faint trickle of blood rolled down her inner thigh. I could see now what she was doing, and at once I felt like I'd been punched in the stomach.

"You wouldn't," I said feebly.

"Yes, we would," she said coldly. "Give in now, and I can make these go away, and I can spend as long as you want making this all up to you. And believe me, I'm really good at making things up to people when I've been naughty."

"Go to hell," I spat at her.

She smiled cheerfully. "I was really hoping you'd say that. I just want to say, I really look forward to working with you. We've got a pool going on, about how long you'll last before you come crawling to me on your knees, begging to lick my toes to make it all go away. I've got you pegged at six weeks. Be strong; I stand to win a lot of money off of you."

Unlocking the door, she started sobbing dramatically and sprinted out into the hallway. I sat on the edge of the bed, trying to wrap my head around what had just happened. They were fools if they thought I was going to give up. I could make it through this, I could be strong, I'd just stick to the truth as best as I could, and hope that everyone would believe me over her.

That feeling of strength and righteousness lasted right until the moment I saw the first stranger's face, curious and a little scared, looking through the open doorway at me.

11.

Mina

"Ben?"

"Yeah?"

"Have you been listening to a word I've said?"

Ben sighed. "We're going to see the guy you knew about who got rejected by the pods before you," he recounted.

"Yes."

"He's the crazy hermit who taught you about Splinters in the beginning. You and a bunch of other people who are already dead."

"Yes."

"And for some reason, you couldn't tell me all this before?"

"Yes."

I was more annoyed with The Old Man than with Ben for forcing me to answer this question on the hike up to the given coordinates. Unfortunately, Ben was the one who was there to hear the involuntary bite in my voice.

At least my head was clear today, clearer than it had

been in weeks. Once we had gotten up into the hills, the distortions to my senses had started fading out, as if all I'd needed was a little space from the town my existence was confined to. There were none at all right now, just my mind, raw and frail and oversensitive, like my body on the morning of a broken fever.

"Okay. You were keeping a promise to him, not telling anyone," Ben added to the summary. "But even though he's still into fighting back and he's guaranteed human, you guys haven't spoken in years."

I didn't like this part of the story. I liked the idea of refusing more of Ben's questions, even implied questions, even less.

"We have a fundamental difference of opinion," I said. "And he withheld critical information from me."

Ben almost laughed. "Is that all?"

"It wasn't like that," I said. "It wasn't someone else's secret, and it wasn't personal. Well, parts of it were, but not the relevant, important part."

"Go on."

"He was in a pod," I repeated. "In the Warehouse. So he *knew* that the people who'd been copied were still alive and what happens if you don't disconnect them the right way. He never saw fit to volunteer that. It wasn't until . . ."

(Shaun) ". . . until a *Splinter* told me that I got him to admit it, and by then, some people were dead, and I was a part of it."

Ben was silent a moment. "Okay, yeah, that's pretty bad," he agreed. "So why are we going to see him now?"

This part was more complicated.

"I told him I couldn't work with him as long as he kept killing Splinters with the people still attached, and that's where we ended things. He is a good person, mostly, and I do owe him almost everything I know. If he's on a hit list, I can't not tell him."

Ben nodded. "And he doesn't get cell reception, I'm guessing?" He didn't seem to expect an answer.

"Tell me the code answers again," I said.

"*Again?*"

"Again."

"His favorite flowers are lilacs, viewed through 3D glasses. His parents met in a hospital in Switzerland after his mother got her foot caught in a wheat thresher. He used to enjoy almonds until he saw a parrot choke to death on one."

"What color parrot?" I hoped I sounded urgent rather than frantic.

"Chartreuse! Whatever that is! And I remember the other two dozen bogus fun facts too! Exactly how is this supposed to keep anyone safe? If I got replaced, my Splinter would know everything I know."

"They're not for asking *you* if you're a Splinter, they're for asking *me*. If I thought you'd been replaced, or might have been replaced, or that you weren't a completely trustworthy human, he'd expect me to give you different answers."

That caught his attention a little. "And then he'd kill me?"

"Yes, or refuse to tell you anything, depending on the answers. There are four different levels of confidence."

"And which one am I on?"

I'd been hoping he wouldn't find that question worth asking, but at least I didn't need to feel guilty about that answer.

"Absolute."

He nodded, not looking overly happy.

"When we get close, don't make any sudden movements," I reminded him.

"Got it."

"And try not to get within arm's reach unless he has his full attention on interacting with you, in case something startles him."

"Okay."

"Don't laugh unless you see one of us laugh first. Don't argue unless you have no other choice. He's missing a hand, and he'll be carrying at least one gun. Don't stare. And *don't* show weakness. Whatever you do—"

"I'll manage," he said.

I hadn't expected him to take the new information or the instructions well, but I had been expecting a little more reaction, a little assurance that his attention hadn't wandered again. He was focusing harder than necessary on the rocky incline ahead, and I didn't think it was simply out of frustration with what I hadn't told him. The way his tongue kept working silently against his teeth, trying to capture an elusive string of words, meant there was something else he wanted to talk about.

"Mina?"

"Yes?"

"You . . . um." He briefly removed his "3 Of A Kind" baseball cap and ran his fingers nervously through his hair before trying again. "I know you're not exactly into gossip, recreationally, anyway, but you hear things, right? If you're always listening for signs of the Splinters, you hear the other stuff, too."

"Yes."

"So, you've heard the . . . stuff? I should—I mean, when I told you to switch Madison's list, I wasn't sure how to say the rest, but you must have heard by now."

The party. Of course. I had made a note of it, when the flood of hate spam had hit Ben on every available public forum, that it would need some talking out, but with the sudden prospect of seeing The Old Man for the first time in nearly three years, that little crisis had completely slipped what was left of my mind.

"Oh, right. It's okay," I told him quickly. He turned and stared at me.

"Okay?"

"Yes. It would have been nice to have someone with his ear to the in-crowd, but that's not why I picked you, anyway. You've got plenty more to offer. We'll make do."

"We'll make do?" Ben repeated. "That's what you have to say about this?"

I thought maybe my voice had been harsher than my intent somehow, as it sometimes is, so I tried to make myself clear. "I'm not blaming you. It's not—"

"I didn't do it!" Ben shouted much too loudly. His voice echoed back off the rocks to where we'd stopped dead in our path. If we'd been within The Old Man's hearing, I didn't know what he might do to us for drawing unnecessary attention to his position.

"I know that!"

I was too loud as well, a few decibels higher than Ben, even, but I couldn't stop myself. The very idea that he found it necessary to explain something so obvious to me was like salt on the exposed nerves the hallucinations kept leaving behind, a kick to my black-and-blue ego, right in the extra tender target that was my defective and failing mental faculties.

"I'm not a complete idiot!" I shouted. "Maybe I don't know every detail of what you mean when you don't say it, but I *do* know you a little! Maybe better than anyone else here does! Better than that! Do you really think I could spend my whole summer with someone the way we did and not be able to tell if he's a monster?"

You mean again?

I wasn't sure if that voice was a regular thought or a crazy one, and I didn't care. "You know what I mean!" I snapped, even though Ben hadn't shown any acknowledgement of the double meaning. "Please tell me you didn't think, even for a moment, that I'd actually believe that you'd—"

"No." I wasn't sure if Ben was really agreeing with me that vehemently or if he just wanted to keep me from finishing the sentence. "No, I guess not. I just needed to—"

"To *what?*"

He sighed. "Nothing."

We continued the climb in silence for a while, his jaw continuing its word-searching dance. As fruitless as I knew it would be, I tried again.

"The rest of the Network won't believe it either," I told

him. "Kevin and Aldo probably know better anyway, and anyone who doesn't will listen to me."

"Thanks," Ben said blankly.

"We won't let this get in the way," I promised. "This is nothing. Really. They're not allowed to copy you or kill you, so they're attacking you with whatever else they've got. In fact, this shows how little they've got right now, that they're bothering to try to make you a bit less dangerous with a lie."

"She didn't just lie," Ben said clearly, as if a few of the right words were finally forming. "And it's *not* nothing."

I glanced over at him, wishing he'd get to the point, say something that made sense, look at me and stop staring so unreadably forward. His hand was tracing the fresh scratches on his neck in a way that gave me the feeling they had come from something other than the simple Splinter fight he'd mentioned in passing when he'd warned me what she was. I gave him the gentlest nudge I could.

"What did happen?"

Just when I thought he might not answer, he did, slowly, describing Madison's stunt in careful, uncomfortable fits and starts, his eyes locked on the ground ahead of us. An unhelpful wave of that too-ready anger broke in my chest and splashed down into my stomach, even though I'd already been given more than enough time to process the outcome, if not the details, of what she'd done.

"And she threatened . . . she said it would only get worse, if I didn't give up."

"Give up resisting them?" I had to make sure. "Give up on me?"

He nodded. "Only I don't know how it could get worse from here, if they can't replace me. They might try to get me arrested or something, I don't know."

Splinters didn't need to try to get someone arrested. The Splinter Council and the human town council together owned Prospero's police, even after the hasty restoration of the human version of Sheriff Diaz. Splinter or collaborator, it made no difference to his interest in truth and justice.

"If they had permission to trump something up, they'd have done it by now and gotten you out of the way," I tried to assure him. "They're just trying to make your life difficult."

"Is that meant to make me feel better?"

It hadn't, even a little. That was obvious.

"It's meant to explain that this isn't an insurmountable setback."

That made no visible difference.

"So you think," his throat sounded obstructed, and he stopped to clear it. "You think this is legitimate, I mean, as legitimate as anything the Splinters do? You think it's coming from the ones in charge?"

"I don't know," I said. "We'll do everything we can to find out."

"Your . . ." his throat clicked again. "Your dad, I mean, obviously not *your* dad, the Splinter one, he said . . . he called himself a lawman. So, if this isn't sanctioned, do you think he could make it stop? Or if it is, maybe appeal . . ."

"You want me to ask my father for help?"

He didn't answer, but the fact that the thought had even crossed his mind after the last time I'd seen the two of them in the same room meant he was more desperate than I'd ever seen him before.

"Ben, what's wrong?"

"What's wrong? Everyone thinks that I—"

"Not everyone," I reminded him.

"Almost everyone thinks it, and you ask me, 'What's wrong?'"

Reputation.

It had taken me a while to understand because I didn't really want to. Once again, this was about reputation, about the opinions of uninformed people of uncertain humanity, a luxury, like honor roll grades, that I'd written off long ago. I'd seen people through the withdrawal plenty of times before, though, so I did my best to recall how.

Unfortunately, that was the moment Ben finally looked at me again.

For a moment, looking into his face was like looking into that alternate reality he had gotten to know so much better than I did. It was written in every tense, minute little contour of his facial muscles, a reality with no Splinters, where a rumor like this could be the most devastating thing to happen in someone's whole school career. A reality that was close enough to being right that it left room for a wrong like this one to matter the way it should.

It was a dizzying view. I didn't know how Ben could stand it as well as he did. I knew that if *I* looked into it for long enough, I'd never be able to look at my world again. If I tried, I would start screaming and flinging rocks off the trail down the cliff face, I would throw my arms around

Ben and try to smooth the angry, scared, sad lines off his face and tell him that I'd make people understand who he really was, or if I couldn't, that I'd somehow make myself enough people for him, so it wouldn't matter.

And then I'd probably set Madison on fire, Splinter or not, right there in the east quad on Monday morning and laugh maniacally while the cops dragged me away, leaving him alone and already breaking my imaginary, otherworld promise.

Obviously, none of those things could be allowed to happen. So I turned and walked straight forward, eyes dead ahead like Ben's had been, so I could talk without the risk of seeing *that* again.

"You realize it was always very unlikely that something like this wouldn't happen?"

"Something like this?"

"Maybe not exactly like this," I amended, "but the Splinters were always going to target you, especially if you helped me. I told you that."

"You didn't tell me *this!*"

"It's not always social. In fact, it's never really had to be. Devoting your life to something most people can't be convinced exists doesn't make you that popular in the first place, if you haven't noticed. Even if the Splinters hadn't decided your peers were worth taking from you, it would have been difficult for you to keep enough in common, and enough time, for those people."

He was about to object again, so I jumped to the sharpest point I could make.

"Remember all the time you spent with the other Haley?

Remember all the energy you spent worrying about what *she* thought and felt and wanted, as if she were human, when all she really wanted was to manipulate us both into the Warehouse? Every time you spend a thought on a stranger or an unverified acquaintance, you could be wasting it on another trap like that."

He actually seemed to give that some fair thought. "If I hadn't cared about the Splinter-Haley, we never would have found the real one."

Then I had to think. My argument was getting all jumbled where I tried to customize it for him. "In that instance, you're right. And I'm glad we did, but you can't save everyone. Definitely not one at a time."

He was staring out over the cliff face, away from me, when he asked, "So what can we do? Please, just remind me one more time, what exactly are we actually doing that's worth this?"

I was saved answering by the reflected flash of movement on the insides of my glasses as an arm darted around me from behind to secure a headlock.

As automatically as tying my shoes, I grabbed the hand by thumb and fourth finger joints, twisted as I dodged out from under the elbow, and tripped the attacker's reflexive, steadying step, sending him sprawling onto the dirt.

Ben turned and drew a stun gun just in time to find it unnecessary.

Even through his makeshift mask and shapeless coat, I recognized my old teacher's presence before I heard his voice.

"You're getting slow, Little Girl," he greeted me.

"You're the one on the ground, Old Man."

Angry as I still was, about a lot of things, I couldn't help returning his grin as I helped him up.

"It's good to see you again, Robin," he said.

12.

TWO LEGENDS FOR THE PRICE OF ONE

Ben

I don't know what I felt more, anger or stupidity. Anger at Madison and the Splinters for destroying my life. Anger at the people deluging me with messages, texts, and voice-mails calling me all sorts of terrible names, telling me to confess, telling me that I shouldn't go to school on Monday because I wouldn't leave alive. Anger knowing that this was only the beginning, and Mina Todd, my closest friend in Prospero, couldn't seem to care less about it.

So far, anger had been the winner in that fight.

Stupidity only started to pull ahead when I saw the man dart out of the forest and go for Mina. I saw him coming. I saw him go for her. I fumbled for my weapon, too slow, too distracted. By the time I had the weapon free, she already had him staring at the sky. If he had meant to do her harm, she'd already be dead.

Mina helped him to his feet. He arched his back, loudly popping his joints into place. He was a large man, tall, and I was pretty sure powerfully built, though it was hard to be sure. He wore thick boots that added at least two inches to his height and several layers of clothing that hid his shape. A long, tattered, black trench coat surrounded him like a superhero's cape, each breast of which was covered in an odd assortment of buttons and pins. I could identify a Dole/Kemp '96 campaign button, a vaguely stained yellow smiley face, and a Prospero Poets pin with its twin masks of comedy and tragedy. There were at least a dozen more too hard to see. His face was completely obscured by tightly wrapped, stained bandages, a pair of reflective skier's goggles, and a faded black fedora. True to what Mina had said, where there should have been a right hand he had a large, iron hook, probably homemade, given its size and the fact that he'd clearly sharpened the outer edge so punching with it would hit like a cleaver.

The Old Man considered me, cocking his head, slightly. His good hand lay casually at his side, though I could see his fingers wavering slightly, considering if they should go for one of the knives or pistols strapped to his chest, or one of the three long-guns that jutted from the quiver on his back.

"This is him," he said.

"Yes," Mina said.

"Put down the stun gun," he said to me. His voice was calm, but firm. Threatening. I made to drop it.

Apparently I wasn't fast enough for his liking. Quickly, he unleashed a bowie knife from a sheath on his chest and threw it, ripping the stun gun from my hand and impaling it to the ground.

The Old Man was on me in a flash, clearing the fifteen feet between us in less than a second. He kicked me in the chest, hard, knocking the wind from me and putting me on the dirt. As my head bounced off the ground and my ears rang, I watched as my old '3 Of a Kind' baseball cap rolled off into the brush. *As if this weekend wasn't going badly enough.*

He knelt down on me, one knee on my chest and the sharpened outer edge of his hook pressed against the base of my throat.

"This isn't necessary!" Mina protested.

"Quiet, Little Girl, you know it is," he growled back at her.

Again he turned his attention to me with that calm, threatening voice. "I had a pet once when I was a boy. What kind of animal was it? What was its name? What did I think of it?"

I remembered what Mina had told me.

"It was a kangaroo with a gimpy leg," I wheezed. "His name was Special Agent Admiral Dog Johnson. And you . . . and you . . ."

With his weight on my chest, I was starting to black out.

"He won't be able to answer you like that," Mina said.

Sighing, The Old Man let some pressure off of me. "Thank you, Robin, I know what I'm doing."

I wanted my arm free. I wanted to slug this man and let out all of my anger and frustration on that bandaged face. I wanted to make sure he was as ugly as I felt on the inside. But Mina was here, and if she was right, he could tell us just what the hell was going on.

"And you . . . you were very fond of him, but you thought he went to the bathroom in your aunt's teapot too much!"

More pressure on my throat. He asked, "You sure about your words, Benji?"

I racked my brain for Mina's exact wording. I looked to her, hopeful, but she just stood off to the side. She wouldn't help me. No, of course she wouldn't. That wasn't what she did.

Then it came to me. "You thought he *crapped* in your aunt's teapot too much!"

At once, he was on his feet with the exuberance of a child on Christmas morning.

"Well shit, Benji, why didn't you say so in the first place!" he said, pulling off his hat and tossing it to Mina. His goggles soon followed. He unwrapped his bandages and pocketed them.

The Old Man looked to be in his early fifties, with a long, clean-shaven face, a thin salt and pepper moustache, and hair groomed with military precision. His eyes were clear blue and utterly cold, but his smile was bright and cheerful.

Even if he didn't have the hook, he would have scared the hell out of me.

He took his fedora back from Mina, propped it back on his head and grabbed me by the hand, yanking me to my feet.

"You scared me for a second, kiddo. Thought I was gonna have to spill your guts just so I could see if they felt like running away!" he said, laughing. He patted my chest and back, dusting me off, and then retrieved my hat from the bushes. "You can never be too careful when it comes to meeting new people. Or old people for that matter, not around here at least. But at least you got sense enough to wear a hat on a day like this, unlike Robin here."

"I don't like hats," she said simply.

"You should like sunburns even less," he said.

He forced the cap back onto my head. Reflexively, and with a fair amount of disgust making me act, I tried to dodge away from the man as he drew close. Before I knew what hit me, he had punched me in the chest. Hard.

"Sorry!" he said, sounding truly apologetic. "You really shouldn't have done that! He really shouldn't have! Didn't you tell him?"

"I did," Mina said.

Going home really sounded good at this point.

"You shoulda listened to her, Benji," he said. "Unless she's a Splinter or she's clearly up her own ass, always listen to your woman. And if you got a good one like Robin here, you can trust she knows what she's talking about, most of the time at least."

"We're not together," I choked out.

The Old Man looked at her questioningly. She nodded.

"Huh," he said. "I see you've learned a thing or two after all, Robin. So, how'd you like my birthday card?"

"That was very sweet of you. Thanks," Mina said.

This one hit me out of nowhere. "Wait, your birthday's coming up?"

Mina shook her head. "Already passed, actually. It was this Friday."

Homecoming. The hits just kept on coming with Mina Todd.

I think I did pretty well holding my frustration at bay. "Why didn't you tell me?"

"It didn't come up," Mina said. This was becoming an annoying catchphrase with her.

The Old Man laughed. "Take it from an old-timer, son, never give a woman a hard time about her birthdays. Reminds her she's not young forever."

I wanted to tell him to shut the hell up so I could ask Mina why she wouldn't tell me about her birthday. I also wanted to ask what this whole "Robin" thing was about. Before I could, he reached to the bag behind his back, pulled out a double-barreled shotgun, and tossed it to Mina.

Though she looked at the weapon with a fair amount of distaste, she smiled up at The Old Man as if the gun had meant something deeper.

"Is it really—" she began.

He nodded, smiling far too enthusiastically for my liking. "You got that right, Little Girl. It's Bigfoot Hunting Season."

As much as my mind wandered between the physical pain that currently enveloped me and the pain I knew I would feel as soon as I checked my computer back home, the phrase "Bigfoot Hunting Season" hit me so unexpectedly that I couldn't help being drawn back to earth.

"Bigfoot Hunting Season?" I asked. "Like, real Bigfoot?"

The Old Man laughed, rubbing his hook through his moustache. "Real Bigfoot? F-, I mean, heck no! There's no such thing. Bigfeet are just good old Creature Splinters with dreams of being something better than they are. They wanna be human, but all they can grab is a possum or a 'coon or a deer and then try and make it look human. What they usually get themselves is a furry giant that don't look quite right, is dumber than a sack of hammers, and will disappear and dissolve into a puddle of Splinter-goo within a few weeks. In that time, they're a menace, and we gotta deal with them."

Mina tossed her shotgun back. "You know I don't like these."

The Old Man smirked at me knowingly and punched Mina on the shoulder. "Recoil."

He tossed the shotgun to me. "You know how to handle one of these, Benji?"

I didn't, but I remembered what Mina said about not showing any weakness.

"I'll manage," I said.

He smiled. "Good boy. You can take a hit, so it probably won't knock you on your ass like it did to Robin here. Just be sure to only ever aim it at something you mean to hit. You got a flamethrower in that magic sack of yours, Little Girl?"

"Of course," she said without the faintest hint of irony.

"Good. Take the northern path, you'll work on covering its retreat. Benji and me here will work on driving it down to Hunter's Lake. If you hear shootin' or screamin', of course come running," he said.

She didn't even question him, pulling a flamethrower from her bag and running up the poorly-marked path. The Old Man pulled a hunting rifle from his quiver and held it in his good hand.

"You worried I'm gonna kill you?" he asked.

Lying didn't seem a good idea. "Yes."

He smiled. "Good boy. Come on."

He was crazy, twitchy, and paranoid, and was covered in guns, knives, and a giant metal hook. Even scarier was how little even Mina knew about him. She'd known him for years, but didn't know his name. Then there was the fact that many of the hunters he'd allegedly trained seemed a lot older than he was. There were scars on the back of his head that he desperately tried to cover with his fedora. And that hook, that gleaming iron hook, so casually holding the rifle up as he stalked through the forest.

"You looking at my hook, Benji?" he asked me without even turning around.

Again, lying didn't seem smart. "Yes."

"You want to know about the hook?" he asked.

I didn't say anything.

"Just say 'yes,' boy. It's my one claim to fame. Just ask about it so we can both get it over with," he said humorlessly.

I gave in. "What's with the hook?"

"Anzio, '44. Found a Kraut nice enough to give me a haircut. Unfortunately, he wanted to do it with a potato masher. He was nice enough to leave enough of me intact to have fun in Vegas and pitch southpaw, at least, and to die quick when I cleaved his head with my shovel," he said.

That didn't make any sense. He'd have to be ninety, at least, for any of this story to be true. He had to be lying.

"They didn't make good hooks back in the day. Coupla Splinter kids ripped my old one right offa me driving off when I tried to get 'em in their car. Got it right in their door handle and zoom, they're off, stealin' my hook. From that day on, I knew if I wanted somethin' done right I was gonna have to do it myself, that's when I started makin' beauties like these."

This was too much. I couldn't help it. Not after everything I'd seen, everything he'd said.

I laughed.

"What's that for?" he asked, his voice icy.

"I'm sorry, I just don't buy it. Maybe your father was old enough to have fought in World War II, but you barely look old enough to have fought in Vietnam," I said.

He shrugged. "I age well."

"Nobody ages that well," I said.

The Old Man stopped in his tracks and turned slightly toward me. "In Prospero, they do."

"And you also expect me to believe that you're The Hook? The urban legend?" I asked.

"I don't expect you to believe anything, Benji, but you should. Just know, if you keep talkin' to me like that, I will bleed you," he said.

"I can hold my own," I said. "I've helped kill a Splinterdeer. I broke into the Warehouse. I killed a Splinter with a chainsaw."

He smirked at me. He actually smirked. "Join the club."

That was it. There was no way, no way in *hell* I was going to let this arrogant old bastard talk to me like I didn't even deserve to be in the same state as his precious Robin. I could fight, I could probably do everything he could and then some.

An inhuman growl in the forest in front of us cut off my

train of thought. The Old Man held his hook up to silence me. I followed his lead, crouching low with my gun held high, slowly making our way through the trees.

We found them in a clearing about a hundred feet ahead. Two of them, each about seven feet tall. They looked like bad parodies of people, too long and hunched over, with flat animalistic faces and covered in long, stringy hair. One had silvery white hair and a rat-like tail that curled around one of its legs, the other had shorter brown fur and a stubby, bushy tail that twitched nervously. True to form, their feet were enormous.

The silvery one ran its fingers through the other's fur, trying to force it to stand upright. The brown Splinter seemed barely able to stand up, let alone stand up straight.

The Old Man chuckled. "A squirrel and a possum. You're in for a treat, Benji."

He whistled like one of the many birds that filled this forest. The Splinters paid it no mind. A returning whistle came from the other side of the clearing. Mina.

The Old Man calmly raised his rifle, aimed, and took a shot. The top half of the Possum-Bigfoot's head exploded; bright red and green matter splattering against a nearby tree. Its eyes looked confused, hurt, as it reached up to feel the spot where its brain used to be, let out a howl of grief and fell over. I knew it wouldn't be dead for long, but it was still a jarring sight.

The Squirrel-Bigfoot knelt down beside its (not friend) partner and let out a chittering howl of all-too-human pain. The Old Man took another shot. This one caught the Squirrel-Splinter in the shoulder. It started to run away.

Before I knew what I was doing, I took a shot at it, blowing a chunk the size of a dinner-plate from a nearby tree. The recoil felt like it would rip my shoulder off.

The Old Man was laughing.

"We got him on the run now!" he cheered, running after the fleeing Squirrel-Bigfoot. "Come on, Robin, clean up here so we can take the last one down!"

Mina darted out of the forest toward the downed Possum-Bigfoot. Its head slowly reformed with crackling, slurping sounds as the splattered chunks crawled back to its ruined skull like a swarm of slugs. It had pushed itself onto all fours and was trying to regain its footing. Mina was on it before this could happen, transforming the howling, screaming creature into a fireball before it could find its feet.

I had no time to take this in. I followed The Old Man as he chased after the Squirrel-Bigfoot. Every so often, he would take a running shot with his rifle, not at the creature, but guiding it with every missed bullet.

It looked despondently at the massive lake we'd led it to. The Old Man had chased it into a position where it could run no longer. The guy may have been completely insane, but I had to admit he knew what he was doing in this situation.

I ran up behind it. The Splinter turned to face me. Its face looked so pitiful, almost human, with beady black eyes, a twitchy, whiskered nose and buck teeth that didn't belong in that face. It looked at me almost pleadingly, just asking for a chance to live.

The crack of a rifle filled the air, a bloody hole ripped

through the creature's chest. Another caught it in the neck. It howled and hissed. It started to transform with that snapping wood sound, tentacles and extra arms bursting from its back and face as it ran for The Old Man.

I fired a shotgun blast at it. I missed again, but distracted it enough for The Old Man to shoot it three times in the chest, knocking it to the ground.

It looked utterly defeated, lying on its back, breathing heavily and feebly trying to pull itself back together. It moaned, almost sounding human.

"Well done, son, well done. There's hope for you yet!" he said. He sheathed his rifle, and made his way to a nearby tree.

"You've got some work to do," he said, removing his quiver and setting it down at the tree's base. "You still have mercy, and you need some time at a firing range, but you could be a hunter yet!"

"I don't want to be a hunter," I said, tossing the empty shotgun at his feet. He smiled, clearing dry bush from the base of the tree to reveal a vintage, military-grade flamethrower.

"Not yet. Give it time," he said, hefting the heavy weapon onto his back.

Finally, Mina joined us. She looked first at The Old Man, then at me with something that might have been gratitude. When I realized she was glad The Old Man hadn't killed me, I felt only irritation.

This is not the life I wanted to live.

This is not a life that should be lived.

This is not a life.

Without saying anything, the three of us walked down to the dying Splinter. Like its (friend) partner, it was trying to get back to its feet. Trying to run away from us, trying to run anywhere it wouldn't be hurt.

Laughing like a loon, The Old Man set the Splinter ablaze. We watched it collapse to the ground, its flesh dissolving into a river of gray ooze and its bones crumbling to ash. With a faint smile, Mina gently took The Old Man's hook in her hand. He smiled down at her gesture of tenderness, then looked at me like a proud father.

"So, who wants some chili?"

13.

SPLINTERS, SLIVERS, SHARDS, AND THE OTHER THINGS UNDER OUR SKIN

Mina

No two things The Old Man cooked ever tasted exactly the same. His "chili" was rarely spicy enough to warrant the name, for which I was glad, and there were too many variables between what he could catch, gather, and loot from his different hideouts at different times of the year. There was enough commonality, though, that the taste of the mountain sage and what I was almost sure was rabbit made me uncomfortably homesick for a string of other shacks much like this one, but not uncomfortable enough to stop eating.

I'd spent as much as I could of the years between nine and fourteen in these hills with him. He burned and rebuilt his shelters at new locations every few months at most, but the basic style of them hadn't changed. This one was made from a fallen metal trail sign, camouflaged with mud and wedged against the top of a small hollow in the rock face as a lean-to, doubling the floor space of what could just barely be called a cave.

The inside contained the usual essentials, a small fire pit with the chili bubbling over it, an old sleeping bag, basic clothes and weapons, cooking utensils, the remnants of earlier non-Splinter hunting trips. Small as the space was, it made me feel smaller, nine years old again, both terrified and bursting with excitement to be there. I hoped it didn't show.

For too many reasons, I couldn't be that anymore.

Ben declined the chili, kept eyeing a couple of the bear traps hanging from the sheet metal ceiling, and, when The Old Man turned to scoop himself another bowl, he leaned over to my ear and whispered, "This is exactly how I always pictured a serial killer's hideout."

He could have been making a better first impression. Then again, I suppose they both could have.

"Close enough, Benji," The Old Man answered as if the comment had been part of open conversation. "Would be, if I were killing humans."

I didn't speak, but The Old Man shot me a look anyway.

"Ah yes, but we still disagree on that point, don't we? This girl was quite the tenacious little exterminator," he reached across to pat me on the head while still watching Ben, "before she went all noble on me. We could have wiped this town clean by now, her and me, if she'd stuck around."

"We would have burned it to the ground by now if I'd stuck around," I said.

"It wouldn't have Splinters anymore, though, would it?"

he barked a short laugh. "You know she killed a humanoid all by herself a couple years back?"

"Speaking of killing," I interrupted. It seemed as good a time as any to dispense with the reunion festivities and get to the point. "I didn't actually contact you for a reconciliation. You're in trouble. Someone's been picking off hunters and sending me the proof. Unless you've got more apprentices you never told me about, we're the only two left from the old days."

Ben looked at me sharply after the last detail, but he didn't complain out loud.

"Sweet of you to worry, Robin. I've got it covered," The Old Man waved the old news away, and I could feel the wasted effort of the climb settling in my limbs.

I'd assumed he'd know. This meeting had only been to make sure; now that I had, I could think of lots of more productive ways to spend a Sunday afternoon.

"It's too bad about the others, of course, but *I've* still got eyes in the back of my head. It's been too long since I got to take down Shards."

"Shards?" I asked him at the same time Ben asked me.

"A *Shard* is what's been causing all this trouble for the rustier hunters," The Old Man explained. "They're like plain old Splinters, only sharper."

I waited for him to finish laughing at his own joke, and thankfully, Ben did too.

"It's what I like to call the ones that come with a little extra kick."

"Extra kick?" Ben asked. "You mean more than the whole

'changing shape and consistency at will, not depending on vital organs' kick?"

"Yep, more than that." He clearly enjoyed the unnerved look on Ben's face.

I didn't ask why he'd never told me about Shards. I didn't think Ben would let me live it down if I did. The Old Man answered anyway.

"Haven't seen one in a good thirty years. Mercenaries. Problem solvers. Vicious sons of bitches. The Splinters only bring them out when they're really riled up about something. Glad it took them this long to bring out another. If I'd had you worrying about those when you were still learning to hold that thing," he nodded at the nearest rifle, resting against the wall at my side, "you'd never have learned to keep it steady."

"I think I would have," I said simply and tried to sound sure.

"I knew one that could move things by looking at them and fly without growing itself wings. There was one that could turn things, not living things, but anything else, to liquid. You could be standing on a nice slab of concrete near this one and suddenly splash through it like quicksand, just like *that*." He illustrated his point quite vividly with his bowl of chili and makeshift wooden spoon and laughed again. Ben visibly disapproved, which was fine. This wasn't the sort of joke we were supposed to laugh along with. Watching them disapprove of each other made something occur to me that struck my feverish brain as disproportionately funny.

Ben turned his disapproving look on me when I stifled the laugh.

"Wouldn't be funny if you were standing there," The Old Man said, dropping his own laughter and pointing to his bowl.

"No, I know, it's just that Ben nicknamed another kind of Splinter sort of the same way."

"Is that so?" The Old Man prompted Ben before I could babble embarrassingly about them having more in common than they thought.

"Slivers," Ben explained. "For the Splinters who don't answer to the main collective."

The Old Man looked back at me with an expression I'd vary rarely seen on him, surprise mingled with very mild curiosity.

"Yes, as long as we're here, we should probably mention that, too," I said. "The Splinters aren't all working together anymore. A few months ago, Ben and I were targeted by a group that's trying to destabilize the arrangements between the Splinters and the Council. The Slivers, we're calling them, actually tried to sacrifice one of *them* to *us* to provoke the regular Splinters against the humans."

The Old Man took another spoonful and swallowed without comment.

"This Shard," Ben asked him, "if you've been keeping an eye on it, have you seen anything like that? Any idea if it might be working for the Splinters or the Slivers?"

The Old Man shrugged. "Doesn't matter. A Splinter's a Splinter, whether it's a Shard or a 'Sliver' on top of that or not. They all want us dead so they can steal what's ours, they all melt when you burn 'em bad enough. If they want to help wipe each other out, that's fine by me. It's not going to slow me down any. Shouldn't slow you kids down either. And don't you dare chalk this up as me agreeing with a Splinter, but let 'em do their worst to the Council. Filthy collaborators."

"There's no reason to invite any kind of Splinters to take the entire town if we can avoid it," Ben said.

The Old Man's face went dangerously rigid, and there was silence for several seconds while I searched for the words to fix Ben's argument. I wasn't quick enough.

"Is this the kind of placating, compromising shit you're preaching to your people now, Robin? Or have you caught the habit of letting rookies preach to you?"

"It's not compromise; it's strategy," I clarified. "He means there's no need to disrupt the only thing holding off a full-scale invasion until we've got more than a handful of people with flamethrowers to fight back with because that's what we're talking about if the Slivers succeed."

"Goddammit, Robin," The Old Man slammed his hook against the recently bubbling pot with a clang. "I knew you'd lose your edge if you left me, but I never thought you could really get dull."

"Coming from a blunt object like you," I could pretend it was my newly weakened mental filter that let those words out, or the fact that if I left Ben room to say anything more, the repercussions were likely to be worse for him than for me. The truth is that, when it came to The Old Man, my filter had always been a little faulty.

"Your mother inducted you into the family business yet?

Is she whoring you out to them already, or is she waiting to sell you off all at once to the highest bidder?" He looked back at Ben. "Is that what this is? Are you two all set to be the next pair of 'peacemakers' like your folks?"

I dropped my bowl half a second before The Old Man dropped his and reached for the gun at my side. He dragged it away with his foot before the chili hit the ground, splattering across half his shirt along the way. I grabbed a Taser from my bag instead and aimed it at The Old Man's chest at the same moment he grabbed one of his own from one of the countless hiding places in the cluttered shack and aimed it at Ben.

I had to hold mine with two hands to keep it from shaking when I wedged myself into the small space between them, uncomfortably close to the fire, my back pressed against Ben, who was pinned to the rock. I remembered that Taser vividly. It hurt.

"What do you need that for?" The Old Man asked with his cheapest imitation of calm. He tapped the side of his head with his hook, where the shrapnel that had forced the Warehouse to reject him was buried. "You know I'm human."

"So is he!" I shouted less composedly than I meant to. "And it'll slow you down long enough for me to get my hands on something stronger." I looked at the rifle he'd kicked away as if we didn't both already know exactly where it had landed.

"You came here because you felt responsible for keeping me alive." He snorted, but it sounded more like a preparation to spit than laugh. "You're not going to shoot me,

Little Girl. You didn't do it for the last Splinter boy, and you won't do it for this one."

"He's human!" I repeated

"Doesn't mean I'm wrong. Sam Todd was human once."

"You are wrong, and a Taser won't tell you what he's going to be anyway! He's human now!"

"I just want to check. It's not like it'll kill him."

I've never used electricity to test Network members. That was the second of The Old Man's policies, after killing human Splinters, that I'd been quickest to abolish on my own. Partly because I prefer not to inflict a sensation on allies that I can barely tolerate myself, but also because it's not foolproof. Electricity will wear any Splinter down eventually, most of them very quickly, but in my time with The Old Man, I'd seen a few take enough to stop a human heart before losing their shape.

"You already know he's human, or you wouldn't have asked me to bring him."

"I thought I knew because I thought I could still trust you, Little Girl."

"I am not a collaborator!" I shouted. "And I am *nothing* like my mother! And even if I were, if I were in bed with a Splinter and planning to keep it alive, why the hell would I risk bringing it up here to meet you? Just because you might not listen to me about the Shard if I didn't follow your instructions to the letter? Do you really think your life would be that important to me then? I don't think there's anyone on earth that dull!"

In absolute silence, without the slightest change on his face, The Old Man leaned in to rest the Taser against my chest—Ben's and mine, really, the way we were crammed together, one conductive circuit—ignoring the way the Taser in my hands jabbed into his sternum when he got close enough. My hand was ready to clench on the trigger in the first convulsion.

It took the whole cavern of my mind to keep my breath and my gaze too steady to criticize.

The Old Man lasted this way for seven and a half seconds before cracking into deep, hoarse laughter.

"Oh, thank God you're still making sense, Little Girl! You had me worried for a moment!"

The moment I joined him, relief slipping out in unsteady breaths that only laughter could conceal, Ben wriggled out from behind me and ducked out through the open doorway.

Saying goodbye to The Old Man was difficult for a multitude of reasons. There were his repeated protestations that I'd "just arrived," that I was "getting too old to run away and cover my ears just because he'd said a few things I didn't like to hear," and that I'd "never be able to lead a successful resistance if I kept letting the pretty rookie boys lead me around by the tit."

All his words, not mine.

There was the involuntary way I kept wondering whether this was the last time we'd see each other alive, and whether I wanted it to be.

And then there was the fact that every second I spent trying to form that goodbye was another step Ben was taking down the trail outside.

My last words were the same as the first time I'd left.

"Let go of me."

Ben didn't slow down for me. Even when I did catch up, it took seventeen of his strides for him to acknowledge me.

"Tell me you don't really think that guy's funny."

"Not at the moment," I answered honestly.

Two more strides.

"What was the point of all that?"

"I told you—"

"Yeah, I know, someone's trying to kill him, and you, and who knows? Maybe me, too! I'm a resistor, aren't I?"

"I never got any threats against you."

"You don't know that!" His pace quickened down the fifty degree incline. "You don't know what 'guess who I'm saving for last' means! Or maybe you do! Maybe you have some undeniable proof! Only I don't need to know about all that until you need me to dupe someone for you, or until he tells you, 'bring the new boy.' I don't even need to know when your *birthday* is, but *him* you'll warn, even if it means spending a day dragging me up here and letting him do whatever he feels like to both of us."

"He wasn't really going to hurt you."

Ben rubbed his right shoulder where the recoil always hit. "Really? Because it sure looked like he was."

"I wouldn't have let him."

"Great. Thanks a lot. That's so comforting after you brought me here in the first place!"

That wasn't fair. I was sure it wasn't, despite my overre-acting nerves. "You're the one who's always complaining about not being included enough," I pointed out.

"Don't even pretend you're starting to listen," he said,

forcing an increasingly uncomfortable pace down through the loose dirt. "You brought me because he said to. How did you ever fall in with a jackass like that?"

"I—"

"Don't lie again."

"I wasn't going to!" I shouted. Without thinking about it, I grabbed him by the shirt to make him stop and turn toward me. He let me, barely. "I was nine years old when I lost my father!"

"I managed," Ben snapped. "Without picking Leatherface for a substitute!"

"You had a mother who wasn't the reason your dad was gone!" Any grasp I'd ever had on tact was gone, but I wasn't finding honesty to be a problem. "Until very recently, *my* mother did nothing about it but tell me I was making it up! The Old Man was the only one who'd listen to me, who'd teach me how to protect myself when they came for me, which they have done, whatever Dad claims the arrangements were! I'd be dead more times than I can count by now if it weren't for him!"

"Well, he sure explains a lot about you if he's basically your dad, I'll give him that."

This produced a pain in my stomach, a compression from more sides than I could consciously catalogue.

"What does that mean?"

"You'd be dead if it weren't for me, too," Ben reminded me. "At least a couple times. Doesn't seem to compel you to leap to my defense at every opportunity."

"You'd be in the Warehouse if it weren't for me! And what do you call what I just did?"

"Damage control," Ben answered, "and not much of it. When we get back down there," he pointed down the hill-side in the rough direction of town, "the Splinters, Slivers, Shards, whoever, are going to go right back to doing every-thing they can to make my life a living hell, and you're just going to sit back and watch! Maybe if you're feeling generous, you'll take the time to tell me to suck it up!"

"What do you want me to do about it?"

"*Anything!*"

The word echoed back off of the hills on all sides, and he waited for me to answer it. How, I didn't know.

"I promise, if there were anything that would make a practical difference—"

That made him laugh, a more painful sound than the most mocking snicker The Old Man could manage. "Never mind, don't bother."

He pushed me, not hard, but far enough to break my grip on his shirt, reached into his backpack for the last full water bottle, and shoved it into my hands.

"Your mother will still pick you up if you call her, won't she?"

The stomach pain tightened.

"Ben, you've been through a lot recently. I'll understand, if you're not feeling rational, if you need to discuss . . . whatever this is, later."

The laugh again.

"No, Mina, that's not what I need."

"Then *what?*"

He took a step backward, zipping the backpack back up.

"Ben."

"What?"

The thin filter let an almost-whisper through.

"Don't do this."

"Why?"

"Because . . ." No tact, no forethought, just instinct and honesty; it was alarmingly difficult to switch off. "I . . . need . . . you."

"For what?"

"There are too few of us already."

"To fight them, you mean? Try again."

For some reason, I was more afraid of this than I ever had been of a Taser. "Please tell me what you want."

Ben lowered his voice, as if he were helping me cheat in class, against his better judgment.

As if he ever would.

"I want an answer that doesn't involve Splinters."

My sore, unkempt brain exploded with nonsensical answers to be sorted and purged and edited, things too jumbled and stupid to be allowed out, especially in my current condition.

Because I'm forgetting how to be without you, and I don't think I want to remember.

That was the closest I could get to an acceptable, coherent thought. I put my hands on either side of my head, as if I could manually squeeze the space small enough to use. "I can't—"

"No," Ben said. "You really can't, can you?"

He took off again, cutting toward a steep wash at the edge, not even a trail, leading down to a lower plateau.

"You'll get lost," I called after him.

"Boy Scout, remember? I'll be fine."

"These aren't regular hiking trails!"

He spun around and pulled out his phone, walking backward unsettlingly close to the edge. "You know where the Warehouse is. Watch my tracker. Or don't. I don't care, just stay the hell away from me!"

Ben's fast, but he doesn't have my stamina or my balance on uneven ground. If I'd tried to chase him through the trees he stormed off into, to whatever parallel trail he ended up finding, he probably wouldn't even have been able to break visual contact. I could have followed his steps until he ran out of breath, and then he'd have no way to shake me before we got back to town.

But then what? Tell him I was sorry for everything I'd already apologized for and anything else he could think of to blame on me, whether it made sense or not? Tell him that I just wasn't feeling myself lately, because maybe I really wasn't myself anymore? Tell him he wasn't the only one who could feel betrayed and abandoned?

Scream?

Hit him?

Hug him?

Cry?

All the things I felt like doing were crazier than the voices and visions that could still reemerge at any moment.

I couldn't do that.

I couldn't follow people around only to beg them to tolerate my presence.

I could handle being pushed away when I didn't fight it. I could handle being alone. I could handle a Taser to the chest if it was absolutely necessary. But I couldn't handle being that helpless, that pathetic.

That hurt too much.

So I fell back to the only alternative I've ever found. I turned toward home, opened the tracker app on my phone as I walked, and through the safe, impermeable surface of the Gorilla Glass touchscreen, I watched Ben walk away.

14.

Ben

The calendar on my bedroom wall read October 28th. It
was a Sunday afternoon. The trees outside my window
were losing their leaves, breaking out in a brilliant rash of
oranges, reds, and browns. I remember thinking, right after
we moved in, that those trees looked so close, so clear, that
I could reach out and touch them if I wanted to.

I couldn't see them now. My window was gone; in its
place hung a semi-clear tarp and the duct tape that held
it in the gaping maw where glass used to be. Jagged, glittering shards littered the floor. Mom was on the phone
downstairs talking to one of the town's few window-repair
places. She'd already called the police, and they said they'd
send someone down to take a report, but I knew that their
efforts would be token at best.

Nobody would spend much time looking out for the
town pariah.

Kneeling down on the floor, being sure to mind the
pieces of glass that still covered it, I finally found it. The

rock had rolled beneath my bed. I grabbed it, rolling the worn stone over in my hands. I was not surprised to see a single word painted on it in bright, white letters:

CONFESS

Probably Patrick's handiwork, or one of his goons'; "Confess" had become one of his favorite words lately.

I tossed the stone in my trash can, too hard. The metal can fell over, spilling odd balls of paper on the ground. A couple rolled toward my doorway. Mom stood there, holding a broom and a dustpan. She forced a smile.

"You know you're going to have to clean that up," she said.

"How long before they can fix the window?" I asked harshly.

Her sympathetic smile disappeared. "How about we try that again with a little less attitude?"

In a heartbeat I was transformed into a little kid with his hand caught in the cookie jar.

She continued. "I know you're having a bad month, but I raised you better than this."

"You did, Mom. I'm sorry," I said. I owed her so much. Through all this, she'd been one of the only people who'd been completely on my side.

"It's all right," she said, her smile returning, mostly. "And to answer your question, they'll be by on Wednesday to fix the window."

"Thanks," I said, taking the broom and dustpan from her. Wednesday would be Halloween, the one day of the year I used to look forward to more than Christmas when I was little. There would be no candy or costumes this year, just barricading in and hoping to survive until the next morning. Like pretty much any day, lately. I didn't want to think about it.

She bit her lip nervously. "That's assuming you still want to be here on Wednesday?"

I didn't say anything. I couldn't say anything.

"I thought that Prospero would be good for us. Would be good for *you*. That clearly isn't the case. We can go back to San Diego. I can beg for my old job, our old apartment. We could try to put things back together, back the way they used to be. God knows you've followed me every time I wanted a change. I think you've gotten old enough to have a say in whether or not we do it again," she said.

It sounded tempting. More tempting than I ever thought it could. Before we'd moved to Prospero, I would have said that I wanted stability more than anything else in life. Now I would have given anything to escape, to leave Prospero, the Splinters—even Mina—behind.

But here, with this treaty in place, escape was not an option.

"It's just high school stuff. I'll survive," I said.

"You're sure?" she asked.

"Sure enough," I said, forcing a smile. I knew she didn't buy a word of what I was saying, but she backed off anyway.

"Just let me know if you need anything," she said.

"I will," I replied.

I hated lying to my mom, but I had to do it a lot these days. She was such a gentle soul; I didn't know what the truth would do to her.

Kneeling back down, I began to sweep up the glass. It

was hard not to see that glittering mess of shards as what my life had turned into over this last month.

If only it were as easy to clean up.

I had no trouble calling it the second-worst month of my life, though with three days to go, it could still make a run for the top spot. The last month of Dad's life—watching him waste away from the vital, strong man who raised me—was still number one; though I was sure the Splinters had a few ideas left.

It started after the party with a barrage of hate online and on my phone. Those were easy enough to ignore. I could change my security settings. I could block numbers.

It's when I got back to school that things really started to go to hell.

Wherever I went, people were quiet, whispering terrible things, looking at me like I was the scum of the earth. Most of them were content to pretend I didn't exist whenever I entered a room.

Then there were those who decided to act on Madison's lies.

Like Patrick.

When nothing happened during that first gym class, I thought I was in the clear. It was when we were changing afterward and most of the class had already left that he, Robbie, and a couple of his other large, scary-looking friends pinned me to a locker.

"You really are a piece of work, you know?" he hissed. "You make like you're the good guy, but you're hiding that you're a real sick son of a bitch."

I tried to protest, to explain. Before I could, he

sucker-punched me in the stomach so hard it felt like I'd been hit by a sledgehammer. My knees gave out, and I fell to the floor, retching.

He grabbed me by the hair and forced me to look him in the eyes. "You stay away from Madison. If I hear about you bothering her again . . . I'll kill you."

I told them I would, but I took Patrick slamming my head into a locker to mean he didn't entirely believe me.

A few days later, I was called into the principal's office, and told that the police wanted to speak to me. At the time, I was thankful when it appeared to have nothing to do with Madison. Apparently someone had given the police pictures of me drinking at the party. They said there would be a fine if official charges were filed, but that I would get some leniency if I gave them some names. I knew Mom would support me no matter what happened (her views on underage drinking were quite liberal), and not wanting to make any more enemies, I said nothing. I told myself I'd get a job if I had to repay Mom for the fine.

In the following days, twenty more people from the party were called into the office by the police. They all got marks on their record and fines; two of them were even arrested. Word got out that I had named names, and much as I protested this accusation, I was now a snitch in addition to a monster.

A week after that, right in the middle of a calculus test, I could hear the skittering sound of a Splinter in the room. I looked around fearfully, trying to find the creature.

Then I looked up.

A small Splinter-drone, a severed hand by the looks of it

(though all the extra insect-legs and tentacles it had grown made it hard to tell for sure), crawled across the ceiling until it was above my desk. Though I wanted to cry out in surprise, I couldn't make a sound. It waved two fingers at me tauntingly, then opened a slit-like mouth on its back, dropping a small, densely-folded piece of paper on my desk. Curious and more than a little afraid, I opened it up. It was covered in mathematical formulas and diagrams.

A voice behind me. "Ms. Velasquez? I think Ben's cheating."

Again I was called into the principal's office with my mom. I failed the test and was told I was lucky not to be kicked out of school, as they have a zero-tolerance policy on cheating. Only the fact that it clearly wasn't in my handwriting saved me.

Add cheater to my growing list of unenviable titles.

Not long after this, my cell phone went missing for a day. I wasn't surprised when it magically appeared back in my gym locker, nor when I was called into the office once again and told to hand the phone over. No, it wasn't particularly surprising that my phone was now full of pictures of girls in various states of undress in the locker room.

To the office. Again.

Police called in. Again.

Mom called in. Again.

Extra counseling sessions and a mandatory sensitivity class next semester. These were new.

Every time something like this happened, I was sure to see Madison not too far away. Smiling, smirking, but still looking oh-so-wounded and afraid from what I might have done to her. No matter what was done to me, they did an excellent job of ensuring that it was something that could be undone if I were ever to surrender. She never had to say a word, she just had to look at me and nod.

I wanted to kill her. I wanted to kill her, and every other Splinter in town, slowly. I wanted to see Mina's dad die in flames. I told myself that I wouldn't break; I repeated it every day, and every day it got more difficult to say.

Soon people started blaming me for any little thing that went wrong at school. Freshman got beat up? It must have been Ben! Someone stole five dollars from the cafeteria cash register? It must be that new kid with emotional problems! The pizza guy is late? It must somehow be Ben's fault! It chipped away at me a little bit every day, and much as I wanted to be strong, I knew that one day I would fall.

I wasn't completely alone, no matter how much I wanted to be. Kevin and Haley did their best to stand by me. They wanted to help. I didn't want them to. If they did, the Splinters would only turn their attention to them too. I wouldn't drag them down with me.

Mom was there for me, of course; Aldo even tried to talk to me once before I sent him away; and Mr. Montresor, my counselor at school, did his best to provide a sympathetic ear. I couldn't be honest with him, not with all the listening devices planted in that room.

Never once, in this time, did I hear from Mina Todd. I don't know if I wanted to hear from her after everything that had happened with The Old Man, but being so easily cut off by her hurt terribly.

I winced in pain as a sliver of glass from the window cut

into my finger. I pulled it out, tossing it into the trash can. I didn't want to think about Mina Todd being right across the street and that she probably hadn't thought about me once in the four weeks we'd been apart.

I didn't want to think about how much her disappearing from my life made me want to take Madison's offer, if just to make this all go away.

"I love what you've done with the place."

Haley stood in the doorway, a couple of shopping bags in one hand, a large pumpkin held under her other arm.

"Get out of here, Haley. You don't want to be here," I said.

She tossed the pumpkin and bags on my bed. "Yes, I do."

"I'm dangerous to be around. If the Splinters find out, they'll—"

"They'll do what? They stole three months of my life. Honestly, what could they possibly do to me that's worse?" she asked.

"Are you here to give me some motivational 'buck up and power through it' speech? That if I just let you guys help me, we can all make it through together?" I asked.

"No," she said.

"Are you here to tell me you guys have come up with some half-cocked scheme to try and get me out of this that will probably backfire horribly?"

"No," she repeated. "Not that killing Madison hasn't crossed my mind."

I looked at her, dubious.

"Hey, I thought she was my friend. When I found out she was one of the people who might've taken me . . . At least Mina talked me out of it," she said.

"Don't say that name," I spat back, too harshly. Even hearing her name hurt.

"Sorry, I won't," Haley said softly.

"Why *are* you here?" I asked.

As if in answer, she pointed to the pumpkin on my bed.

"I'm here to carve a jack-o-lantern," she said.

I looked at her, silently.

She continued. "Your mom knows the kind of pain you're in now and that you won't accept any help from her, so she called me. Now I don't know if what you need is a shoulder to cry on, or someone to vent to, or someone to be around who just doesn't hate your guts. You may need all of that, you may need none of that. But if there's one thing you do need, it's a jack-o-lantern. Your house is seriously lacking Halloween spirit, and I know *that* is something I can help with."

Her smile was confident and firm.

"There's nothing I can say that will get rid of you, is there?" I asked.

"Nope," she said, almost perky. I wanted to hate her for staying here when I wanted to be alone, but it was hard to say no to her.

"Then you should probably grab a knife and some garbage bags. Let me clean up this glass first?" I asked.

"Sure," she said.

I cleaned. She gathered supplies. I was numb, angry, and confused, but feeling slightly calmer with her there.

The floor clean of glass, Haley spread out a few trash bags as a makeshift operating area for the pumpkin. She gave me a marker and tasked me with the design. I'm not an artist; I can barely draw stick figures, but I did my best to make an appropriately fierce jack-o-lantern face. As I did this, she looked for Halloween music in my iPod. She was less than thrilled at what I had loaded.

"Styx? Crowded House? Derek and the Dominoes? Don't you have anything from this century?" she asked, skeptically.

Dad's music. I tried to play it off casually. "I'm a sucker for the classics."

Dissatisfied with my selection, I saw her pick at random, clearly wanting something in the background. The opening guitar chords of "Layla" filled the room.

"Sad song," Haley said, listening to the lyrics.

"Then change it," I said. It was a personal favorite of mine, but its words filled me with a sadness I wasn't quite prepared for.

"No, I think I like it," she said.

"So, what's in the bags?" I asked, trying to distract myself.

"Some fake cobwebs, a couple plastic tombstones. Can't have the jack-o-lantern alone out there, can we?" she asked.

"No, I guess not," I said.

"I even got you a costume," she said, a little bashful.

"That was a waste of money," I said.

"I figured you'd say something like that," she said, sitting down beside me. "First, I got it on sale, so I didn't waste that much, and second, I know you don't want to go out because you don't want to be seen, but this is Halloween. Everybody gets to be somebody else, and if you wear this, nobody has to know who you are."

I looked into the bag skeptically, saw the elaborate

werewolf mask and gloves and knew that she lied about getting these on sale. Not that her offer didn't sound tempting in the back of my brain, the part of me that still remembered how to be Ben Pastor.

"Besides, I've got some ulterior motives with this," she said.

"Oh?" I asked.

She nodded. "I'm working the 'Ghosts of the Miracle Mine Haunted Hayride' up by the old historical cemetery this year. You know, hide in the trees wearing scary costumes, jump out when the tractor comes by, and scare all the housewives and kids. We're shy some bodies, and we could really use your help if you don't have any other plans."

"You need a werewolf with your ghosts?" I asked.

"Hey, I never said it was a *good* haunted hayride, but we make do with what we can," she explained.

"I'll think about it," I lied.

"You do that," she said, handing me the knife. "So, where do you want to start?"

I looked at the knife. I set it down.

I had to say it.

"So you've talked to her?" I asked.

She didn't need me to explain who I was talking about. "A couple times. Mostly just checking in, seeing if there was anything I could do to help. I think she's trying to dodge me."

"You're not alone," I said.

Haley looked at me sympathetically. "You mean, you haven't . . ."

I laughed bitterly. "Not since I told her to get the hell

away from me. I thought she might try to call me still, maybe try to apologize, and that I'd come to my senses and we'd be able to work things out. But she hasn't. I told her to leave me alone, and in that goddamn compartmentalized brain of hers, she's done just that. I only see her at school when it can't be avoided, and she never says anything to me. At first I didn't call her on principle, but now, I don't even know if I could stand to talk to her."

The tears were coming. I didn't know if I'd be able to hold them back.

"You know, I actually started to think she was my best friend?" I said. "I haven't had one of those in . . . forever, I think. The way we moved around, I never tried to make one because I knew it wouldn't last, but with this, even as messed up as it is, I thought I could finally make a connection. I knew she was weird, but I thought I understood her. I thought that no matter how bad things got, I could get through it if I had her on my side. I thought that if she was here, she'd find a way to keep me from giving up."

The tears rolled freely down my cheeks. I should have been embarrassed, but I didn't care.

"I hate her so much right now, but there's no one I want to see more. How screwed up is that?"

I fell apart there on the floor, holding my head in my hands and sobbing. I could feel Haley wrapping her arms around me. I could hear her telling me that everything was going to be all right, but by then I was broken.

They were winning.

15.

THE SECOND WORST NIGHT OF MINE

Mina

It had become quite evident that Ben's absence, even in large doses, lacked any quantifiable curative properties whatsoever.

In the following weeks without him, the hallucinations continued unabated, and the pain in my stomach spread up to my chest and lymph nodes and settled there.

Grief is my least favorite sensation, one notch below electrocution, even, but I have a lot of experience feeling it while maintaining maximum functionality.

My weakened brain stung and shuddered when I clenched it protectively around the compromised part of itself, around my relevant memories and aching body parts like a layer of cast-iron armor, and for the moment, it held.

It was my own fault. I'd known when I'd stayed in contact with Ben after the Warehouse that I was risking this again. And I'd gotten lucky this time. If things between us had become any more intense, the pain would have been more intense too.

I directed my eyes and hands through ordinary tasks, waiting for them to become as effortless as they should be again. I sifted through the counselor's computer files and did my best to compile a list of Shard suspects. It wasn't easy to narrow. In fact, the inconclusive nature of all the evidence put Courtney pretty close to the top. There was Madison, too, of course. She'd been a Splinter for about the right amount of time judging by her records. The only problem was the way she'd been assigned to reveal herself to Ben. A Shard's secret was likely to be better guarded than that.

Cayden had been flagged for unusual mood swings recently, and he would be a smart choice if I was on the hit list, since he had always lunched almost within earshot of me. But then he'd been going through dramatic, moody phases for as long as I'd known him.

Almost the entire theatrical society was worth watching out for, too, of course. They were always under close Splinter watch, and a few of them had had emotional outbursts at school recently, but with artistic personalities, that wasn't too unusual.

I also tried to figure out just what this Shard's ability was. Based on the deaths so far, particularly the one with the barricaded freezer, my best guess was some form of teleportation, something that would allow the Shard to kill, dress up the deaths according to pattern, and be gone without a trace, even if there were witnesses seconds away.

Unfortunately, there was still one more thing I had to do that required opening my mental armor enough to think about Ben, just a little.

I thought once he'd separated himself from me, the Splinters would stop the smear campaign, leave him to what little peace could be found in Prospero, and spare me this one particularly daunting task.

They'd done a lot of damage, so for a while I convinced myself that Ben's relief was still coming. When it still hadn't arrived on the evening of October 30th, more than a month after our separation and only one day from the second most vicious prank day of the high school calendar, I finally dragged together what I could of my strength and my mind and knocked on the open door of my father's workshop.

Mom was working late, so there had been no need for us to meet and make conversation over our separate, improvised dinners. He turned to look up from his workbench with convincing surprise.

"Mina, sweetie, I can't remember the last time you came to join me in here!"

He had to know that the imitation of innocent fatherly affection was useless, but he had an unsettling way of making me feel almost like he wanted it to be true.

"Need help fixing something up?"

"You could say that," I said, then regretted it because it made him smile. "Did you really authorize a harassment campaign to coerce Ben into disassociating himself from me?"

The smile and innocence vanished. I wished they'd take the fatherly affection with them.

"I'm sorry, sweetie, you really didn't leave me much choice."

The phantom iron around my internal organs went

surprisingly cold just then, as if I'd actually been hoping he'd deny it. "*I* didn't leave you a choice?"

"I do want you to have friends, believe it or not," he said. "It's what you do with them that's the issue. And you do it a little too well with him. It had people frightened."

"You mean Haley? We talked about this. You said you'd made a deal for us. This wasn't part of it." I kept my voice steady through my own uncomfortable implication that I'd actually expected him to keep his word.

"You didn't stop," he said. "We have word you interfered with a replacement on your first day at school together."

"This is about *Courtney*? Those weren't even your people who were after her, were they? Your people are better at it than that!"

"Yes," Dad agreed calmly, "we are. But if it had been my people, would it have stopped you two?"

I couldn't pretend it would have.

"We haven't broken the treaty," I said.

"Neither have we," Dad pointed out. "Sweetie, if I'd insisted on keeping the two of you untouchable *and* together after that, I'd have had a riot on my hands. One of my people would have turned vigilante on him by now no matter what I said."

"So you decided to provoke the humans into handling the vigilantism for you, is that it? You're trying to keep your hands clean?"

"The humans aren't going to kill him!" Dad exclaimed, as if this were absurd.

"Just make him wish they would," I finished.

"Exactly! And when he's had enough, we'll make it stop, I promise."

"'Had enough'?" I repeated. "What are you asking him to do now to prove he's 'had enough'? Do you want him to help kidnap humans for you?"

Dad looked appalled. "Don't be ridiculous, Mina. Didn't he even tell you our terms?"

A small pulse of stomachache leaked through the iron as I understood.

"You mean to tell me that he hasn't even promised to stay away from me for good yet?"

Hopeful, much? One of the more frequent voices in my head spoke up, louder than my own voice in the quiet workshop. It was male, young, and low. Beyond that, I couldn't have identified it even if I'd cared to try. It felt like an amalgam of every young male voice I'd ever heard. I was sure one element was just slightly stronger than the rest, but I couldn't put my finger on it.

Shut up, I thought back at it as loudly as I could without it showing on my face.

"Not yet, but he will," Dad said. "He's a stubborn boy. I can see why you like him, but he'll break, and once he does, he'll be fine."

Not yet, though, huh?

Shut up.

"We'll give him the best life we can here in Prospero. He can have anything he wants, except geographic mobility and, obviously, you. I know it'll hurt him at first, but we'll set him up nicely, I promise."

The corners of the workshop were becoming fuzzy and sparkly, and I knew I was on the verge of an episode more severe than an irritating voice in my head. I didn't have much left of this coherent moment, not enough to argue properly for Ben the way I wanted to, but it had just occurred to me that there was one more quick question it couldn't hurt to ask, for him and for me.

Running on impulse, I pulled the full stack of obituaries, envelopes and all, out of my bag and handed them to Dad.

What the hell are you doing? The male voice got sharper, almost panicked.

Shut up. ·

"Did you authorize this, too?" I asked. "And can you also promise me that it has nothing to do with him?"

Dad's eyes narrowed more the further he read.

"Yes," he said slowly, "and no."

"What do you mean, 'yes and no'?" I prompted, hoping he'd answer while my ears were still only slightly glitchy.

"I mean yes, I'm aware of the purge of your old faction, we had to do something to show the other colonies we can still keep our house in order, and yes, Ben should still be fine, but no, I didn't authorize this." He pointed to my name on one of the envelopes. "You were not to be targeted, informed, or involved in any way."

"So if I am, then Ben could be too," I finished.

Wow, out of what he just said, that's what bothers you? Shut up.

"Sweetheart, listen to me very carefully." Dad stood up from the bench and put a hand on my shoulder. "I'm going to put a stop to this. You are *not* an authorized target. If anyone tries to hurt you, if anyone threatens you again, you tell me, and I'll come down on them hard."

"Great. Thanks."

"I'm not finished," said Dad, tightening his grip slightly when I tried to back away. "No one's going to hurt you just because they think they can get away with it, but that doesn't mean you get to be stupid about this either. *Do not provoke the assassin.*"

"I get it."

"No, you don't. This isn't something you take under advisement. This is something you *do*. The people we use for this, they're not like me."

"I know that."

Slight surprise crossed his face again. "Do you? I don't know what you've seen or heard this time Mina, but our assassins, our specialists, they're dangerous, even to us. Sometimes they're the only things strong enough to get the job done. What we have to do to make them strong enough—" he broke off and started over. "They're not stable. They're not reasonable. You can't bargain with them, and you do *not* want to get in their way."

What's wrong with you, Mina? The voice hissed. *Are you actually listening to this guy? The one who as good as killed your father? Grilling him about Splinter plots is one thing, but taking his advice?*

"Okay, Dad," I said and pulled away, making a note to decide what really was and wasn't okay later.

"*Please* be careful!" he called after me while I navigated

the glowing, rippling carpet to the stairs. "And you don't have to wait so long to talk to me next time you have a problem!"

The stairwell to my room was dark, much darker than it was supposed to be, and the room itself was pitch black. Even when I fumbled my way through the thorny, Splinter-bat-infested nets my skin and ears were convinced were hanging in my way, when I turned on both the desk lamps, and leaned over the heat of one of the bulbs, I couldn't see.

Darkness lacks boundaries. There are no edges to pack things in and make them sensible and orderly, so I can't say exactly how long I stood in it, trying to think of anything it couldn't prevent me from doing, before I felt a different hand on my shoulder.

Light returned as I spun around and secured an arm lock. The colors in my room were too bright and the edges too soft, but otherwise it was almost exactly as it was supposed to be. There wasn't even a crowd of dead people in it.

There was just one dead person, the one I least wanted to see.

"Hi, Mina."

I dropped the hallucination of Shaun Brundle on the floor and proceeded to the newly visible desk. I didn't think about how long it had been since I'd seen even a photograph of him, or about how his resemblance to Kevin always made it feel more recent than it was. I didn't try to comprehend how he could look exactly the way I remembered him at fourteen, same floppy, dirty blond hair covering his ears, same gawky-tall frame, same nose and Adam's apple that he hadn't quite grown into yet—would never get the chance to grow into—and simultaneously still feel exactly my age.

A drawer opened behind me, and I didn't need to turn to tell that he was digging through the old stalker-shots of Ben that I hadn't felt up to cleaning out yet.

"Nice to see you've missed me."

"If I didn't miss you, you wouldn't be here," I snapped, and then tried to pretend I hadn't just spoken to myself out loud again.

"Same old Mina," he laughed. "Can't stand to give a compliment unless you can slap someone with it." He closed the drawer again. "It's cool. It's not like I didn't expect you to move on."

"You didn't expect anything." Just like when he was alive, it was hard not to answer where he left an opening. "Your capacity for expectations ceased when I set your Splinter on fire with you still in its pod."

"I forgave you for that, you know."

I swiveled around in my desk chair. "No, you didn't!" I hissed. "You didn't have time to forgive me because you were dead! You're still dead! The thing I'm talking to is just a bundle of my own misfiring neurons, trying to make me feel better!"

He smiled the sad, serious smile he'd always had in reserve. Serious enough to trust with life and death, but still a smile, a real smile, as if there was nowhere he'd rather be. "Under the circumstances, is that so terrible?"

I turned back to the desk and started trying to guess which of the crawling, Splinter-arachnid icons on the screen would reopen the spyware. Shaun wrapped a very solid pair of arms around me from behind, and I didn't validate their existence by trying to shake them off. I just stared at the incomprehensible screen and waited for them to disappear, trying not to feel their familiarity or the warmth of his breath on my ear.

The iron around my torso started to crack, and wherever I tried to visualize it rejoining, more of it crumbled away, flaking like burnt out charcoal.

The tears it had secured in my chest leaked out, and I let them.

I'm alone, this doesn't count. It's just me and the rest of my brain.

Shaun squeezed me tighter and kissed my quickly soaking cheek. I very nearly turned my head to kiss him back.

"It's okay. Hey, can we at least agree that I would have forgiven you?"

My diaphragm gave an involuntary spasm, and tears splashed onto my keyboard and my chest, washing away streaks of the unexplained grime.

"It's been hard on me too." He glanced, and I followed his gaze, to the kitchen paring knife I kept next to my keyboard for emergency defense, the same one I'd stabbed his Splinter with. "To be honest, I kind of thought we'd be together again by now."

I turned then, sharply enough to elbow his stomach.

He looked back at me steadily. "Mina, look at you. You've done all you can. You've given everything. There's nothing left. There's no shame in that. When will you finally feel you deserve a rest?"

We both looked back at the knife, and, for just a moment, it sparkled, reflected back a ghost image of both of us, and it was absolutely beautiful.

As I've said before, it's occasionally obvious, even to me, that it's time to call for help.

Shaun leaned in to kiss me properly. I tipped my desk chair over backward to get away. I briefly considered screaming for Dad, but for all I knew, there still might be nothing genuine in all his expressions of concern. I couldn't risk dealing with him while I wasn't myself.

I grabbed for my phone instead.

"What are you doing?"

By the time I opened my contacts folder, the screen had turned to glittery gibberish again. Luckily, the name I needed would be the one at the top.

"You're not Shaun," I told him again.

He protested. I stopped him.

"If the real Shaun still existed, any part of him, in any form, *he'd be the first one to tell me to fight this!*"

The hallucination looked sheepish, and for a moment, I almost expected it to concede to my logic and vanish.

Then it cocked its head to one side, then the other, with two horrible, Splintery, wood-snapping sounds, and grinned at me, suddenly colder than Shaun's face, even the Splinter Shaun's face, had ever managed to be.

"Can't let a guy be romantic just once, can you, Mina? Can't take it slow and smooth, gotta get right down to business. Okay, fine!"

He lunged at me, and on blind instinct, I grabbed the knife and turned it on him. It passed through his chest as if it were made of smoke—less than smoke—made of *nothing*, but the hands he closed on my neck felt perfectly real.

"That isn't where you need to stab me," Shaun laughed, only he didn't sound quite like Shaun anymore. It was that vague, familiar, male amalgam of a voice again.

I listened to the ringing of the phone, hoping I hadn't missed and hit the next name down. If the acuteness of my condition correlated at all with my emotional state, which seemed likely at that point, I might not have survived the sound of Ben's voicemail message. But the voice on the other end was live, and it was the right one.

"Now isn't a good time," Aldo whispered. There was an indiscernible raised voice in the background.

My phone was elongating itself, becoming uncomfortably scaly. The earpiece hissed and snapped at me so suddenly that I almost dropped it.

"I need you to come over," I wheezed from a foot away.

"Um, like I said—"

"Please." I brought it closer, and it latched its fangs into my ear. "*Please*." I heard my voice crack, and I didn't pretend to cough it away. "I just need . . . a couple of hours. I just need someone to watch me and make sure I don't . . ."

"Why don't you say it?" Shaun squeezed harder. What was it you used to call it, Mina? The ultimate failure? The S word. The S-U word. Worse than submit. Worse than surrender. S-U-I-"

"Make sure I don't die," I compromised with the last of the air in my lungs.

If there was an answer, my brain wasn't capable of processing it.

"Aldo?" I shaped the name, but no sound came out. After a few moments of silence, I dug the phone's teeth out of the side of my face.

You can't be strangled by your own imagination, I told myself firmly. *Take a breath.*

I could, just barely. My throat and lungs fought the contradiction every inch of the way.

On a sudden inspiration, I jerked the knife upward, toward Shaun's left hand. It connected with nothing, but the hand flashed briefly intangible like the rest of him when the blade got close enough, long enough for me to twist away. I made a grab for the window.

It retreated, further away the harder I reached for it.

"You can't run from me," Shaun told me calmly, standing on stationary ground beside me while I scrambled ineffectively toward the far side of the room. "And you can't hide, not even in a head as big as yours."

It will end, I told myself in my pathetically quiet little mental voice. *It always does. I'll wake up in the morning, I'll go to school, and everything will look normal for hours at a time.*

"You know how this ends," he said.

The knife in my hand was getting bigger, harder not to look at.

I don't do that. I'm not a coward. I have responsibilities.

"Responsibilities?" he snorted. "To what? Humanity? You don't even like humanity, Mina! Not that you can do anything for them when you try!"

That's not true.

I was suddenly at my desk, in front of the compilation of my life's work.

Shaun was leaning over me from behind again, this time with unnatural, Splintery angles in the arms he wrapped around me. "Name one thing you've accomplished! One person who was worth it!"

Aldo.

"You can't protect Aldo from Splinters! You can't even protect him from the lousy humans he lives with! You never even cared enough to try! One phone call, one mention to the school counselor, that's all it would have taken, but you couldn't do it because you knew that if it worked, they'd take him away from you, along with all his fancy tech toys!"

That's not what he would have wanted.

"He's a child! He doesn't know what he wants! You might as well trick a hatching duckling into thinking you're its mother! He's not old enough to understand that you don't really love him!"

I . . .

"Can't even contradict me!"

They're all worth it. Humans are worth it. The Network's worth it. They need me.

He pushed me closer to the board. The maps, the lists, all the words on them perfectly legible for the moment. The pushpins dug into my hands when I tried to steady myself against it.

The short, sterile obituaries were all displayed there in a row.

"How long do you expect before you're one of these?" he asked. "'Died suddenly,'" he read to me, "'died in her home,' 'is predeceased by no one worth mentioning, survived by no one at all, so let's skip that depressingly empty paragraph and pretend that her life was about hunting, or genetic research, or whatever other euphemism we can find for her obsession with a project so hopeless that no one even knows about it! In fact, why not just skip the obituary altogether, since no one can find anything to say about her!'"

Just because a life wasn't public doesn't mean it was pointless.

"So what was your point, Mina? Shaun is dead! The Old Man will be dead in days, and even you know he'll deserve it! Haley will grow up a broken woman just like you would, if they even let her! Your mother considers you an inconvenience! Your father's never coming back! Even if you could find him, he'd be nothing but a shell! And even if you could revive him, do you really think he'd be proud?"

Courtney's face flashed across the board, indignant and betrayed, typing in the code to bring up my less than heartwarming criminal record.

"How long has it been, Mina? Since you felt close to someone? Any kind of someone? Was it this?"

I was in Shaun's room, before it had become an extra home office. He was kissing me, and I was kissing back, my body locked into the motion it had followed before. It had happened. It couldn't be changed.

"Or was this *closer* for you?"

I was wrapped in suffocating Splinter, its sharp tendrils under my skin, between my bones, closer than close in the worst possible way.

"No wonder Ben couldn't get through. Poor guy never stood a chance after that, did he?"

Ben.

For some reason my mind latched onto his name as if it supported my argument.

"*Ben left you!*" The drawer of his pictures opened, sending them fluttering across the desk. The map became a giant phone screen, his tracker storming away. It took up my entire range of vision. "He wants nothing to do with you! Name one reason why he would!"

I couldn't.

"Even if you could have made him happy, how long could it last? Do you think The Old Man was too paranoid about your mother? You think she wouldn't make you trade him away for some Splinter diplomat the way she did?"

I would never—

"Not to save the town? Save the world? To stop whatever else they threaten you with and then do anyway? You caved to that treaty, didn't you? You think putting some dying Bigfeet out of their misery and annoying some Slivers the Splinters want to stop anyway makes you a hunter again? You're hiding, Mina. Even when you're not busy having psychotic knife fights with the dead Splinter of your dead boyfriend! You're cooperating! You're beaten!"

Next we were sitting on my bed. I'd utterly lost track of where my body really was in the room, if I was even really in my room. Shaun cornered me against the edge that touched the wall. I closed my eyes, but I could still see him.

"In eight years, you've accomplished nothing, and no one cares. What do you have to stay for?"

In a fit of pure, futile rage, I jumped at him, knocked him backward on the mattress, and sank straight through, right into the middle of him. He solidified while we occupied the same space, rubbery sheets and misshapen masses of Splinter instantly bisecting my entire body, and suddenly I was the one on my back.

A piece the shape of a circular saw blade ran from the right side of my neck, right through the carotid down through my chest right next to my heart, all without drawing blood. A scalpel-edged wedge wrapped thickly around the inside of my left hip bone. We were so folded and twisted and layered together, like half-kneaded dough, that I could have lost track of where I ended and he began, if every Splinter part had not then made itself violently and inescapably known with a paralyzing and thoroughly realistic electrical charge.

Only one part of me was free; the hand with the knife.

You want to kill me, Mina? I'm right here. I'm inside of you. Let it happen. Let it in. It'll be easier. Quicker. Over.

The offer was very nearly irresistible.

I don't care about quick and easy.

That's what I like about you.

The knife tip was two and three quarters of an inch from my skin when the window opened and something real, someone real landed on my bed. The relief was distressingly indistinguishable from disappointment when Aldo twisted it out of my hand.

"Mina, what the hell?"

16.

DAY OF THE DEAD

Ben

I shouldn't have been surprised that they found me. Every day I had to find a new quiet stretch of hallway or hidden cul-de-sac near a building where I could eat in peace. I couldn't use the same place twice, not if I wanted to stay hidden. I'd been pretty lucky so far.

On Halloween, that luck ran out.

I was eating lunch in a small alcove just off the science building when I heard them coming. I tried to look like any other student.

It didn't work.

"That's him!" one of them said.

"Come on, droogs, let's get 'im!" Patrick cried gleefully. They started to run for me.

I set my lunch down and stood up. If this was going to happen, I was going to be on my feet.

I was thrown to the ground in a flurry of punches and kicks by Patrick and three of his friends. I kept my arms up, covering my head and neck.

The beating felt like it lasted for a few hours, but it

couldn't have been more than a minute or two. If it had been a few hours, I wouldn't have survived.

"He's not fighting back," one of them said, confused.

"He will," Patrick said, dragging me to my feet. I stood. Barely. I could taste blood, feel one of my eyes swelling shut.

"Come on," Patrick said. "You just gonna take this, or are you gonna fight?"

My voice came out raspy, hollow. "I'm gonna take this."

Patrick laughed. "But don'tcha see? You don't have to. Just confess. Just walk right into the police station, tell them what you did, and take your medicine like a big boy."

"I didn't do anything," I said. I tried to sound firm, but probably only pulled off tired.

"Bullshit," Patrick said, knocking me down and attacking me with even greater ferocity. Yelling, cursing, kicking me to the ground. A few weeks before, he had threatened to kill me if I ever bothered Madison again. I hadn't believed him at the time.

I believed him now.

Faintly, I could see his friends shifting from helping him to nervously trying to pull him away. Being a head taller and fifty pounds heavier than the rest of them, he could easily throw them off.

A loud, authoritative voice called out. "Hey, stop that!"

His friends ran for it, but Patrick was blind to them.

"This doesn't concern you," Patrick said as he continued to attack me.

"You got that wrong," the voice said, approaching Patrick and grabbing him by the shoulder. Patrick whirled on his attacker, punching him with all his might.

Patrick howled in pain as he broke his hand against the Good Samaritan's chest. As he stumbled away, I was able to see that my savior was an honest-to-God knight in shining armor, covered from head to toe in polished steel plates and wielding a vicious looking pole-axe. At that moment, cradling his swelling, shattered hand, Patrick was angrier than he was smart. He rushed the knight. My rescuer just took a casual step to the side, swinging his pole-axe in a wide arc and sweeping Patrick's legs out from underneath him. Patrick landed on the ground in a heap.

The knight walked over to him, holding the spear tip of his weapon right above Patrick's throat.

"Keamy, I don't know what's more stupid, the fact that you just attacked a teacher, or the fact that you just attacked a teacher wearing full plate armor and *wielding a flippin' halberd!*" the knight said.

"I'm sorry, Mr. Finn," Patrick said through tears of pain.

Mr. Finn. He'd been boasting about having an awesome homemade Halloween costume for the last few weeks.

"You could be expelled for this, you know that, right?" Mr. Finn threatened.

"I'm sorry, Mr. Finn," Patrick repeated.

"Good. You just saved your school career," the knight said. If I could see his face, I knew he'd be smiling. "Now apologize to Pastor here."

Patrick looked at me with pure hate in his eyes. "I'm sorry. Can I go to the nurse's office now?"

"Feel free," Mr. Finn said, helping Patrick to his feet. "Now if anybody asks . . . ?"

Patrick's hand had swollen to almost double its size. "I fell down."

Mr. Finn nodded. "Good boy. Don't want an 'assaulting a teacher' charge on your permanent record now, do you?"

"No, Mr. Finn," Patrick said, limping away.

Looking back to me, Mr. Finn pulled up the visor of his helmet. "You all right there, Pastor?"

"I'll live," I said, getting back to my feet and dusting myself off. I was pretty bloody, but nothing felt broken.

Mr. Finn smiled. "Well, if Keamy there did you one favor, it was giving you the best damn zombie costume in the school."

I didn't laugh. Mr. Finn didn't seem to care.

"I'd say you should head to the nurse's office, but with Keamy there probably looking for a round two, I wouldn't advise it. Come on down to the shop with me. My first aid kit's stocked better than most ambulances."

I didn't want to follow him; I was plenty content to just wallow in my misery, but part of the old programming kicked in, the programming that said I had to listen to my teachers. Slowly, I grabbed my backpack and what was left of my lunch.

Mr. Finn walked ahead of me, using the halberd as a walking stick of sorts to compensate for his limp.

A little sheepish, he said, "Also, I'd appreciate it if you didn't spread around what I did to Keamy there. The little prick had it coming, but that doesn't make it better in the administration's eyes if you know what I mean?'

"I didn't see anything. I was just eating lunch," I said.

Mr. Finn clapped me on the back with one of his heavy gauntlets. "Mr. Pastor, I think this is the beginning of a beautiful friendship."

His first aid kit wasn't so much a kit as it was a filing cabinet full of enough supplies to treat a classroom full of severed limbs. I didn't need much more than a bottle of peroxide, some gauze and a few large Band-Aids. Mr. Finn provided the mood music, popping a mix-tape of surf tunes into an ancient-looking boom box, warbling along with the Beach Boys as they mused about how nice it would be to be older.

They didn't know how right they had it.

"So should I be asking about why Keamy there wanted to rearrange your face?" Mr. Finn asked as he polished the blade of his halberd.

"It's nothing," I said.

He didn't buy it. "Nothing like the mess your life's become lately?"

I looked at him questioningly.

"People talk, and you're hardly keeping a low profile these days," he said.

I didn't say anything. I couldn't confirm it, nor would I deny it, not to someone who didn't understand. Someone who couldn't understand.

"Well, say something or say nothing, either's fine by me. Let me tell you, I don't believe a word of any of those rumors," he said.

"You don't?" I asked. My voice was faint, but there might have been some hope in it.

"Look, if you did one bad thing, maybe I'd believe it, two or three, still possible, but at the rate your evil deeds are stacking up, you're looking less like Charles Manson and more like Job. Small-town people love to have their pariah, and when one isn't readily available, they'll make one on their own," Mr. Finn said.

He hobbled over to a mini-fridge by his desk. Opening it up, he pulled out a couple of bottles of root beer and tossed one to me.

"Thanks," I said.

"No problem," he said. "Nothing but the best for Mrs. Finn's pride and joy. And present company, of course."

I took a sip. I tried to ignore his kindness as I had ignored Kevin and Haley. It wasn't as easy.

"So why'd you ask me, if you already knew?" I asked.

He shrugged, which was no easy task in his heavy armor. "Give you a chance to get it off your chest? Sometimes when life's treating you like an outhouse, it helps to talk."

"I don't want to talk about it," I said. I'd been saying that a lot lately.

"Fair enough. Mind answering a different question then?" he asked.

"Why not?" I said.

"Did you let yourself get beat up there because you're feeling sorry for yourself and thought you deserved it, or because you knew by fighting back you'd stand a good shot of getting kicked out of school? Please say it's because you didn't want to get kicked out; makes you sound like less of a dumbass," he said.

I didn't say anything. I wanted to give him the easy answer, but he knew the truth before I could even get those false words out.

"Got it. You're a dumbass," he said.

"I don't think you're supposed to call students dumbasses," I said.

"You're also not supposed to use power tools without wearing safety goggles, but what can I say, sometimes I feel like taking risks," he said. "By the way, I ever catch you using power tools without goggles, you're failing that assignment. Besides, sometimes calling someone a dumbass when they're being a dumbass is the best way to get through to them."

"I don't need getting through to," I said. "And I don't need any more first aid. I can take it from here."

I got up from my stool painfully and started to walk to the door.

"Would it make you feel any better if I told you that things won't stay bad if you don't let them?" he said.

I stopped in my tracks. Those words were too familiar, cutting into too many recent wounds. I grabbed a chisel from a nearby work station and turned to him.

"Are you a part of this?" I asked shakily. "Are you here to see if I've broken yet? Are you reporting to Madison or Sam? If you are, you can tell them that they don't have me!"

Mr. Finn didn't flinch.

"What is it you kids don't get about the whole armor and halberd concept?" he asked.

The weapon felt pitiful in my hand compared to my shop teacher, the walking tank. Still, I held the chisel threateningly, prepared to give whatever kind of fight I could, if I had to. Mr. Finn looked unconcerned, but I noted his grip on the halberd had tightened slightly.

"Answer the question," I said, trying to sound threatening and failing abysmally.

"Fine, if it makes you feel any better. I'm a part of a lot of things. The United States Marine Corps, honorably discharged, the Prospero Parent Teacher Association, the Split Infinitives Bowling Team, but Pastor, I'm not your enemy. I'm not a part of whatever it is that's going on in your life right now. I'm a teacher, and I'm concerned that one of my students is about to do something very stupid with his life. I've been where you are; you're not the only one this town's nearly killed. I want to help," he said.

Splinters are good liars. Billy was an exceptional one. Right up until the end, I thought he was someone I could trust. I didn't want to let my guard down again, but for some reason, I did with Mr. Finn. Maybe it was because he was a teacher, or because I just couldn't hold it up any longer, or maybe even because he reminded me a little of my dad. I set down the chisel and took a seat.

"What happened to you?" I asked.

In answer, he removed the armor from his left leg and rolled up his jeans underneath. Just under his knee there was a terrible, jagged scar that looked as if someone had tried to remove his leg with a chainsaw. No wonder he limped.

"Just after I got out of the Corps, I was on a hunting trip in the woods just outside of town with some buddies. I was out on my own for a bit, when this . . . thing came out of the forest. Not sure what it was, it walked on all fours, had thick patches of fur and scales, more eyes than I could count, and a mouth that looked like a blender. If you wanted to call it a monster, I don't think you'd be that far off. I tried to run. It didn't want me to."

He rolled his jeans back down, started to reattach the armor. "Don't ask me how I fought it off because I don't rightly remember most of what happened that day. I remember a lot of hollering and pounding and the feeling of my leg going down its slimy, toothy throat. I even remember my buddies getting me to the medical center. Now, I didn't serve during wartime, but I'd seen some combat. I'd thought I could handle pretty much anything, but seeing that thing . . . It snapped something in me, something that ought not have been snapped."

Mr. Finn took a swig of his root beer and tossed the empty bottle at a nearby recycling bin. He almost made it. Considering the other odd pieces of broken glass that covered the floor by the bin, I didn't imagine this was his first attempt.

"I knew I had to warn everyone about what I'd seen. Sure, some people would listen to my story in the good old humoring sort of way. They'd laugh, pat me on my back and recommend a good place where I could get a tin foil hat. But then there were people who wanted me to shut up. They said that I was bringing 'unnecessary attention' down on this town. They tried to bribe me at first, but when I turned that down, they just started to threaten me. They said that if I didn't play ball, they'd take everything from me. Friends, family, the life I'd built."

This sounded a lot more familiar than I would have liked. "So what did you do?"

He laughed humorlessly. "I didn't let them push me around. I told the truth because it was the right thing to do. And that's when things started to go downhill. I lost my job, my apartment, and my girlfriend in the stretch of a week. I got blamed for a hit and run—it wasn't my fault, but they had enough to lock me up for a few weeks. A paperwork mix-up even had me put in a psych ward for about a month, pumped full of drugs and surrounded by loons. By the time I got out, everybody in town thought I was crazy. A lot of my friends, some of my family, even, wouldn't talk to me anymore. I thought I was alone. I wanted to be alone. I hated myself so much that I thought maybe if I just gave up, maybe if I ended it all, that everything would be better."

"But you didn't," I said.

"Obviously," Mr. Finn responded. "Because I realized that, as much as I hurt, killing myself would be damned selfish and would hurt the people who still loved me a lot more than I was hurting myself at the time. So I got out of my pit. I found my friends who hadn't abandoned me. I still got attacked plenty, but knowing I had people who would stand by me no matter what made it easier. And after a while, simply by standing with them and not giving up, the attacks started to taper off. I was still 'Crazy Old Leslie Finn', but nobody bothered me anymore. Life went on in Prospero as it always does, and I now have my cushy teacher's salary to show for it."

His words hit me like a ton of bricks. I didn't know if he knew about Splinters, not really, not the way he was talking, but it was clear he'd been through what I was going through.

I'd been going about this the wrong way. The Splinters weren't taking my friends away from me; they were making me do it for them.

"Thanks, Mr. Finn," I said.

He smiled broadly, stroking his large chin with one of his heavy gauntlets. "Now, I'm not gonna say I can fix your life, that's your problem, but I can at least help you out with your lunchtime problem. I got a side job, making furniture and replica medieval weaponry; good money. I do most of my work during lunch and after school, and I keep myself locked in. However, for you, the door's open. You can lunch in here if you want, any time you want, avoid Keamy's wrath—or half-wrath if that hand's as bad as it looks—but I'm gonna work you. You work with me, and you earn a fair percentage of each piece you help me complete. Sound good?"

It did. It sounded real good. I liked building things, and I could learn a lot from Mr. Finn.

"Sounds great," I said.

"Good. Now, the bell's gonna ring in a few minutes and I got a class to get ready. Think there's something you need to do before lunch is out?"

I nodded, running for the door and thanking him profusely as I went. I felt almost like my old self again, and it felt good.

Real good.

Things would be tough, at least until we figured out how to deal with Madison and the rest of the Splinters.

SHARDS

If I could reconnect with the world, at least I wouldn't be fighting this fight on my own.

I had to talk to Kevin.

I had to talk to Haley.

More than anything, I had to talk to Mina.

I just hoped it wasn't too late.

17.

ALL HALLOW'S EVE
Mina

Silly question: do you want to talk about it?

Except for class, Aldo hadn't let me out of his sight all day until his dad had come to pick him up from school, but we hadn't talked much. He seemed to be hoping I'd say something first, so I'd managed to avoid this silly question until now, after dinner, when it popped open a video-free Skype window that we would both pretend wasn't hiding whatever part of his face needed to heal before tomorrow. The illusion from the night before was gone, but that didn't mean I was any stronger or nobler than it had given me credit for.

Not really.

I'd asked him to watch me for a few hours. I'd slept for nine. I couldn't remember the last time I'd slept for nine hours at once. I wasn't sure when I'd last slept for *two* hours at once.

Aldo's typing icon flicked on and off for a while before the next message appeared.

I almost woke your parents last night, you know. I almost

thought you'd be safer in the med center. Of course, then I realized that's INSANE, but I thought about it.

I'd woken up fully clothed, with full sunlight streaming in through my window, my face stiff with dry salt, every potentially lethal object in my room gathered and locked in the closet. Aldo had been propped up, bleary-eyed at the head of my bed with my glasses folded safely over the neck of his shirt and his fingers resting in my hair.

And I might have become aware of all this thirty or forty seconds before I opened my eyes and had to push him away.

I'm glad you came to your senses, I typed.

Uh, yeah. You, too.

I'd lectured him the entire time we were cleaning ourselves up for school about not waking me sooner, about how much unnecessary trouble he'd be in for staying out all night. It hadn't made me feel any better.

I was too grateful to feel better.

The screen was still for a moment. *Seriously, what happened to you?*

I started to type "nothing," felt ridiculous, deleted it, and settled for,

I don't know.

Are you okay now? Not going to go all Evil Dead II on me again tomorrow?

I don't know.

Silly question 2: Can I help?

I don't think so.

My phone vibrated for the twenty-third time that day, and for the first time since lunch, I forced myself to look at it. When it displayed a message with Haley's name on

FJR TITCHENELL & MATT CARTER

it yet again, I very nearly deleted it unopened. As always, the compulsive need for the advantage of maximum information won out.

Need help, PLEASE. Ben and Kevin aren't answering. At the historical cemetery haunt. Hurry.

A jolt of adrenaline forced its way out of my reconstructed mental armor. The productive kind.

Back to work. I wasn't sure I was up for it, but an entire night stuck on the *receiving* end of Network protection had me itching to be useful again.

Besides, Haley and whatever was currently menacing her didn't care whether I was ready to protect again or not. I had my bag already fully restocked and on my shoulder when I turned back to the keyboard.

Going to the cemetery, duty calls.

I can't go, Aldo typed back, eliciting another stab of guilt.

Not a problem. I'll handle it.

Good luck, be safe, take no shit and all that.

I debated for a moment before pressing Enter on my sign-off.

You, too.

Prospero holds its Halloween Haunt at the historical cemetery because apparently gold-rush era graves are considered creepier than fresh ones. The historical cemetery is also much larger, more hilly, and more heavily wooded than the active one, making it less than ideal for fighting Splinters at night.

I half expected to arrive to find that the haunt had

devolved into a full-fledged Sliver massacre with Haley and maybe a few other humans barricaded in the nearest sturdy structure, but when I set my bike in the rack and started to scout out the edges of the festivities, it looked like any ordinary gathering of humans and well-hidden Splinters on the one ridiculously irresponsible night a year when no one even considers coming to help when someone screams.

· Emanating from the maze were the ordinary flashes of light, laughter-punctuated shrieks, and other sharp noises, mostly metal on wood.

I scanned the crowd quickly for Shard suspects and other possible threats. The only ECS I could see was Madison, standing in line at the caramel apple stand, wearing bunny ears and far too little else for the temperature, cooing over the plastic pirate sword her dazed-looking date was carrying.

I was ready for the surge of anger, ready to contain it. It wasn't until I recognized the edge of disappointment in it that I realized how much I'd been hoping that she'd be the one I'd get to rescue Haley from, the more violently the better.

I shook off the unproductive thought.

Patrick was near one of the edges, surrounded by some of his usual associates, pretending not to stare at Madison. His costume was dirtier than it had been at the beginning of the school day, and he had a fresh cast on his right hand. I was going to have to look into that later.

I spotted Julie in her elaborate witch's costume at one of the photo-op sets and almost approached her for backup, before I saw Zach, her ten-year-old brother, making faces for her camera. She'd never forgive me if I involved her with him around.

Courtney, professional-looking as ever, was manning a ticket booth for the haunted hayride, which meant the perimeter of the activities was wider than what I could see.

I checked the tracker archives for Haley's phone on mine. It hadn't been near the Warehouse, and it was still somewhere in the cemetery. I just had to hope it was still on her.

Where are you? I texted back.

I only waited a few seconds.

Girl's bathroom. Stone building by the back of the maze.

I circled the outside to reach it, hand on a Taser in my bag, ready for a trap. I'd convinced her when we'd first gotten her back to put a password on her phone, but if someone was threatening her, there was still every chance she wasn't the one texting from it.

There were a few people milling around near the bathrooms, but not many. Theater kids and someone I couldn't identify behind a Sci-Fi spacefarer mask. Robbie glanced away from the cluster of girls who were admiring what I guessed was his attempt at a vampire costume, the new kind with the fangs and cloak replaced by messy hair and makeup that made him look like a syphilis patient. For a moment, I could have sworn I saw him looking at me in that improbably interested way I'd imagined in class last month, but then he was back to whatever joke he'd been telling them.

The bathroom itself had one of those dark T intersections, perfect for an ambush, but I made it to the door on the girl's side without incident.

It was ajar, almost pitch black inside. It opened outwards.

I pulled, shielding myself with it, and shone my flashlight around it into the room.

"Haley?"

Movement.

Haley, sitting on one of the sinks in her pale, bodiced, Old West ghost costume, bent over her own glowing phone screen, looking hopefully up at me.

I beckoned to her.

She beckoned pleadingly to me.

I wanted to get out of those dark, stone corners as fast as possible, but if she wouldn't move, there was only one option. I swept the corners quickly with the light, checking the empty floors of the two open stalls, and went in after her.

"What happened?" I whispered, looking her over for injuries or restraints. There were none.

I heard him, saw him out of the corner of my eye, just as I got too close to Haley to run back to the door in time. The boy in the mask, sprinting down our side of the intersection. I lunged, grabbed a notebook from my bag, and jammed it in the door just as he slammed it shut.

"Sorry, Mina."

The sound of the voice behind the mask froze me just long enough for him to kick the notebook away, latch the door and click a padlock over it.

"*Kevin?* Kevin, unlock this door!"

"Not a chance," he said, still apologetic. "I'll be back when you two are done talking things out."

I kicked the door once, testing its formidable sturdiness, then turned on Haley.

"You said you needed my help!"

"I do need your help!" Haley got down off the sink and stepped toward me, squinting against my flashlight. She gestured around the dank, unpleasant-smelling park bathroom. "Does this not scream desperation loudly enough for you?"

"I thought you were being attacked!"

"I'm sorry!" she said, without the slightest sign of relenting. "I'm *sorry* I had to resort to this, but I did have to. Now, since you took so long getting here, I have to get back to scaring the riders in fifteen minutes. You can either spend that time hearing what I have to say, or shocking me with that thing in your purse. It might make you feel better, but I told Kevin to give us some space, so if you're thinking about trying to make me scream for him to open the door to rescue me, you're out of luck."

She announced all this with an absolutely straight face, without a single quiver that I could detect by the light of my flashlight and the echo-y acoustics.

I removed the hand that wasn't on the flashlight from my bag and showed it to her under the light. Empty.

"Speak," I said.

She took only one breath to gather herself.

"First of all, you need to know that Ben has been a complete wreck lately, and that I, for one, am absolutely disgusted that his best friend doesn't want to be there to see him through it."

My armor dented but held in place. "Ben doesn't want

to talk to me," I said as neutrally as I could. "You already know that. But he doesn't mind talking to you. Maybe you should be 'seeing him through it' instead of wasting my time with false alarms."

"Oh, believe me, I'm trying, but what he needs is you."

I couldn't categorize this statement as either true or false without cracking through the iron, so my brain simply rejected it unanswered, leaving me momentarily mute.

"Yeah, that's the second thing you need to know," Haley continued. "At first I thought you just didn't care. I didn't think someone as smart and brave as he's always saying you are could really be stupid enough not to figure that out, or chicken-shit enough not to do anything about it. Then it hit me, when Ben told me you were just doing exactly what he told you to do, that maybe you really don't get it. Maybe you actually need someone to tell you that he didn't mean it."

I needed to be somewhere private to think about that. "Thank you for the information," I said. "Are you finished?"

Haley stared at me hard, waiting for something more. I didn't give it.

"That was the really urgent part," she said. "But as long as I've got you here, there are a few things we've needed to talk about for a while."

"Such as?"

"Such as why you don't like me."

There were too many things wrong with this question.

"You mean other than the way you just lured me into a park bathroom under false pretenses?"

"Yes, other than that."

I searched for a new way to deflect.

"How I feel about you doesn't matter."

"It matters to me how you treat me," she said pointedly. "And don't give me that 'I have a mental condition that makes me a bitch to everyone' bullshit. I know you're not the same with everyone. You talk to Aldo. You used to talk to Ben. You even talk to Kevin. Maybe not as much as they'd like, but at least they don't have to pull a stunt like this to make you acknowledge that they exist! And don't give me your 'trust issues' speech either because I know you've been watching me every minute since you two rescued me from the pod. You know I'm human, so that's not it either. Have I done something to offend you?"

"No."

"Is it because of Ben? Because this part, the you-and-me part, has nothing to do with him!" she exclaimed. "If you think this is all about crowding in on your friendship, or some pathetic attempt to be more like you for his sake—"

"I would never think so little of you," I said honestly.

"Then what is it?!"

Her knuckles were white where her hands folded over the strap of her purse, shaking with a terrible *need* that I understood too well to trust it.

"I think you feel too much," I said.

"For Ben?"

"For everything."

The glare she gave me didn't help. She looked exactly how I'd felt eight years ago. I'd made a lot of mistakes thanks to feeling like that, mistakes that no amount of advice or supervision could have kept me from. I'd survived them through sheer luck.

"A little anger is good," I explained. "A little fear, a little pride in your associates and your species, that's necessary to keep you going, but you've got too much. It goes too deep. They hurt you too badly, and you're not going to be able to handle it."

Haley folded her arms, almost stopping the shaking, but the desperate rage was still obvious on her face.

"So you're the only person they've hurt who's allowed to fight back?" she demanded.

"You don't want to be like me, Haley."

"No! I don't! But it's already too late for me to just go on with a normal life, and I'd rather be like you than be hurt and helpless!"

If there'd been another way to make her understand, I would have used it. Instead, I rolled my right sleeve up to the elbow and turned my flashlight on it.

Haley stared for a moment at the thick, twisted, discolored gouges circling my arm before recovering herself. "You can't scare me away just because I might get hurt. I don't care—"

"Believe me, the two surgeries and four skin grafts it took to save my arm were the easy part. The hard part was burning the Splinter who did it alive."

"I could kill a Splinter," Haley insisted.

"It's not just the Splinter!" I said. "Look, the only other people who know this are Kevin and Aldo, and I'd like to keep it that way, okay?"

She nodded.

"I killed the person it took, the one who was still in the pod. We were involved. Romantically."

Haley swallowed hard, still staring at my scar. I could see her adding up the timeline, the only disappearance that matched up.

"You don't mean . . . Shaun? Oh God, Mina, I'm so sorry."

I turned the flashlight back on Haley and advanced on where she'd cornered herself between the sinks, wanting to shake her, wanting to cut through her anger and sympathy to what had to be inside, to what was always inside mine, to the little nine-year-old girl who still wanted to go hide under her bed and wait for all the monsters to go away.

"I don't want you to be sorry! I want you to think about doing that!" I shouted. "I want you to picture it! Think what would happen if the Splinters took someone you . . ." I took a breath to brace myself for the word, "someone you *love*."

I hadn't pronounced it out loud for two years, not since Shaun. And before that, not since I'd been able to say it to my father. But for Haley's sake, I had to be absolutely clear.

"If it were Ben, or Kevin, or your mother," she winced just slightly when I reached the last suggestion, so I jumped on it, "if one of them looked like your mother, sounded like her, smelled like her, remembered things only she could know, could you kill her if you had to?"

Haley was shaking a little again, and for a moment I thought I'd won, but when she answered, it was with absolute certainty.

"Yes."

That was when we both heard the unmistakable crack of a Splinter transforming, just outside the door.

"Kevin?" we shouted together.

No answer. But we turned out not to need him to let us out. Two strikes of what must have been a transformed Splinter appendage—it was heavier than a rock—and the door swung open, the warped remnants of the padlock falling to the concrete below.

I drew a flamethrower and positioned myself in front of Haley, waiting for the Splinter to come in and find us cornered.

And waited.

Nothing entered.

"What are we waiting for?" Haley asked from behind me, pulling out a pitiful bottle of mace and trying to push past me. "It's right outside!"

I grabbed her by the flimsy top of her costume with my flashlight hand and held her back. The beam fell across her face at a distorting angle.

"See, this is the problem! You think you could kill a Splinter of your mother if you had to? Okay, let's try a harder one. Could you not kill her if you didn't have to?"

Haley just looked confused. I repeated the question.

"Could you let the monster that stole your mother's life keep on living it, if that was your best move?"

That one she couldn't answer so easily.

I explained as quickly as I could through this momentary gap in her raging deafness.

"Love is dangerous when you live among Splinters." I paused and wrapped my tongue around the second forbidden word as indifferently as I could, the one I'd added to the list when I left The Old Man. "Hate is just as bad.

And the worst part is that you can never get rid of them completely. They're like a cancer that goes into remission and keeps on threatening to come back. But you have to keep medicating them away, however you can. You can't let them take over."

It was strange how this seemed to be getting easier to explain, even as it got harder and harder to demonstrate.

Haley gave the door a longing look.

"I'm sorry, Haley. You and I don't get the quick, clean, easy revenge story. We don't get to just grab a gun and shoot a few bad people before the cops take us down. This doesn't end that easily. There isn't just one Splinter who hurt you, and if you destroy one, another one will break off and take its place, and they'll barely feel the difference. If you fight them, you fight all of them, the whole infestation, the whole machine, and you can't do that by knocking off the heads of nobodies in public whenever you feel like it. It's a big, long job, and to make even a dent in it, you have to settle in, pick your battles, hedge your bets, and keep *your head together*."

Haley bit down on her lip, and I hoped she might simply cry, run off, fall into Ben's arms, and never speak to me again, and that would be the end of it.

Instead she nodded and looked at me, utterly clear-eyed. "I can do that. I promise, but we do still have to find out who broke the lock, right?"

"Yes," I let go, stuck the flashlight in my bag, and started for the door. "I do."

Haley kept pace right beside me as I followed the sound

of the next crack out of the bathroom and further out into the periphery of the cemetery, toward the hayride track, heavily decorated, currently vacant, and shielded from the center of activity by a broad stretch of wooded hills and darkness.

The broken lock, the undisguised sounds—it was obvious I was being deliberately led. I couldn't pass up the chance to see the Splinter's face, but whoever it was would be ready. Not a good time to have an amateur along.

"You'll draw attention," I accused her.

"I'll draw attention?" She pulled something out of her purse, a headband with a pair of cat ears on it, and placed it on my head. "There. Now you sort of look like you belong. There are different ways to be inconspicuous, you know."

I felt the hallucination coming a moment before I saw it, the entire cemetery scene ahead turning green and purple, the dirt of the old graves moving, grey hands clawing their way up, and the shudder it sent through me made me wish harder for some way to lose Haley.

Not again, please, not again.

Then Haley screamed.

It was a small scream, followed by a frantic effort to recover her composure for my benefit, but she was still staring at the graves, intently enough to give me the nerve to ask,

"You can see them too?"

She nodded.

"And they're not part of your show?"

She shook her head.

"That's . . . interesting."

"What is this?" she asked.

But I didn't have time to speculate with her because, at that moment, a fireball rocketed out of the trees, forcing us both to dodge and roll.

I looked up to see where it had come from.

The man in the distance had to be a hallucination, and not only because he was mounted on a jet black horse with red eyes. His costume was much like the rest of the hayride cast, an old west gunslinger all in black with a low, wide-brimmed hat, but his arms were far too long to be human and too rotten for the theatrical society's makeup skills. A Splinter could have shaped those arms, maybe, but no Splinter I'd ever met could have worn a face like that. I could swear it was made of fire; it was black and green, emitting absolutely no light, except for the two bright yellowish points that passed for eyes.

The horse started toward us at a canter, and the gunslinger twirled his lasso over his head once, twice. The rope brightened with red fire with each revolution until it hurled another fireball at us like a sling.

I grabbed Haley and rolled behind the nearest tombstone for cover. The fire ricocheted off of it. I could hear the tap of hooves coming around, ready to make another pass at us.

After my last episode this vivid, I was not at all sure that survival was reasonable to assume.

Haley stayed crouched beside me, looking up, waiting for some kind of direction. "If you repeat this, I'll deny it," I warned her, and then I had no choice but to let the rest slip out. "The irrelevant fact is that I do like you, Haley. I never wanted you to do anything that would screw up my life's work and make me change my mind about that, and I also didn't want you to do anything that would result in me scraping charred pieces of you off of someone's lawn."

Haley nodded as if these were the most reasonable considerations in the world.

"Thanks," she said. "I guess. But, see, the thing is, I'm going to be fighting back. It's just the not-screwing-up-and-dying part I could really use your help with."

I may not be able to read faces the way normal people can, much less the way people like Haley and Ben can. Not everything is written in those quantifiable micro-expressions I have to look for and rely on, but it didn't take any special, vague, elusive instinct to know that she was serious.

It certainly didn't feel like eight years since I'd given The Old Man the same ultimatum, just as sincerely.

I pulled out an extra flamethrower and handed it to her.

The gunslinger was almost on us again, and together we dodged sideways to a broader tombstone with a better angle.

"What do I do with it?" Haley whispered. "Against this, I mean?"

I thought about how I'd briefly made Shaun's hand intangible with the knife. The whole concept of fighting things that weren't there was frustratingly imprecise.

"I don't know, probably believe in it really hard, or something equally ridiculous."

One of the dead hands burst out of the grave beneath us and wrapped around Haley's ankle. She summoned a look of intense concentration and gave it a burst of fire further up the arm. It shriveled almost instantly away.

"Got it!"

We'd picked good high ground. There was no clear path through the graves, so the gunslinger had to back up and take a running start. Haley and I exchanged a nod, ready to blast the horse's underside together as soon as it got close enough.

It was three graves away, two graves.

And then it vanished. The world flickered and returned to normal, the green and purple tinges gone.

The only thing out of the ordinary was the guy on the ground next to us—Robbie, I realized when my eyes adjusted—trying to crawl away from the figure looming over him.

It looked like another boy, another one in a full mask, something hairy and monstrous. He was carrying a tree branch and looked very much like he'd just clubbed Robbie over the head with it.

Robbie found his feet and sprinted back toward the parking lot without glancing back.

The figure started toward Haley and me, crouching down over us.

I steadied myself against the stone and kicked hard for where its nose should have been. It keeled over onto the grass, but before I could get in another shot, Haley jumped between us.

"Wait!"

She pulled off the monster mask before the guy wearing it could find the wherewithal to do so.

"Ben?"

Ben nodded up at me, still cradling his nose, which, for reasons I would have to look into, had already been bandaged. "Hi."

"What are you doing here?"

"I asked your mother where to find you," he admitted.

"Why were you fighting with Robbie?"

"I saw you two freaking out, and he was just standing there with this creepy look on his face, and . . . and it seemed like a good idea at the time!"

I looked back at the crowd where Robbie had disappeared. With an almost uncontrollable fit of nausea, I understood which voice was strongest in the amalgam I kept hearing.

"It was," I said. "He killed the hunters. He's the Shard, and he did this to me!"

"He's what?" Haley gasped.

It had been him in my head all semester. It hadn't been myself that had tried to kill me. He hadn't needed teleportation or some other physical ability to make the others look like suicides. He had made real suicides.

It took every ounce of what was left of my will not to chase him through the cemetery, his own turf, with no preparation. The urge was almost as strong as the one to hurt Madison in that fair, alternate world. It brought bile to my teeth, standing still, following the essential advice I had just given Haley.

Ben was standing there, watching me, Haley watching us both with a mix of dawning horror and hope. I allowed myself to wonder if what she had said about Ben wanting to hear from me was true.

Ben was trying to say something, maybe to ask what I was talking about or quite possibly preparing another verbal kick if I left myself open again, but compared with the past month, that couldn't frighten me enough to stop me from speaking first.

I couldn't watch him leave again no matter how quiet I could be.

"He made me think I was going insane," I explained. "It's complicated, but I promise, I'll explain everything, if—"

"If we're still . . ." Ben paused as if trying to remember the right word in a second language, "allies?"

"No."

I'd told Haley two of the three forbidden words, but only in the abstract. That didn't really count. The third word, the one I hoped would prove to be the smallest and most harmless, I said for real. I said it because, whether it was a good idea or not, it was inescapably the one I meant.

"No, only if we're still friends."

18.

GETTING THE BAND BACK TOGETHER

Ben

None of us should have been there. Not after all this. We should've been scattered to the winds, and maybe we would've stayed that way, too, had Mina and I not gotten back together on Halloween night and started working out our differences. Maybe then we wouldn't have all been gathered around Haley's kitchen table sharing horror stories.

It had been almost a week since Halloween. We had the house to ourselves for now; Aunt Christine was out on a date with some firefighter, which, if he was as handsome as Haley said, probably meant we had a good amount of time to work this out. We were able to pull together Aldo, Haley, Kevin, Greg, Julie, and even Courtney.

Unlike the last meeting, this one was almost entirely Mina's show. She took the lead in explaining everything that had happened, from Courtney's near-kidnapping and our theory on Slivers to Madison and my month in hell to Robbie being a Shard assassin working for the Splinter

Council. The only thing Mina left out was The Old Man, but I was willing to give her that one secret.

I wish I could say things were easy after Halloween night, but I'd be lying if I did. I was upset with her for abandoning me. She had defended herself, saying she thought that was what I wanted. I told her not to take me so literally and next time to ask me what I wanted instead of assuming. I was also beating myself up for not being more sensitive to the fact that she had clearly been going through some tough times of her own (with the help of Robbie York's mental powers). Over the past several days, we had yelled, we had cried (okay, maybe replace that *we* with *I*), we maybe even laughed a little. In the end, we worked out a lot of our problems.

The way friends would.

After that, it was a matter of figuring out a plan. We had worked out a lot of ideas, some simple, some not-so-simple, and it was clear that we would need to get everyone together. It took a lot of pleading, a lot of bargaining, and the promise of some fresh brownies for Greg (thankfully, Kevin's a pretty good baker) before we were finally able to pull it off.

The room was silent as Mina finished telling them of Robbie fleeing into the darkness on Halloween Night.

Greg broke the silence.

"War. They want a war, we give them a war," he said.

"Greg, sweetie, that ain't exactly going to fix nothin,'" Julie said. Her pigtails and nails were orange and black now, fitting for both Halloween and Thanksgiving. Through her white makeup and black lipstick, I could see her concern.

"No, but it'll feel good," he said, exasperated, pulling a joint from his jacket pocket.

"Not in here," Haley said quickly. "My mom's gonna get back in a couple of hours, and I don't want you smelling this place up anymore than you already have."

"You saying I smell?" Greg said, offended.

"You do, hon', not showerin' for a week at a time and smokin' reefer every day's no way to make friends," Julie said.

"Who says I want friends?" Greg asked.

Courtney spoke up next, irritated with the conversation's turn. "Far be it from me to advocate a course of action like this, but I'm afraid I have to agree with Greg."

"Thank you," he said. She ignored him.

"What they do violates all of our fundamental human rights, and I cannot understand how you stand by and simply do nothing. They have kidnapped us! They have stolen our lives! And what have we done? We have stayed quiet, we have allowed them to put fear into our hearts. We can fight them. We can kill them. You have proven that, Mina. Show us what we need to do, and we can send them straight to hell where they belong!"

Mina shook her head. "That's not how it works."

Greg pointed a finger at her emphatically. "Then show us how it does work! Show us how to end this!"

He looked to Courtney for validation. She didn't give him any.

"You can't end this. You can't fight this. Don't you realize that yet?" Kevin said softly.

"Why are you even here, collaborator?" Greg asked.

Kevin slammed his hands down on the table. "I am NOT a collaborator! They've destroyed the lives of my friends! The Splinters killed my brother! They kidnapped the woman I love!"

Haley stared awkwardly at the table, face slightly pink, and didn't comment.

"I hate the Splinters with every fiber of my being!"

"Then why won't you fight?" Courtney asked.

Kevin laughed. It was not a pleasant sound. "Because Haley was right. I am a coward. I'm afraid. I've seen what they do when you let them into your life. It's not something you can come back from. I don't want it to happen to me again. I don't want it to happen to anyone."

He was looking at Mina as he said this. She didn't let it get to her.

"Nobody at this table is a fan of Splinters. We've established that," said Mina. "But can we all agree that our most pressing problem at the moment is the Shard of Robbie York?"

This point didn't bring up any arguments.

"Has anyone seen Robbie since Halloween?" Mina asked.

Nobody had an answer for that. Haley said, "He's been out sick. Rumors going around say he's got mono."

"I heard the clap," Julie added, getting a few snickers around the table.

"He's a Splinter, a *Shard*. He doesn't get sick. That's just a cover," Mina explained. "He had every intention of killing us that night, but when Ben intervened and broke his cover, he must have gone into hiding. He hasn't once tried invading my thoughts since then."

"You say that like it's a bad thing," Aldo said.

"It isn't . . . and it is," Mina said. "While I am glad to no longer have an outside party violating and manipulating my thoughts, having him quiet worries me even more. We don't know where he is, or what he is planning, and I believe that makes him more dangerous now than he ever was before."

"So what do we do? Track him down and kill him?" Greg suggested.

"There's an idea," Haley said dryly. I had a hard time telling if she was snidely commenting on Greg's suggestion, or if she was serious. I knew she felt pretty betrayed by Robbie turning out to be a Splinter. Kevin did too, though he was better at hiding it. He was good at hiding a lot of things.

"That's not our best move," Mina said.

"Why not?" Greg asked. "If he's faking sick, he's gotta be in his house. We can just burst in there and take him out. Or better yet, why not just burn the place to the ground?"

"Because that'd be frickin' stupid!" Julie said, twirling a finger through her black pigtail. "You wanna spend the rest'a your life in jail on an arson-murder rap? You're cute, love, too cute for that and ya know it. Besides, if his mind-powers are anywhere close to as strong as what Mina and Haley say—"

"They are," Haley interjected.

"Then you wouldn't get within a hundred feet of that place before he made you cut yourself open because you think you got spiders under your skin," Julie finished.

Greg turned white, unconsciously rubbing his wrists

through the long sleeves of his shirt. "Don't even joke about that."

Julie shrugged. "You started it."

"Even if we could get to him and get away with it," I said, "if we kill him, the real Robbie dies."

Greg shrugged. "Well, the real Robbie's a dick."

Kevin, Mina, and Haley all stared daggers at Greg.

"What?" Greg said. Julie smacked him in the back of the head.

"Thank you," Haley said.

"No problem," Julie said.

"Can we take him from the Warehouse?" Haley suggested. "You got me out of there all right."

Again, Mina shot the idea down. "Also not an option. We were able to get in last time because Billy and your duplicate let us in. Now that they know we know, they'd be expecting us."

"So we can't kill him, and we can't rescue him. What *can* we do?" Courtney asked.

Mina and I had talked about this point for many a long hour over the past few nights.

I didn't exactly have high hopes for my sales pitch.

"We play by their rules," I said.

I was expecting either dead silence or a violent uproar when this was proposed. I was glad when dead silence won out.

"What does that mean?" Kevin asked, almost too quickly. I wondered why he was the first one to bring it up, but considering the number of times he'd been called a collaborator, I could see why this subject might make him edgy.

Mina said, "The way I see it, the Splinters have given us two options. We cooperate, or we make an effectively hopeless last stand. Now, you all know I'm not one to cooperate lightly with Splinters, and I'm not much for letting the whole town succumb either. So, I've given this a lot of thought. I've discussed it with Ben, and—"

Greg tried to interrupt, but Mina shot him down.

"Ben is mentioned by name in the treaty. And don't say we're not consulting you because that's what this meeting is for. Anyway, Ben and I agree that for now, the question is just how blind and unconditional the Splinters expect our cooperation to be. If they plan to be reasonable, at least according to their own rules, it may be worth using that to our advantage, to keep holding off war until we're better prepared."

"At least long enough to do something about the Slivers first," I explained, but Greg continued to glare at both of us.

"Exactly," said Mina. "We have a dangerous common enemy. But if the Splinters are not willing to be reasonable, if they plan to continue taking whatever they want whenever they want regardless of any promises they make to us, then an immediate stand may be the only option. Robbie York is both the greatest immediate threat to us and the ideal test. He has been hired by the Splinters to eliminate Splinter hunters. My father has made it very clear that I am not to be touched, but Robbie has tried to kill me at least twice already, meaning that he is either working with the Slivers or has gone completely rogue."

"Or that your Splinter-dad is lying, and he wants you off-guard when the Shard shows up to kill us all," Greg cut in.

"Yes," Mina agreed. "Or that. That's what we want to find out."

"You can't be serious!" Aldo blurted out suddenly, obviously realizing what Mina had in mind.

"I am," Mina said calmly.

"What?" asked Haley. "What's wrong?"

Aldo pinched the bridge of his nose, irritated. "Mina's planning to provoke Robbie into attacking her again, then call her dad in to catch Robbie in the act and ask him very nicely to do something about it! Is that about right?"

"That, or bringing him before the Splinter Council," I said.

"WHAT?!" Aldo yelled.

"Relax, we've got a plan on how to find them," Mina said. "Calling a meeting with them may be more difficult, but I've got some ideas that I might need your help with."

Aldo sat down with his head in his hands. "Do you have any idea how many things can go wrong with this?"

"Lots," I said. "But really, this isn't as crazy as it sounds."

"It isn't?" Aldo said, looking frantically for support around the table and getting none.

"It's the only way we might save Robbie. Over the summer, Mina and I found that a Splinter had secretly taken over Sheriff Diaz. After we revealed him, he had his . . . episode. Stumbling through the street, acting confused and disoriented, his memory not exactly what it used to be."

Haley shuddered. She knew that experience well. I squeezed her hand.

"If they don't want you anymore, if it's not too late, they

spit you out. I've felt that happen to people I was in there with," she said.

"What if Mina's dad *doesn't* care if the Shard breaks the rules?" asked Julie.

"Then we know the treaty isn't really giving us any protection," I explained and tried not to be annoyed by the way Greg's face started to light up. "And killing Robbie may be all we can do."

"That's assuming anyone survives Robbie's next attack long enough to get to Sam!" Aldo shouted directly at Mina and me. "Did she tell you?" he asked me. "Are you going to tell them?" he asked her, jerking his head at the group. "What he's capable of? What he did to you? Are you going to tell them that afterward you needed me to watch you sleep? Or about what you were trying to do when I found you?"

"Enough," Mina snapped at him.

I was prepared to physically hold Aldo back if I had to, even though I didn't want to. What he said, it was a cheap shot, but if I hadn't had these couple of days to get used to the plan, I could easily understand being desperate enough to sink that low.

"Robbie didn't just show me scary pictures," Mina said. "Everything looked and smelled and felt completely real. And they weren't just things that would frighten anyone. He used things against me that I've never talked about to anyone outside this room. There were details no one could have known, even some things that came after I was in the pod, so he couldn't have been working just from the information it gathered from me. I believe he has the ability to reach into a person's mind, to find out what scares her, or him, most, and then bring it to life."

Her matter-of-fact tone didn't do much for the group's confidence.

"I'd like to say that the result is just an illusion, that it's no big deal, that it's something any one of us could shrug off, but I can't. I won't lie to get any of you to help me. I will point out that ignoring Robbie won't make him any less dangerous, and that both Haley and I are only alive thanks to the timely intervention of an unexpected extra party. It seems probable that the involvement of more people makes his job more difficult, and since he's already attacked two unauthorized targets, there's no guarantee he won't get around to the whole Network eventually, one by one. But if we work together, I believe we can stop him."

Everybody looked at Mina, standing at the head of the table, waiting for anyone to join her. Despite all the problems we had had, I knew without question that I would be with her for the long haul. I would be the first one to stand if I had to.

Kevin beat me to it.

"I don't believe that what you're doing is the answer, but I do believe that this Shard that has Robbie is too dangerous to let run freely in this town. I will help you," he said.

I stood next. Julie and Haley weren't that far behind. Julie punched Greg in the shoulder. He just looked to Mina.

"So let me get this straight," Greg said. "You want us to help you act as human bait to draw out Freddy Krueger—"

"Robbie York," Mina corrected.

"Right," Greg continued. "To draw out a psychopath who can get in our heads and make our worst nightmares come to life, just so we can try to capture him and turn him over to his own people who we'll have to assume have a sense of justice and will make things right again?"

"Something like that, yeah," I said.

Greg laughed, standing with Julie. "Hell yeah, I'm in."

That left Courtney and Aldo.

"You know this doesn't guarantee that anything will end, right?" Courtney asked. "That they could very well just send in a replacement for Robbie, someone they think they can control more, and that this will almost certainly start up again right after?"

"Of course," Mina said.

She shook her head, muttering something in Lebanese that I guessed was a bad word.

"Well, I'm not going to be left in the dark after those things came after me, so I guess that means I'm staying close to you guys. But if you want me to help with anything, I want to know exactly what we're trying to do before we do it, and I want full access to any information I help you get."

Mina nodded. "On a case-by-case basis, agreed."

Courtney clearly didn't like that last qualifier, but she stood with us.

That just left Aldo.

"Aldo?" Mina said.

"Can't you think of some other way? Some other way that doesn't involve you just waiting around for this psycho to strike?"

"Aldo, we have to do this," Mina said firmly. He sighed.

He clearly didn't want anything to do with this plan, but he stood with us.

With everybody on board, the meeting broke up quickly. Mina was still brushing out some of the details for how we would track down the Splinter Council's meeting place and promised she would give everyone details on the plan within the next few days, so we could finally put it into action. Haley pulled me off to the side.

"Why didn't we talk about you more?" she asked.

"What about me?" I asked.

"About you and Madison! It's fine that we're looking to protect ourselves from Robbie, but what are we going to do about Madison destroying you?" she exclaimed.

I sighed. "It's not something we can fight. Not now, at least."

"She drags your name through the mud and all you can say is you can't fight?" she said.

"Madison doesn't want me dead. She just wants me to suffer. I have it on good authority that this will blow over eventually," I said.

"That's not how it works," Greg said as he sidled on over to us.

"How what works?" I asked.

"Dead agenting. Lying around and taking it totally isn't gonna help you out here," Greg said.

"What's dead agenting?" Haley asked.

Greg smiled, clearly glad for the opportunity to explain something. "Dead agenting is the fine art of attacking your attackers. Say someone is a threat to you, or they're exposing you in a way you don't want to be exposed, you put your resources toward making them look even worse. Dig up some dirt, or if there's no dirt to be dug up, just make some up and smear it all over them. Cults do it all the time. It's pretty damned effective, isn't it?"

He directed the question to me, and though he was smiling, I could swear I saw some sympathy in his eyes.

"So what can you do about it?" Haley asked.

Greg shrugged. "If killing them isn't an option, there's always seeing what dead agenting can do for you. Like you said, Eagle Scout, we could always play by their rules."

I could see over Greg's shoulder that Mina was done wrapping things up with the others.

"Excuse me," I said, feeling bad for leaving Haley behind with Greg as I made my way to Mina. She looked up at me hopefully.

"So, that went well, didn't it?" she asked.

"It did," I said, watching Haley and Greg continue to talk. They were joined by Julie, and soon after, Haley waved Aldo over. Now that was an interesting group.

"Do you really think this is the right idea? Bringing them all into this with us?" she asked.

"I do," I said with a smile. "God help me, but I really do."

The smile she flashed was almost worth all of Patrick's beatings.

19

MY KINGDOM FOR A DIGITAL VIDEO RECORDER

Mina

Things had been better in the days after Halloween, for everyone, maybe for me most of all.

For the first time since I'd come out of that Warehouse alive, I'd gotten a reprieve. Reality was actually better than the probable scenario I'd spent the last month trying to accept.

I had Ben back on my side, and if it had been another of my recent reckless highs that had made me call us friends, I hadn't come down yet. I hadn't taken it back. I'd even said it a few more times for good measure. So far there had been no shattering, cosmic retribution. It wasn't as if I'd offered to sell out our species for him or have his children or let him take me away from all this. We were still resistors, still allies against the Splinters, and we were also friends. A small risk, a small happiness, like stealing from Dad's candy stash as a kid. After so long following the rules and losing so much anyway, it felt frighteningly good.

Ben still had to hide at school, and for appearances' sake, we still had to avoid being seen together, but we kept in near-constant messaging contact, and all signs indicated he was also in much better spirits. Haley and Kevin helped shepherd him from class to class, and he allowed it with only minor protests. Haley had also started to visit Aldo and me occasionally during lunchtimes, when we'd talk her through whatever we happened to be working on at the time. Aldo was uncharacteristically welcoming toward her. He actually seemed to be enjoying her company, and if I was honest, so was I.

I was actually having trouble deciding which was better, having Ben back, or having myself back. As sickening as it was to know that my brain had been tampered with, it was also a tremendous relief to know that it hadn't simply decided to collapse on its own. I wasn't unsalvageably defective after all. I was not doomed to death or uselessness by rapid, unstoppable mental deterioration.

However, I wasn't quite back in peak mental condition. My nightmares were more frequent and vivid than usual, always featuring the Shard-Robbie and that one particular night in my room. There were also odd moments, even during the daytime, when bits and pieces of it would resurface in response to ridiculously tiny reminders.

The recollections usually stole a few seconds from me, a few breaths' worth of violently gagging on nothing and feeling that imaginary grime as if it were still layered under my skin, before I could put them aside again.

But this was far from the first incident that had given

my brain these kinds of processing errors. This was no new, dangerous, potentially fatal malfunction. I knew it would fade out after a while into the ordinary background nightmare rotation.

All we had to do was neutralize the Shard-Robbie, and eventually I'd be okay.

Of course, all our plans on that front were pretty serious long shots, but I'd take a long shot any day over no plan at all.

So, with my whole Network in position for the boldest move we'd even considered since the latest treaty signing, I counted it the beginning of a pretty good Saturday morning when Greg and I leaped the fence into Alexei's backyard.

Alexei's house is fairly small, suitable for the drama teacher he masquerades as more than the high-ranking Splinter he is. I've only broken into it a couple of times, and I wasn't planning on adding to that tally today. All I'd ever been able to do inside was bury a few temp bugs and run. It's impossible to search it for anything worth finding, even an electrical outlet, without leaving evidence. The garage alone gives a clear enough preview of what's inside, with its ceiling-high stacks of knickknacks and photographs, and books on baffling subjects, supported by sheaths of mildew-encrusted cardboard that don't live up to the technical definition of the word "box" anymore. But, thankfully, there's just enough space between them for Alexei to park the front half of his car. Greg and I were able to duck under the half-rolled garage door with no picking or breaking and start work on the car itself under nearly full cover from the street.

When I shone my flashlight through the window, it reflected off the screen of a big, ostentatious GPS, ridiculously advanced for anyone human to keep in an insular little town like Prospero.

Perfect.

I kept the flashlight trained on the window while Greg slipped in the artfully-sculpted coat hanger, more for my benefit than his. I wanted to watch. This was a skill I still hadn't quite mastered on my own, partly because whenever Greg did start to explain what he was doing, he tended to get sidetracked.

"See the manual lock down there? This kind you just have to rock to one side, and they make it as easy as possible so it doesn't feel jammed up already when it's brand new. But you can do that with those smooth vertical ones too, the ones that are a bitch to lift up no matter how low friction the workings are, so why doesn't everyone just use those instead?"

I didn't need to offer so much as a shrug for Greg to continue with, "I'll tell you why. Four words: most stolen vehicles list. Sounds like a bad thing, but it's like the Oscars of cars. The more often a car gets stolen, the more people will think it's worth stealing, so it must be worth buying. And that's partly true, but the savvy car companies know they can boost their numbers with shitty security features like these."

The lock clicked open as if to underscore his point.

"Now, GPSs, those are really sinister. I mean, if we can use them to track people without their knowledge with just a few modifications, can you imagine the government and marketing spyware they have to come preprogrammed with?"

"Is the chatter really necessary?" Courtney piped up over the party line. "I can't hear myself think."

"You're on lookout duty," Greg answered her as he opened the door for me. "What do you have to think about?"

I climbed in past Greg and turned the flashlight back on the GPS.

"You with me, Aldo?" I asked.

"Is it one of the cheap attachable ones, or is it wired in?" Aldo skipped to the point. I could picture him waiting in my room, surrounded by his collection of instruction manuals.

"Wired in."

"Okay, you're going to have to start the ignition."

"Pop the hood," Greg prompted me immediately. I did, he disappeared under it, and after approximately six-ty-seven seconds, the engine started with a roar.

The GPS booted up, and I read Aldo the model name that flashed across the screen.

"Passing mark A," Kevin announced from his spot three blocks north, concealed in a borrowed, tinted minivan from his dad's lot.

Greg cursed from under the hood.

The timing was always going to be tight. Alexei had a fairly predictable schedule, but it very rarely separated him from his car. His Saturday morning walk to the used bookstore was all the time we were going to get.

"We'll make it," said Aldo. "Go to 'Account Settings' and add the new email," said Aldo.

"Mark B," Ben alerted us from his spot in the tiny gas

station convenience store, less than a block away, within view of Haley's intercept point.

"Done."

"I see him," said Haley. There was a crackling sound as she dropped her Bluetooth into her purse, out of sight.

"Now 'Customize Alerts,'" said Aldo.

"Mr. Smith!" Haley exuded her usual theatrical society abundance of enthusiasm. "I'm so glad I ran into you!"

"Oh, hello, Haley!" Alexei greeted her with his usual excessively lengthened vowels. "Are all things alright-ing?" he gave one of his skin-crawling Splinter chuckles at his own poorly constructed half-rhyme.

Haley giggled along. "Oh, everything's fine. I just wanted to talk to you about the spring production! We're still doing *Measure for Measure*?"

"Yes, yes, it will be great fun!" There was a shuffle of footsteps as Alexei tried to pass Haley and she blocked his way. The GPS froze for a moment while I fiddled with its settings, and my breath caught until it moved again.

"But I had an idea about casting Mariana!"

"Oh, Haley! You knooooow I cannot show favorites! You will have to audition like always!" By the way her Bluetoothed purse knocked against her, it sounded like he'd thrown a conspiratorial arm around her shoulders. "And that is not the whole problem! How am I to have *Measure for Measure* without you for my Isabella?"

"No, I don't mean me for Mariana!" Haley assured him with another giggle.

"Oh, good!" Alexei sighed with exaggerated relief. "But we will talk about the others later, okie dokie?"

Another shuffle of feet.

"It's kind of important," Haley stopped him. "I have a friend—"

"Oh, Haley, you know how you and your friends are planning too much these days!" There was a tiny edge under his unnatural geniality. "Life is most easy when you can let things happen."

Haley's voice lost all trace of giggle. "Humor me," she said.

It was the closest the drama teacher and his star student had ever come to breaking character, dropping pretense, acknowledging their opposing sides, and for a moment I was afraid the effect would snowball until she was screaming about how she'd trusted him before he'd been party to her replacement, until he was dragging her back into the woods to repeat the process just to quiet her.

But then there was another set of steps, longer, more in tandem, the heavier ones following just behind the lighter ones, meaning that Haley had pulled Alexei around the corner, just one more short turn from his home street, but also directly across from Ben's vantage point and into the second ambush.

"This is Abby," she introduced the girl waiting there. "We're old pen pals, and she's visiting because her parents are thinking of moving to Prospero, but only if I can prove there are enough activities around here for her to get really involved. It'd mean a lot if you two could just talk a bit today. I know she'd be perfect for the troupe!"

The party line went dead silent, all seven live

mouthpieces catching a sudden absence of breath while we all waited for Alexei to smell a rat and call Haley out.

But the ploy worked, and the friendly, odd drama teacher façade clicked instantly back to full power for the human stranger's benefit.

"Oh, of course! Why did you not tell me so? Hello, Abby! It is a treat, always, to meet Haley's friends!"

"Didn't think so when you voted to stick me in a pod, did you?" Ben muttered.

Abby gushed convincingly for a while about her theatrical experience, and Alexei interrupted with bizarre irrelevancies with his usual regularity.

With a small purr on the line, Kevin started the van.

Just as Aldo finished talking me through the parental controls settings, there was an extra-long, awkward lull in Alexei, Haley, and Abby's conversation. "How soon is your mom expecting you?" Haley asked, tapping her purse, right on the microphone, asking for a sign.

"How's it looking?" Ben asked me.

"Shit," said Aldo. "Send the validation email again. Screwed up the 'are you human' code. Letters were too distorted. Looked like it was asking for gamma, epsilon, and the 'Artist Formerly Known as Prince' symbol."

"Sending," I said, and started another agonizingly long progress bar.

"Milk Duds it is," said Ben, and I heard the slightest breath of recognition, disguised as recollection, as Haley saw him press the "more time" candy box signal to the gas station window.

"Oh, I forgot!" said Haley. "She wanted to know if the troupe counts for any school credit, right?"

Such bland formalities wouldn't hold Alexei long. Greg raised an eyebrow at me.

"Start picking," I told him. He nodded and knelt by the door that led from the garage into the house. I still didn't like the idea of going inside, but the way things were going, we were going to need every possible escape route open. "If you can't, don't break it until I give the word," I warned.

Greg snorted. "You seriously overestimate this freak's taste in locks."

"I am so sorry, girls!" Alexei finally exclaimed. "But I really must be gone. It is almost story time! You know missing one minute of *Search for the Sun* means never catching up!"

"Seriously?" Aldo moaned. "He watches soaps *and* he doesn't have a DVR?"

"How bad?" I asked, and thankfully, Aldo didn't answer with an analysis of daytime television.

"Transferring data," he said. "You're done pushing buttons. I just need you to keep it online a few seconds more, maybe thirty."

"Just one more question!" Haley tried.

"But we will talk so soon! I must insist!"

"Got it," said Greg, propping the door open to a view of a perilously dark, narrow, and paper-strewn path of maroon carpet.

"Two houses from the corner," Ben warned us. "One house. Around the corner, six houses from you. He can see the front walk."

"Done," said Aldo. "Get out of there."

Greg cut the engine, fumbled the wires back into place, and shut the hood.

"Two houses, perfect view of the front," Ben said, struggling to keep his voice neutral and factual. "Mina?"

"Get under the car," I whispered to Greg. "I'll keep him off you, and the first chance you get, you run to the pickup point."

He paused just a moment before nodding and stepping back to let me into the house.

"Was it enough?" Haley's voice got louder as she hitched her Bluetooth back onto her ear.

"Get to the pickup point," I told her.

"Was it enough?" she repeated.

"Mina, what's going on?" Ben hissed in my ear "Are you two out of there?"

"Should I move?" Courtney asked. "What are we doing?"

Greg rolled all the way under the car just as Alexei's legs came into view on the driveway, the last thing I saw before closing the door on myself.

The smell inside the house was overpowering: years' worth of mold and fermenting dairy and backed-up drains. The junk was packed so tightly against most of the walls and windows that even now, in the middle of a sunny day, there was barely enough light to maneuver by.

I tiptoed across to the one unobscured pane of frosted glass set into the front door and watched Alexei's silhouette coming closer through the front yard, right between the two entrances.

This way, I thought at him, for all the good it would do. *Not the car, don't check the car, this way.*

But Alexei's silhouette veered off in the garage's direction anyway.

So much for getting away clean. I took a steadying breath and pounded on the front door from the inside.

That changed his course pretty quickly.

He made straight for the front door, and I ran back toward the garage and skidded to a stop when the door refused to open under my hand. I turned the latching mechanism in the center of the knob, and it moved with too little friction, broken and disconnected somewhere inside. Maybe Alexei only used this door for coming in, or maybe if I wiggled the latch just right it would catch the inner workings, but I didn't have time to figure out how because the front door's knob was already moving. I opened the nearest interior door and scrambled through it, closing it behind me just as the front door opened.

Footsteps pounded distant pavement. Greg, I hoped.

"Picking up Courtney," Kevin said in my ear. "Headed your way, Mina. Where are you?"

The low information stream of the Bluetooth felt like a siren signaling my position.

"Pickup point," I whispered once more into it with the softest possible breath. Then I hung up and stuffed it into my bag.

In the dim light, judging by the raised, soft-looking free space in the middle, I guessed I was in Alexei's bedroom. There was a window high in the wall, covered only with a stack of books and overlooking the backyard.

I stepped slowly toward it, choosing the quietest-looking sections of floor coverings, listening to the creak of floorboards back in what passed for the living room. They progressed too quickly in my direction along the hallway toward the bedroom door, and I had to stop and wedge myself out of sight, four feet up the wall, between two overflowing boxes of paperwork.

I didn't need Robbie nearby to make me feel the skittering movements of vermin in the refuse beneath me.

The door opened, and I watched through a pencil-width gap between boxes as Alexei entered the room.

I half expected him to start tossing boxes this way and that, searching and digging for the obvious intruder, but he simply pulled his jacket off, the pasty white arms underneath Splinter-cracking into whatever inhuman, elbow-less shapes made this process easier, and threw it on the space I'd taken for a bed.

"Kit-ty-cat?" he called out, pronouncing each syllable as if he didn't know where the gap went between the words. "Kit-ty-cat? What did you knock over? It's okay, I still love you!"

With my slow, quiet breath of relief, I examined the stench in the air a little more closely. Of course there'd be a cat or two in here somewhere.

Alexei stood there, looking around, for twenty seconds, twenty-five, before he wandered back down the hall, leaving the door open behind him.

That relief slipped away when I heard the mewing in the box beneath me.

Go on, I thought at the cat. *Go find him. Don't make him come to you.*

"Kit-ty-cat?" Alexei called from the other end of the house, turning back.

With the tightest fist I could form, trying not to imagine what I was about to get stuck under my fingernails, I punched through the layer of cardboard beneath me, into Kit-ty-cat's hiding place.

There was a yowl, two claws grazing my wrist, and a ball of long, patchy grey fur rocketed out of the front of the pile to meet its owner at the far end of the junk canyon, past the living room, in what I guessed was the kitchen.

I watched for a few seconds, more out of an irrational inability to look away than fear of being noticed, as Alexei formed his left leg into some twisted shape in the dark. A cat's scratching post, I realized, when Kit-ty-cat leapt up into the newly formed tunnel where his knee had been.

During the last few wood snaps of the transformation, I found the sense to shift the stack of books behind me away from the window. If Alexei noticed, Kit-ty-cat would have to take the blame for that too.

There was a tearing sound from the kitchen, like cardboard or very thick paper, and I realized what Alexei was ripping into and turning over—a bag of cat kibble—just in time to wrench the stiff window open under cover of the sound and hoist myself and my bag through.

I was back over the fence and sprinting for the pickup point on the street behind the gas station almost as soon as my feet hit Alexei's back lawn.

Kevin pulled the van forward to meet me, the side door sliding open.

Ben and Haley pulled me in by one hand each.

"What took you so long?" Greg was very conspicuously wiping motor oil off his shirt as he asked me this.

"Minor detour," I said. "Mission accomplished."

Haley squealed with delight and Ben insisted on high-fiving me, though it looked like he was suppressing a stronger gesture of relief.

Even though I'd known she would be there, I did a double-take when I glanced into the back seat and saw the utterly unmemorable, unrecognizable, nondescript "Abby," just before she pulled off the plain brown wig, gratefully shook out her black and orange hair, and leapt into Greg's lap.

"Still freaks me out when you do that," he said when they broke off an adrenaline-heavy kiss that briefly forced me to look away.

"Yeah, me too," she agreed, pulling out her compact and black lipstick and urgently repainting all the features that distinguished her as Julie. "Has its uses, though. I mean, other than not embarrassing my mom at Temple."

Aldo had the GPS records open in eight separate windows on his laptop when we joined him in my room to review them as agreed upon, all at once, all together.

He was still busy cross-referencing them with my records of Dad's movements to create a list of likely Splinter Council meeting places when Courtney asked me to "help her upstairs," as if she had anything to do upstairs in my parents' house.

The front door opened and closed while I followed her to the kitchen in the hopes of getting whatever problem she was having out of the way. Someone must have gone outside. I made a mental note to check the bushes for the remnants of joints. That was the last thing I needed to explain when my parents got home.

Standing on opposite sides of the kitchen's glimmering white tile island, I waited for Courtney's latest cutting ethics lecture.

"That was sloppy," she said finally.

"It could have been tidier," I conceded. "Thankfully, we succeeded, and everyone survived to go over notes on it for next time."

"Do that," she said. "But I don't mean them, I mean you."

That annoyed me, but I was confident it didn't show. "Would you like to elaborate on that?"

Courtney briefly unfolded her arms in a gesture of placation so graceful and dance-like that it looked like she practiced it in the mirror ten times before breakfast each morning. "I'm not here to usurp you, Mina," she said. I tried to figure out if this was one of those times when people say the exact opposite of what they mean.

I shrugged. "Good."

"And I'm not saying you're a bad leader."

"But *you* could do better," I finished for her.

She shook her head. "No, I couldn't. Not for this crowd," she said. "But you could. They were looking to you, and you left them hanging."

"I knew they'd manage."

"You could have helped them manage better. You could have made them feel engaged, instilled them with a little confidence. I understand need-to-know, believe me, but your definition is severely limited. You have skills," she said. "In fact, you must be pretty amazing to have this many natural loose cannons this loyal to you."

"I'm not, really," I said, and Courtney actually looked surprised. She stopped and waited for me to explain.

I remembered drawing the exact same conclusion about The Old Man and realizing much too slowly how wrong I was. I couldn't exploit the same fallacy, not even with her.

"Ben's the one who knows how to talk people into things and make them get along, not me," I told her. "I stumble my way through every single pep talk. I've never even had this many allies in the same place at once before. People only do what I tell them because they know I know what I'm doing, because I've been doing it for a long time. There isn't a lot of competition in my field, and I happen to be the best."

Courtney accepted this explanation with a curt nod. "You may be right," she said. "Doesn't matter. Whether you deserve it or not, these people won't accept any leader but you. You owe it to them to *lead*."

If I'd tried too hard to answer this somehow, I might have missed the door opening again and the identifying set of footsteps returning.

Ben.

"Everything okay?" I called out to him.

"Fine," he called back. "Just thought I heard something."

20

LOOKING FOR HELP IN ALL THE WRONG PLACES

Ben

The Prospero Public Library was on the edge of town, about as close to getting out as you could go without leaving the city limits. I didn't know if he had gotten my message or if he would even be able to interpret it once he did get it, but I had a feeling that I was worrying about nothing.

He would show. He couldn't keep himself away.

I continued pacing the library's aisle on manufacturing and building books, occasionally pulling one from the shelf and flipping through it. I'd taken to woodworking quite a bit in the last couple of weeks with Mr. Finn. Considering that I would probably never leave Prospero, maybe I had a future to look forward to in carpentry, assuming, of course, I had a future.

Footsteps nearby. I slipped the book I'd been looking at back on the shelf and looked for the source of the sound. Just a few girls—freshmen, middle-schoolers maybe. They'd been laughing, but as soon as they saw me, they got a look of disgust on their faces that would've hurt me deeply a couple of months ago.

Things had slowed down slightly since Halloween. Maybe it had something to do with Mina making sure I had an escort almost round the clock, but Madison and whatever other goons the Splinters had on my case were laying low. The few new accusations that came my way were shot down pretty quickly since I had a ready supply of alibi witnesses. Patrick, especially, had gotten quiet after shattering his hand on Mr. Finn, with rumors of how he had broken it making him a laughingstock around school.

Still, the old accusations were more than enough to keep most people avoiding me. You'd think that would have made the privacy I needed today easy to come by, but my constant escorts were nearly impossible to avoid unless I was in the bathroom or sleeping. To pull this off, I had to figure out when everyone would be most busy (Thursday afternoon when Mina, Aldo and Julie checked the GPS data, Haley had cheerleading practice, and Kevin volunteered at the rec center), deliver my message, show up, and hope for the best.

I checked my cell phone. 4:30, on the dot. He wasn't here. *No,* I corrected myself, *just because I can't see him doesn't mean he's not here.*

I looked back to the bookshelf and made to pull out another book when I saw it.

The jaunty, stuffed kangaroo I had tossed over the fence of Mina's backyard after we'd broken into Alexei's car sat in a gap in the bookshelf at about eye height. It still wore the bright yellow t-shirt that proudly proclaimed, "READING IS FUNDAMENTAL," and the code I had written beneath it.

1115 1630 694

I picked the kangaroo up from its gap between the books and was not surprised to see his steely eyes staring at me from the other side of the bookshelf.

"Hello, Old Man," I said.

"Hello back, Benji," he responded.

"Glad you could make it. I didn't know if you'd get the message," I said.

"Date, Time, Dewey Decimal location in the library. You couldn't have made it clearer if you'd screamed it. You also couldn't have picked a worse location for a meet," he said.

"I thought you'd like the privacy," I said.

"I do, but the Prospero town fathers don't much like me in town," he said.

"That's funny," I said. "They don't like me out of this town. So we got that in common."

He chuckled. "And there's you. You know this is the kinda place where you stand out like a sore thumb. How many kids your age hang around libraries these days? Now me, I can get away with lookin' like a homeless person flipping through the art books looking for porn; plenty of free tits or Greek boys to go around there. You, you don't fit. There are so many more inconspicuous places you could've picked, Benji. I'm disappointed."

"You're also here," I said. "So you can't be that disappointed."

I couldn't see him well on the other side of the bookshelf,

but I could tell by his voice that he was amused. "Call me intrigued. Why'd you call me here? And no witty answers this time; I know you hate me."

"I don't hate you," I clarified. "It's not like I like you very much either."

"You 'don't like me' 'cause you think I broke little Robin and made her into the mess she is today. If you'd seen her when I first met her, you'd be thanking me for all I've done for that girl," he said.

"Well, I didn't," I said bitterly.

"So again, why am I riskin' my neck for you today?" he asked.

"I came here to ask for your help," I said.

"You don't need my help," he said. "Robin's as good as they come."

"Yes, we do," I said. "We've got way too much to deal with right now, and we could use every bit of help we can get. We've got a Shard who can get into our heads, we've got Slivers trying to kidnap people, probably so they can incite a war, and the regular Splinters are doing everything possible to destroy my life. You've fought them for a really long time. You know how to deal with Shards. Help us."

He laughed. As usual, it was not an entirely pleasant sound.

"What?" I asked.

"Well, I've been working on one of your problems for a while. You know how long I'd been following Robin, waiting for your Shard, Yorkie, to show up? He finally makes his move out in the open on All Hallow's, and you have to go and foul things up. He ran away. Kid can't hide forever, though, and I'll take care of him for you. Just worry about your high school shit and let those of us who know what we're doin' take care of this," he said.

I didn't even know where to start with what he said. He'd been hunting Robbie, using Mina as bait? I knew we were doing basically the same thing, but at least Mina was in on our plan. Then there was Robbie.

"We don't want to kill Robbie. We want to save him," I clarified.

He laughed, again.

"Benji, I can tell you're a good kid, and I know Robin likes you, so I'm willin' to cut you some slack, but I gotta say, you can be really thick sometimes. When are you gonna realize that there's no difference in Splinters, and they're all part of the same problem? When you realize that, you'll see that there's only one solution."

"One easy solution," I shot back. "We've found others."

"Right, the Perkins girl," he said. "So you saved one girl. A girl who might just live to a ripe old age like yours truly because of what the pod did to her, watching her grand-children die of old age, assuming of course they didn't void her womb. Don't you see? You can't save 'em all. Hell, only the ones who've been in the pods less than fourteen months really stand a chance at coming back, and even then it isn't for sure. After that, they're too far gone."

I thought back to the Warehouse, seeing some of the bodies that looked shriveled in their glowing pods while the images of their hosts appeared to be healthy and vital.

I said, "Even if we can't save them all, there are still people in there who deserve a fighting chance."

"Maybe they do, maybe they don't, but I can say with good, personal knowledge that when you're in one of their terror pods, you don't want to be saved. You don't want to be human again because being back in the world is agony after what their pods have done. You welcome death. Killing them all is the best way to save them. It's merciful," he said.

Again, I thought of Haley. I had not seen her welcome death for one moment since we had freed her from the Warehouse. Sure, she still had her jumpy moments, but she was glad to be alive. She wasn't whatever had made The Old Man this way.

A sudden, stupid urge hit me. It's one I would have held back months ago, back before I had been worn down by the Splinters' campaign against my life, but now, I couldn't anymore.

Now it was my turn to laugh unpleasantly.

"What's so funny, Benji?" he asked.

I couldn't stop laughing. It hit me too hard, too quickly. "I'm sorry, it's just, after everything Mina told me about you, the way she built you up, I never expected that you'd be a coward!"

He glared at me through the bookshelf, his eyes staring into my soul.

"You're lucky I like Robin as much as I do, son, or I'd kill you where you stand," he said evenly. "And I am *not* a coward. I'm just here to make sure they pay. They have to pay."

"They have to pay?" I repeated. "That's all you've got to say? You just say 'kill 'em all' because they put you in a pod for a while?"

"No," he said, angrily. "They have to pay because they

took everything from me. They stole my life! Tell me with a straight face that whenever anyone looks at you like a goddamn rapist because of what they did that you don't fantasize about killing them all!"

He pounded the bookcase powerfully with his hand, so hard I worried that he would tip it over. I held on to it to steady it. Of course, he was right.

"I did. I still do, sometimes. But I would never do anything about it, not knowing there was still a chance to save the person they took. Everybody deserves a chance," I said.

"You say that now. Stay here long enough and you'll change your tune," he said. The earnestness, almost sadness, he said that with gave me a chill.

"I thought like you, once. Back when I was a more responsible man. I had a wife. I had the two most beautiful daughters a man could have. A house with a white picket fence. I didn't know how I got so lucky. After the war, I wasn't in a good place, but Gertie, she made me human."

We barely pretended to read anymore, locking eyes through the bookcase. I didn't know if I wanted to hear the rest of his story.

"One day, she took our kids over to see her sister in Milton's Mill for the weekend. *They* came for me that night. Looking like my friends, people I knew from town, but not them. They dragged me out of my living room, beat me, tied me up and tossed me in the back of a truck. Dragged me down into the mine and hooked me up to a pod. I knew pain and fear and not much else, surrounded by thousands of voices calling to me, screaming for help, asking me to join them. After some time—it felt like it was a day or two but was closer to four months—I got out. It just vomited me out like it didn't want me anymore. I fought my way to the surface, back to town, back to my girls.

"They were glad to see me, they'd thought me dead. They nursed me back. They didn't know what to think of my story. I didn't know what to think, but I knew it was real, and I knew it was wrong. I knew I had to do something to fix it, I thought I could save those people inside. I thought if I could get out that I could get them out too. I made plans. I gathered weapons. Gertie thought I was crazy. She said that if what I said was true, we had to get out of town. I told her I had to save those people, that it was the right thing to do. Three weeks passed."

He gulped, clearly uncomfortable about telling this part of the story.

"They came for us in the night, shining their car headlights in all our windows. They didn't come looking like people this time. No, they came wearing those damn gray faces they wear when they don't want to be recognized. A man came to our door. Artie Koppin, a judge, a friend. He came with an offer, said that I knew more than I ought to, and if I just let them talk to me, that we could all come out ahead. Things didn't have to get any worse. I knew he was lyin'. He still lies. You watch out for him."

"I don't know who you're talking about," I admitted.

The Old Man chuckled dryly. "Artie Koppin died back in the mid-eighties. He's got a new body now, but the smile, those eyes, are the same. You know him as Sam Todd. That name ring a bell?"

It did. The offer he made sounded about the way Sam worked, too.

"He'll smile and make nice and seem like the most reasonable guy in the world, but Sam Todd is one dangerous son of a bitch, Benji. He'll cut your throat, anyone's throat, even the throat of any Splinter in town to get what he wants. If you ever wind up on his bad side, you can either watch out for him, or you can kill him. Only that last choice'll get you anywhere because no matter where you are, he will find you. When he came for us, I decided to fight."

That dull glow of anger in my chest had been replaced by a faint sickness. I knew how this was going to end.

"It wasn't a fight. It was a slaughter. They were on the house all at once. I sent my girls into the basement. My guns did nothing to the Splinters. I shot them, I stabbed them, I threw boilin' oil fresh off the stove at them, and they just kept comin'! They set the house on fire, there was smoke everywhere. I tried to find my girls. I tried to help them, but in all the smoke, the fire . . ."

He pulled up the sleeve of his jacket that covered his good arm, showing skin that looked like a scarred roadmap of pain.

"I ran outside. They got me again. They didn't want to bargain this time, but they also didn't want to kill me. Artie, Sam, whatever his name is, used his sway as a judge to have me committed up at the old Braiwood Institute. I had to hear in a padded room that my family burned to death. My Gertie, my Carol . . . my Robin."

"Robin was your daughter?" I asked.

"Mina looks just like her," he nodded. "I never claimed to be a sane man."

"I never accused you of being one," I said, trying to let that sink in. "Does Mina know?"

"Of course she does. Can't hide anything from that one, Benji. She's special, you know that, right?"

I nodded.

"If I was a broken man goin' in there, I was a shattered man after that. I knew that mercy was pointless with these sons of bitches. They all had to die. They all had to pay for what they did. I healed. I broke out, and I've been huntin' them ever since. Mostly alone, sometimes with the help of a lost soul whose world's been upturned almost as bad as mine. But I've fought the good fight, and I'll tell you Benji, it's been a good, long fight."

I was shaken, but I kept myself together.

"Look, I'm really sorry for what's happened to you. I've lost someone close to me, too, but that still doesn't change the fact that we need your help here," I said.

He looked at me through the bookcase, thoughtful.

"Are you ready to admit that all Splinters are the same, and that they all deserve to die?" he asked.

I shook my head.

"Then you're not ready for my help," he said. "I'll be doing what I've been doing for the past sixty years. If we happen to be fixing the same problem at the same time, then you might find me helping you. If you ever get in my way . . . get out of it. Quickly."

"What happens if I don't?" I challenged.

He laughed. "You're a smartass, I'll give you that, Benji. I can see what Mina sees in you. I always told her, her biggest problem, aside from havin' a monster for a daddy, is that she doesn't laugh enough. Keep her laughin'. She might keep you around."

"She keeps me around because we're friends," I corrected him.

He laughed even louder. "Keep tellin' yourself that, Benji. Take a word of advice from an old man, son; you best be in this for the cause, because if you're in it for her, you're going to be sorely disappointed. I raised her better."

I meant to counter him, but before I could, he was gone. I ran around the edge of the bookcase looking for him. He had completely disappeared. The art book he had been flipping through lay on the floor, a small box on top of it. I picked it up, saw that it contained hot pink sidewalk chalk. On the back of it he had written a simple note:

T IS FOR TROUBLE
I'LL FIND YOU.

Well, that certainly sounded like a more efficient means of finding The Old Man than tossing a stuffed kangaroo over Mina's back fence, but it didn't help me here.

I'd meant it when I said we needed his help. Mina knew a lot about Splinters. He knew more. He'd been to war. We hadn't. There was so much he could do a lot more safely than the rest of us, but it would come at a price.

A price I wasn't ready to pay.

He was right. I did hate him. Maybe not as much as I hated the Splinters, but pretty close. He had no regard for human life, and he treated everyone he came across as garbage because he believed his fight made him morally superior to the rest of us. Even those he claimed to care for, like Mina, he was ready to dispose of at a moment's notice. It was hard, considering everything he had been through, not to feel bad for him. Maybe we really were better off without him. Maybe we shouldn't have considered him an ally. Maybe Mina would be better off if she never saw him again.

I considered the box of chalk in my hand. There was a trash can ten feet away. I could throw it in there so easily, completely wash my hands of The Old Man.

I could have, but I didn't. I forced the chalk into my pocket as I walked from the Prospero Public Library. I may have hated The Old Man, but even with that hatred I couldn't write off the fact that there might come a time when we might need him.

After I got a couple blocks from the library, I turned my cell phone back on. There were easily a dozen messages from Mina asking where I was. I texted her back, telling her I was fine and that I just had to take care of something.

STILL HUMAN?

I took this as her attempt at a joke. Remembering The Old Man's frustration with my resistance to killing all Splinters and the people they were attached to, I had no problem typing back, *YES.*

21.

Mina

In the hallways between Ms. Craven's classroom and Mr. Finn's, I did my best to emulate what my face would look like if I were on my way to have a raging argument.

Aldo more or less imitated my demeanor as we walked, serious, always keeping himself to the busier side of the hallways, shuffling me toward the wall.

I wasn't sure when this had started between us, him walking like the bodyguard instead of the client, challenging my riskier plans to the Network. When exactly had my lost little puppy learned how to morph into a snarling German Shepherd of a guard dog?.

I didn't try to stop him. He could handle himself, and I could still pull him out of the way quickly and easily enough if it came to that.

My knock on the classroom door sounded convincingly irritable.

Ben opened the door only a crack. I saw the smile flash across his face before it went serious again. Luckily, no one else was standing that close.

"What are you doing here?" he snapped abruptly, producing a very tiny, irrational pain in my chest. As usual, his act was absolutely flawless.

"Believe me, I wish I were somewhere else," I said. "We need to talk."

"Now you want to talk? Fine. Talk."

Hoping I wasn't moving too quickly, I looked over both shoulders at the passersby who were beginning to stare. "Inside," I said.

With a dramatic sigh, Ben opened the door just enough to usher Aldo and me quickly inside.

Mr. Finn was turning off the power saw and removing his goggles, and Kevin sat in the corner rubbing something with sandpaper, visibly trying not to laugh at us.

As soon as the door was closed, Ben's smile came back, and one of his hands moved toward me and then uselessly back to his side. It was as if he'd been about to hug me and then stopped himself. Old instinct made me fold my arms and step slightly away from dangerous, strategy-clouding, unnecessary contact. The moment passed, but I was sorry when it did, sorry enough to make me think that maybe if another one like it arose, I wouldn't let it go the same way.

For the time being, I let myself return his smile with every bit of the enthusiasm I felt.

"So this is the girl they've been trying to take away from you?" Mr. Finn asked him, squinting across the room at me. "Good for you, dumbass."

I was pretty sure this was meant to be nice, to both of us.

It took just a few minutes of looking around to realize that I liked the woodshop. Everything in it was more sturdily built than in most of the school. There were plenty of innocent-looking tools lying around that could make excellent weapons if needed, and the intricate patterns of the stray wood shavings and the deep gouges in every surface made it easy to absorb it all clearly.

"No Haley?" I asked. I'd assumed she'd be there if she wasn't with Aldo and me, especially if Kevin was here.

"She said she had some kind of project," Ben said in his normal voice, but quieter. "So, really, what are you doing here?"

"I came to remind you to check your email," I said.

"What? I checked ten minutes ago." But he was already hurrying through his phone, expecting to find a new disaster there. He stopped at the message I'd just sent, with the subject line 'The Need-to-Know-Newsletter', and I had to prod him.

"Open it."

He scanned it with wide eyes. "This is . . . a lot."

"The first of many," I told him. "I'm thinking once a week to the whole Network unless something major comes up."

Kevin warily pulled out his own phone to check his copy.

"It started with the information I promised Courtney, and I thought, if I'm giving it to someone as unverified as she is, there's really no reason not to give it to the rest of you," I explained. "And then I thought, if I'm putting that in an email, there are some other things that are just as important and not that much more dangerous to the cause, like the lists. That's what made me think of weekly updates because the lists are always changing, I mean, they've already changed a lot since the last time we handed them out, and keeping them up to date will help everyone keep themselves safe."

I didn't blame Ben for being speechless. I'd been speechless when I'd realized I was even considering this. "It's still risky. In the wrong hands, this could tell them exactly whom to use against us." I didn't like this next part, but I said it anyway. "Courtney said my definition of need-to-know was too narrow. You've been saying . . ." I stopped trying to explain how hard I was trying to accept, even celebrate this dangerous, yet liberating, idea of working with friends. "After a lot of careful consideration, I'm starting to think you may both have been right."

"I think it's a great idea," said Ben, but there was some distraction to his excitement. I could guess by his look as much as the color of the screen's reflection off his eyes that he'd scrolled back up to the newsletter's top story, the Splinter Council meeting place we'd narrowed down from Alexei's GPS data. "Foxfire Collectibles?" he read. "Your dad's shop?"

"I'd call it ninety-eight percent certain," Aldo told him. "Alexei and Sam were both there while we were patching up Haley."

"It explains why I could never pinpoint any suspicious locations from my dad's car alone," I said.

"This all sounds terribly important and interesting," Mr. Finn cut in, "but are you kids going to pull your weight, or are you going to spend the whole hour talking in cryptic whispers?"

Ben looked back at me, and his face had those tense corners it gets when he's about to try to ask one thing by asking something else. He held up the phone.

"Was this all you wanted to talk about?"

I had to guess that I was answering the other question correctly, not just losing him valuable points at his one lunchtime harbor, when I pulled out the new deck of cards I'd bought the day before on yet another circuitous and solitary walk home.

"Actually, Aldo and I were just going over the rules of five-card draw, and I couldn't quite explain all the subtleties the way you can. He's pretty convinced he could beat us both."

Aldo rolled his eyes, but didn't argue with me.

Ben gave Mr. Finn a look that might have qualified as pleading.

Mr. Finn sighed. "Your loss. The kind of guy who commissions an authentic fifteenth-century catapult for his wedding can usually be counted on to spare no expense."

I didn't think I'd ever seen Ben smile so much in such a short space of time. "Thanks."

Kevin joined us to form a circle on the cleanest section of floor, and soon the four of us were arguing over the somewhat subjective denominations of the crumbling wood chips we'd gathered to gamble with, shouting our bets over the swells of noise from the buzz saw, then shushing each other whenever Mr. Finn turned it off.

Ben and Aldo seemed to derive a great deal of enjoyment from heckling each other over every single betting round, and Ben and Kevin kept conferring with each other, ana-lyzing Aldo and me for tells—as if Ben hadn't spent the summer before the Warehouse incident accusing Kevin of being a Splinter because of some messy issue involving Haley's attention that, as far as I could tell, still hadn't entirely been resolved after her rescue.

When I was dealing, Kevin even asked me for cards as if he found me just barely uncomfortable to look at.

As if I weren't the reason his brother was dead. As if we hadn't had to mourn him awkwardly alone together while the rest of the town had still been calling him "missing." As if I hadn't forced the unwelcome knowledge of Splinters into his life. As if he'd never run away.

It was almost as if none of us ever had.

The only problem was the one I always had when playing cards with Ben, the way it somehow allowed time to slip away from me. The whole hour passed in what I could have sworn was only half that.

Ben and I had our next classes in the same direction, so we had to make some quick arrangements for our exit.

"I'll go south first," I offered, "when we storm off in oppo-site directions. I can loop around the east corridor."

"Okay," Ben agreed. "Crap. I forgot."

"What?"

"We might need to work on our act, some stuff other than running separate ways."

"What stuff?" I thought I'd been acting natural enough in the mock extension of our feud, but there was always the chance that I'd missed some critical detail, something

someone like Ben could spot from across a crowded hallway but that I'd need embarrassing amounts of practice
to get right.

"My mom wants to have you and Haley and your parents
over for Thanksgiving dinner," Ben said almost apologet-
ically, "to thank the families that got us settled. Basically
to prove that we can get along with someone around here.
I think your mom already accepted."

Of course she had. It would look unwelcoming not to.
I even felt a brief, absurd flicker of hope that she'd done it
partly to annoy Dad.

"So, when your mom's watching," I whispered my guess,
"we're three inseparable best friends, heartstring-tugging
enough to make keeping us together worth all the broken
windows and car keyings Prospero can throw at her, so
she doesn't get herself and you killed trying to escape. But
when she's not watching, and my dad is, we can barely keep
from strangling each other, let alone keep up the selfless
charade we've concocted for your mother's safety, and we're
certainly not in any shape to pose a threat to the Splinters
together, so there's no need for them to do anything more
drastic to you than they have."

"Sounds about right," Ben agreed.

"Glad I didn't help 'settle' you," said Aldo, still smirking.
"Makes Thanksgiving at my place sound almost relaxing."

Kevin clapped Ben and me on the back before shifting
to Ben's side of the doorway, ready to storm off his way.
"Might want to ask Haley for some pointers," he said.

Mr. Finn couldn't have heard the whole exchange, but he

waved us off with a sigh of, "Oh, the drama, the deception, the intrigue. You know, sometimes I miss high school."

"Ready?" asked Ben.

In answer, I opened the door to let Aldo through first and then slammed it back before Ben could follow us.

Ben ran out a few steps behind, clutching his elbow much more dramatically than the sound of the door hitting it had warranted, Kevin watching with convincing concern from a safe distance.

"You know, for a genius, you really suck at rational discussions!" Ben shouted.

"Just because *you* couldn't infer a valid conclusion to an Aristotelian syllogism to save your life!"

"Freak!"

"Traitor!"

"Spaz!"

"Sellout!"

I wished as soon as we were out of sight of each other that I'd asked for the shorter route after all.

I had to duck into a bathroom on the way to class to wait until I could stop smiling.

22.

THANKSGIVING

Ben

"You can do this."

"I know."

"You've done it before."

"I *know*."

"Then why are you having so much trouble?"

I wished I had a good answer for that. "Look, it's been a while, all right?"

Haley looked at me in the mirror and smiled. "You've fought a Splinter deer, beaten a Shard with a tree branch, and broken into the Warehouse to rescue me, and you have a hard time tying a tie?"

"Mankind has never created a more oppressive garment," I muttered.

Haley did not look amused. "Try wearing women's clothing sometime. Then we'll talk."

"Point," I said as I untied the knot I'd managed to fumble my way into and went back to square one. Haley smiled again. She wore a nice dress of autumn colors and had her hair tied back with a bow. As usual, she looked beautiful, a fact made more uncomfortable by her insistence on wrapping her arms around my neck as she helped me with the tie.

"How bad do you think this is going to be?" Haley asked.

That was a good question. Having Mina around other people was always a risky proposition, and having her parents around with her—one of them a Splinter collaborator, the other a leader of the Splinters who was personally responsible for ruining my life—had the potential to be a really unstable situation.

"It could be bad. It could also be perfectly pleasant. Splinters are good at playing nice," I said.

"And you'll be okay with that?" she asked.

I scowled. "I'll play nice if they play nice. What about you?"

Her smile faltered, briefly, but she quickly recovered and looked as happy as ever. "I'm a good actress."

Looking at that smile, I believed her. You could hardly tell that she hated Splinters as much as, possibly even more than, Mina.

I tried to find some silver lining. "Well, at least there's gonna be good food."

"Better than usual," Haley said, her fingers nimbly fixing my tie into something presentable.

"Oh?" I asked.

She nodded. "Most years since Dad left, it's just been turkey sandwiches and cranberry juice on Thanksgiving. My mom's never been the most imaginative cook."

I laughed. "My mom's the exact opposite. Old Wisconsin farm family. I always thought Thanksgiving was supposed to be one of those family sorts of things, you know? I mean, after she moved away from her folks, Mom never really liked making it about the big family thing, she tried to keep it between the three of us, and the two of us after Dad died, but she always used to cook enough food for ten people. It was one of those things to look forward to, and it was never something I thought I'd have to share with . . ."

"The enemy?" Haley said.

"Yeah."

"It's not going to be easy for any of us," Haley said.

"Except your mom. And my mom. At least they get to be blissfully ignorant," I said.

"Should they be?" Haley asked, finishing my tie. "Perfect."

"They have to be in the dark," I said, turning to face her.

"Why?"

"Because the more they know, the more danger they're in," I said.

"They're in danger simply by being related to us. If the Splinters think they can use our moms against us, they will. So why not tell them?" Haley said.

"Because . . ." I didn't want to say it was because I didn't think my mother could handle it. Aunt Christine was tough. She might be able to handle it if we told her honestly, maybe providing some proof.

"Because they'll think we're crazy. I think this is something that they'd have to see firsthand in order to believe. It took a lot for me to believe, in the beginning," I said.

Haley sighed. "This sucks."

"Tell me about it," I said.

The doorbell rang downstairs.

"Ben, honey, can you get that? We're a little busy in here!" Mom called from the kitchen.

"I got it!" I called back. I looked at Haley. "Are you ready?"

"As ready as I'll ever be," she said, giving a light twirl on her feet. "Am I presentable?"

"Very. Me?" I asked, pulling on my dad's old sport coat.

"Dashing," she said. I held out my arm theatrically, and she took it in kind, her hand trembling very slightly. I hoped that she wouldn't feel how nervous I was, too.

"To dinner with the enemy!" I proclaimed loudly, getting one last laugh out of her before we went downstairs.

To be fair, we were able to stay on our best behavior for close to an hour.

That was a lot better than I was expecting.

Haley and I let the Todds in, playing gracious hosts, showing Mina, her mother and her father around and introducing them to our respective moms (though, being a small town, they all knew each other anyway). Mina had told me that her mom wasn't a particularly good cook, and the store-bought pumpkin pie she carried in proved that theory. She tried to make up for it with a few bottles of wine for the adults and sparkling cider for the rest of us. My mom couldn't tell one type of wine from another for the life of her, let alone pronounce the name of the vineyard the bottles came from, but she took them gratefully, cracking one of them open and sharing it with Aunt Christine and Mina's mom. They stayed in the kitchen talking, even laughing some. I didn't know if that was a good thing or not.

I didn't know what to make of Mina's mom. On the one hand, she was a collaborator on the town council who actively worked with the Splinters to help keep their presence hidden. On the other hand, she had nearly divorced Mina's dad after finding out that he'd snuck a Splinter into the town council, and she looked at him as if she could barely stand him. She didn't strike me as a friend, not with her cold demeanor and calculated appearance of friendliness in front of the other moms, but she didn't strike me as an enemy either. That would have to do.

With them out of the way, Haley and I were forced to give Mina and her dad the grand tour of my house, not that it was particularly necessary since they had known the previous owners. Haley and I kept up our act pretty well, doing our best to ignore Mina while I answered whatever inane questions her dad had about what plans we had for the place, as if he weren't my jailer and the architect responsible for my social shaming in Prospero.

I had to remind myself that soon we might have some leverage of our own to even the playing field. I knew Mina had to be thinking the same thing. She seemed focused on some far-off place, probably uncomfortable in the colorful dress and sweater her mother forced upon her, keeping a careful cold shoulder to us both. Haley was having a harder time. It was hardly visible, but I could tell she was already struggling to restrain herself.

Finally, Aunt Christine called us back in, saying that dinner was almost ready. We came back inside and took our seats at the dining room table. Soon enough the moms came out of the kitchen carrying large dishes of vegetables, mashed potatoes, yams, and corn bread. My mom apologized for the turkey, saying it would still need more time in the oven.

Time to be friendly with Mina.

Mr. Todd led dinner with a brief prayer, thanking God for his family, friends, and the life he'd been allowed to lead. *The life he'd stolen.* I bit my tongue. Haley bit hers. Mina looked pretty used to this. Once he had finished, to the approval of my mom and Aunt Christine, we dug in to the first dishes on the table.

Like most holiday meals I'd attended, most of the early conversations were separated between the parents and the kids. Mom was asked about moving in and her job in Town Hall, Aunt Christine about school and her new boyfriend (apparently it had caused quite the scandal when she'd broken up with the school counselor, Mr. Montresor), and Mina's parents about the various goings-on in Prospero. Mina, Haley, and I couldn't talk about anything honestly, so we made a good show of talking about school. I told them about building furniture with Mr. Finn, and Haley spoke of the school's upcoming Winter Holiday Showcase as if she was looking forward to it more than anything in the world.

I almost started to think we'd be able to pull this off without incident.

Then Mr. Todd turned his attention to me.

"So, Ben, I haven't really seen you around the shop recently," he said, pleasant as ever.

"I haven't really had the time," I said.

"School, huh?" he said, smiling.

I smiled back, trying to hold the venom at bay. "You could say that, yes."

My mom stepped in. "It's been a rough adjustment, moving here, but I think we're finally getting settled in."

I nodded in agreement. Mr. Todd smiled, stroking his beard. "Really glad to hear that. I mean, people just have this way of spreading some real mean rumors sometimes. When I hear them talking about you, I just up and say, 'Ben Pastor? I think you must be mistaken. He's a good boy if I've ever seen one. He'd never get in trouble.'"

"Thank you for your vote of confidence," I said, gripping the tablecloth tightly. I wasn't the only one. Haley looked about two steps away from jumping over the table and throttling him. Mrs. Todd simply downed the rest of her wine glass and poured a new one.

"Don't mention it, Ben. You've got people who believe in you, real friends out here, all you have to do is ask for our help and we'll be there for you," he said with a smile. I couldn't believe his arrogance, the audacity of asking me to surrender, in front of my mother and friends on Thanksgiving!

"That's real sweet of you," my mom said, smiling. "I keep trying to tell Ben that he's not alone here, but he doesn't want to listen."

"Teenagers," Aunt Christine said with a theatrical roll of the eyes before shooting me a wink.

My mom laughed softly. "It's just been so tough for him—"

"Mom, do we have to have this conversation?"

She shushed me with a raised hand. "It's just been so tough for him here, with all the stories going around, that I'm just really glad to see he's got friends like all of you."

The table was silent. Only Aunt Christine took her comment for the sweet remark it was intended as. Haley looked at Mr. Todd furiously. Mina was tensing up. Mrs. Todd choked a bit on her wine as if suppressing a laugh, but composed herself before she could make a mess.

The beeping of the kitchen timer couldn't have been better timed.

"That sounds like us," Aunt Christine said.

"Need any help? I'm pretty handy with a knife!" Mr. Todd offered.

"No thanks, we've got it," Mom said, leaving for the kitchen with Aunt Christine, leaving the three of us with Mina's parents. sMr. Todd drummed his fingers on the table distractedly, clearly hoping for one of us to fill the silence. He looked to his wife, then to Mina, then to me, clearly unsatisfied with our enthusiasm for casual Thanksgiving conversation. Finally, he looked to Haley.

"So, Ms. Perkins, I hear you're quite the actress," he said, conversational.

"Yes," Haley said, taking a bite of mashed potatoes. "Almost as good as that Splinter bitch you replaced me with last summer."

He dropped his fork. It clattered loudly against his plate.

"Wait, we're telling the truth now?" Mina asked, surprised.

"Seems like it," I said.

"I'm fine with the truth if you guys are," Haley said,

continuing on without even asking for our approval. "I can't keep this act up anymore."

"That's fine with me," Mina said.

"Me too," I said.

Mr. Todd tried to clear this problem up. "I really don't think this is the place—"

"You didn't wipe her memory?" Mrs. Todd asked. "Isn't that what you got that blonde bimbo for, whatsername?"

Mr. Todd was flustered. "First, her name is Marie, and for the thousandth time, dear, she's a respected colleague, and there is nothing going on between us, nor has there ever been. Second, it was deemed imprudent to 'wipe her memory' given the fact that Mr. Pastor and our daughter were watching her like hawks after freeing her from the Warehouse and would have gladly refreshed her on whatever memories we removed."

"And you couldn't break that up?" Mrs. Todd asked. She looked between me, Haley, and Mina, all our pretense of being anything but solid friends and allies shattered. I couldn't tell if her smirk was irritated or amused. Probably both. "No, it certainly seems you couldn't."

"Actually, I'm glad you didn't remove my memories," Haley said firmly. "No, I'm glad I could see what you were doing with my body while you'd stolen it. I'm even more glad to remember how she felt when Ben killed her. Do you want to know how she felt?"

"I'm sorry. It's going to be a few more minutes! We got a really big bird this year! We'll have it out soon, I swear!" my mom called from the kitchen.

"That's okay. We're having a fine time in here!" Haley

called back. Then, dropping her voice so only those of us at the table could hear, "It hurt. A *lot*."

"Look, Ms. Perkins . . . can I call you Haley?" Sam asked.

"No," Haley replied.

"Okay, Ms. Perkins, I know you've been through a lot lately, and I—"

"Did you choose me?" Haley asked.

"It's not that—"

"You're on the Splinter's council, you guys run everything in town, choose who gets taken over, right?"

"That's one of many things we—"

"Then were you the one who decided to steal my life? Who should I thank for that?" Haley said.

Mr. Todd sighed, exasperated. "I didn't nominate you, and I'm not going to tell you who did, it's not my department. But if it gives you any feeling of vindication, I did vote for you to be a vessel for one of my people, as did the rest of our council. Does that make you feel any better?"

Haley started to stand up, and I pulled her back into her chair again, trying to change the focus.

"So what is your department?" I asked. "Strong-arming and extortion?"

"I'm a lawman," Mr. Todd said.

"Not a very good one," his wife muttered. He ignored her.

"I've kept order in this town since before your great-grandparents knew how to walk," he continued.

"So siccing Madison on me, is that how cops work where you come from?" I asked.

"A little help, dear?" Mr. Todd said, looking to his wife.

"You dug your own grave on this one, *dear*," Mrs. Todd

said, tipping her wineglass in his direction in a mock toast and then topping it off yet again.

"Madison may take too much enjoyment in her job at times, but only because she is very, very good at it. I think we have explained ourselves more than adequately as to why her presence is necessary," he said.

"Bullshit!" Haley exclaimed. I half-expected her to jump out of her seat again. She didn't.

Mina did.

"You didn't have to take it out on Ben!" she said angrily. "He didn't want this life. I practically forced him into it. Your problem is with the hunters, and Ben is not a hunter."

"He did kill me, kinda," Haley corrected.

"Well said, Ms. Perkins," Sam said humorlessly, without taking his eyes off Mina. "You may not think of him as a hunter, but whether you like it or not, you have introduced him into the lifestyle. In the eyes of my people, he's just as bad as you, or The Old Man, or any of the others after what he did to our Haley."

"What Old Man?" Haley asked.

"It's a long story," I said, trying to keep his secret protected.

"We'll explain it to you later," Mina said firmly. Now *that* was a surprise.

Mrs. Todd gave her daughter a sharp look at the mention of that name. "The Old Man is dangerous, Mina. I can't believe you still spend time with that lunatic."

Mr. Todd's eyes narrowed when Mina didn't immediately deny this, and he seemed to do some very quick thinking. "Believe me, Ben, Mina, Ms. Perkins, we don't want this situation to be any more inconvenient for you than it already has been. If you just turn The Old Man over to us, I can offer all of you protection."

"Turn him over to be killed, you mean," I said. "Like you killed his family?"

This comment got a brief look of surprise on his wife's face.

"He didn't tell you he burned The Old Man's family alive?" I asked her.

She shook her head. She didn't look very surprised anymore. Surprise had given way to anger in the blink of an eye.

I continued. "So would you kill him, or would you let Rob—"

He pounded his fist on the table angrily. "LOOK! There're a lot of things I'm not proud of in my life—"

"You mean Sam Todd's life?" Mina said firmly.

That one hit him like a punch to the gut. He looked at Mina, hurt, almost begging for forgiveness.

"Go on, though, you were saying there's a lot you weren't proud of? Which were you less proud of, ruining Ben's life, or letting a super-powered psychopath into my head so he could get at The Old Man?" Mina asked, voice full of acid.

Now it was Mrs. Todd's turn to interrupt. "What was that?" She looked at her husband angrily. He tried to keep calm, but had a hard time not letting a little fear through.

"Now, Diana, after the incident this summer, we needed to bring someone in to help deal with the hunter problem."

"And you let him into her head?" Mrs. Todd said, trying very hard to keep her voice low.

"He got a little overzealous. I have told him to stay away from our daughter!" Mr. Todd said.

"I'm not your daughter," Mina said, angry.

Mrs. Todd glared at him. "We're going to have a talk about this later."

Again, he sighed. "That, my dear, I don't doubt."

"Turkey's ready!" my mom called cheerfully, bringing the bird out with a smile.

In a flash, we all pretended to be happy and smiling, as if the rather unorthodox holiday fight hadn't happened. My mom and Aunt Christine sat at the table, completely unaware. Mr. Todd tried to look cheerful, doing his best to ignore the anger coming from his wife. Considering how much of our plan to take down Robbie revolved around having him on our side, I realized that we maybe should have been nicer to him, but at the time it felt liberating to let loose on a Splinter responsible for so many of our troubles.

It felt even better to no longer pretend that the three of us were on good terms with each other, and actually just be on good terms with each other. We laughed together, we shared our family-friendly stories, and we ate until we were stuffed, content with this minor moral victory.

It was a happy Thanksgiving after all.

23.

Mina

There was a time when I truly dreaded my bi-monthly counselor's appointments, the professed pity and disappointment, the thinly-veiled threats, the subsequent lectures they inspired from my mother.

Over the years, as I'd come to realize how little power and interest Mr. Montresor really had, and as Mom had come to accept a plateau rather than a spike in my accumulation of write-ups as cause for celebration, the appointments had become just one more of the many minor inconveniences hampering my work.

As usual, the countdown calendar was on his desk when he called me in, a set of tear-off sheets with descending numbers under a picture of a terrified-looking kitten in a party hat.

Two hundred and eighty-two.

Almost Christmas now.

Two hundred and eighty-two days until my eighteenth birthday.

Two hundred and eighty-two days until the record goes blank and all the new blotches stick for good.

Two hundred and eighty-two days left to straighten up and fly right. As if that had ever been an option.

As little consolation as it would be to Courtney, I was glad that the bug in this room had finally allowed me to confirm that he did in fact keep such a countdown for a few people other than me.

"Shall we go over the record again?"

I shrugged. Mr. Montresor adjusted his wire-rimmed glasses, tidied the almost spiky haircut that tried and failed to conceal a few of his thirty-four years, and opened the file with the list of my known transgressions—the fresh ones he hadn't yet covered marked in neon pink highlighter. He began the usual ritual with tired eyes, looking almost ready to join me in acknowledging its pointlessness.

"Seems you've had a quiet year."

I didn't offer him the clue of laughing at him.

"Getting nervous? Just six counts of trespassing since May? One of breaking and entering, four of theft—"

"Three," I corrected. Mr. Montresor likes to combine all the complaints against me, substantiated or unsubstantiated, made to the cops or directly to the school, into a single list to make the numbers sound bigger. He also sometimes inflates the numbers further, hoping I'll lose track, mix up what I've been caught doing with what I've actually done, and confess to something extra. It's never worked, but it does force me to pay a little attention.

"You're right," he pretended he'd misread the number. "Three. *Five* counts of attempted fraud."

That's his way of making it sound serious when I get caught logging someone else into the computer lab to make it less obvious I've been there. Other people log their friends in all the time to make it look like they have been there when they're ditching. None of my counts of successful fraud ever make the list.

"One of harboring a runaway."

I put a hand automatically to the bridge of my glasses for a moment to hold in the discomfort of that one. I'd never thought Aldo's parents would get the authorities involved.

"He wasn't exactly a runaway," I said.

"He?" This was clearly a thrilling surprise to Mr. Montresor. "It was Miss Perkins' personal physician who expressed concern that you might have endangered her life by indulging her delusions after her second episode, instead of alerting her mother immediately."

Keeping Haley long enough after her rescue to get her ready for an hour with a personal physician instead of a night in the med center had probably saved her life.

"Is there a young man we should be concerned about as well?" Mr. Montresor asked, and to my own shock more than his, I hesitated three whole seconds.

"No."

Mr. Montresor tried to stare me down, but after only a few seconds, a sudden, sharp yell from outside startled us both.

"Oh my God, oh my God, you gotta see this!"

Then, Patrick's voice. "No, it's some kind of mistake!"

Laughter. Squeals. Hooting.

Mine was one of the last counseling appointments of

the day. The last classes had let out, the lawn and sidewalk out front were crammed with people, and something had them very, very excited.

There was a short burst of a police siren.

"It's not mine! I've never seen it before!"

Madison. Scared and furious. I left my chair and reached the window just in time to see the officer tighten the cuffs behind her back.

Ben and Haley were in the crowd, close to the sidewalk. They couldn't see me, but I could see that they were among the laughers.

What it was that wasn't hers and why the Splinters were allowing all this, I had no idea.

Then the officer shut the squad car's back door on her, cutting her off mid-sentence.

"I didn't do—"

Slam.

Ben's voice flooded back to my ears, shouting the same words. "I didn't do it." The desperate, helpless awfulness of that day in the hills suddenly felt further away than it ever had, compared with his shocked, nervous, laughing face across the grass outside.

And for one short, stifled breath, I laughed too.

Mr. Montresor cleared his throat behind me.

"Mina, I can't help you if you won't pay attention."

I forced myself back to the chair.

"And that, of course, brings us to your grades. Now, I won't say you're the worst student we've got. I just can't see what's stopping you from being the best. Your standard-ized test scores are among the highest this school has ever seen, and we are quite an impressive school. You can tell me, Mina. I am on your side."

He gestured to the placard on his desk that read "Counselor," as if that somehow supported this statement.

"Would it really take that much extra effort to finish all of your assignments and turn them in on time?"

I returned my usual shrug and waited for him to ask me three or four more times in increasingly helpful, flattering, and irritated ways, but he didn't. He opened his mouth to ask for the second time when he turned his head sharply toward the window.

I took the opportunity to turn and look again too, wondering if Madison's scene had escalated to something that demanded even his attention, but she had already been hauled away, and whatever he had seen was already gone. There was nothing there but a few clusters of excited students catching each other up on the news.

He snapped my file shut well ahead of schedule and stood up.

"Give it some thought," he advised me vaguely, eyes still on the window. "And remember you can come and talk to me any time."

"Okay," I said, getting up as well. "Do you want me to send in the next appoint—"

"No!" He recovered himself quickly. "No, I'm going to go sneak a quick bathroom break first. I'll call him in myself."

Mr. Montresor grabbed his coat, without explaining why he expected to need it in the bathroom, and hurried out of his office through the small adjacent waiting room without looking back.

I gathered my things and followed.

The waiting room was empty except for one boy in the chair closest to the door, examining a "LOST DOG" poster on the bulletin board over his head. When he turned and I registered his face, I choked like an amateur on my own intake of breath.

Robbie York smiled and held something long and thin to his lips—a Pixie Stick, I realized after a few surreal seconds.

"Shhh," he breathed, as softly as if I were a crying baby, shifting his backpack, a heavy, hiker's one, casually in front of the door. "Shhh-sh-sh-shh. Not like last time, nothing like last time. I'm just here to talk. We're just two people talking, okay?"

He looked around as if afraid of being observed in the empty room, then offered me the Pixie Stick.

I needed to leave. I needed to find Ben or Aldo or Haley, anyone who could call for more help if this became the night in my room all over again, or at least make it feel less like that night already. I needed someone to make my skin stop generating imaginary grime and my esophagus stop tying itself in painful, swelling knots simply by making me not alone with this monster.

But more than that, I needed him not to see how much I needed a way out. He had seen too much of me already.

I latched onto the first ridiculous greeting I could think of that didn't involve screaming or crying or vomiting or clawing fatally slowly for the door.

"You're not supposed to eat in here," I said.

Robbie shrugged and ripped open the stick. "I'm trying

to live fast." He poured the whole tube of loose, acidic sugar into his mouth.

I hope it stings, I thought.

"I can still hear you, you know." I felt the faint echo of his words, projected onto the back of my mind as well as spoken. "And it doesn't matter if you're home in your bed or hiding out in Florida, or Montana, or Madagascar. With a little extra peace and quiet and concentration, I can still hear you, and I can still make sure you hear me. I'm just trying something new." He enunciated each word as if he weren't perfectly proficient at speaking out loud already. "In fact, I'm trying a lot of new things."

He reached into the backpack, and I readied one hand to reach into my own bag, for all the good my school-friendly supplies would do, but Robbie only pulled out an enormous red apple. The bag rustled with plastic, cardboard, and foil. Food, lots of it. He bit a large chunk out of the apple and pulled a sour face.

"These are not all they're cracked up to be," he decided, then tossed it to me for my verdict. I sidestepped and let it bounce off the wall behind me and roll under one of the chairs. "Like talking," he added.

"Funny," I said, mostly to keep from forming revealing thoughts. "You certainly do a lot of it."

He laughed much harder than the joke deserved. "It's alright, I guess. I just don't like the way it distracts you."

"Distracts me?"

Distracts me distracts me distracts me, I focused on the words, on sounds without meaning, trying to block out everything of more substance, but the space the sounds filled only made everything else a shade sharper.

"Call me old-fashioned," said Robbie, "but when I talk to a girl, I'd like her to think about me."

His mouth closed, but his voice continued.

Not about the range of the bug she's got planted in the next room over.

Anger, disappointment, another flash of fear, all as exposed and obvious as if I'd never spared a thought in my life to keeping such things out of sight.

I had to speak again and speak fast, something without feeling, without thought.

Live fast, my brain repeated at random. *Live fast, die young.*

"How old are you really?" I blurted out.

He liked the subject. I could tell.

That depends on how you measure it. If you count all the time since the day I was born, a few thousand years; if you count all the time I can remember, a few hundred; or if you only count the time I've actually lived, instead of having to suck an old, cheap recording of it out of whatever body I've been given to use, I think I'm just a little bit younger than you are, Mina.

He pulled a Snickers bar out of the backpack, tore open the wrapper, and closed his eyes as he took the first bite. I wondered if it was the first bite of a Snickers he'd ever had, but the thought inspired no pity.

"Is there something else I should call you? Since we're not pretending you're Robbie York anymore?"

Oh, I can think of a few things. His eyes were bright with glee when they opened, and there was a smear of chocolate left on his teeth when he grinned. *I've been Phobos. I've been the Bunyip. I've been the Bogeyman, everybody loves that one.*

"I'm not calling you the Bogeyman." I tried to laugh. I couldn't.

Then Robbie will do for now, he said. *He's a pretty dashing guy, don't you think?*

My mind flicked briefly to when Mr. Montresor might want his office back.

Don't hold your breath, Robbie told me. *It'll probably take him hours to decide he didn't really see his geriatric grandmother wandering the streets alone. Looks like he might have to reschedule my appointment. And it's already been pushed back so many times for all my sick days.*

"Where have you been?" I asked. I was running out of non sequiturs, and I couldn't take the chaotic, thought-swirling silence.

At least that question seemed to kill the pleasure of the candy for a moment.

You want to know something that does sting, Mina? Strychnine. It's like the worst muscle spasm you've ever had, in every single muscle in your body, your body that is also on fire. It won't kill one of us, of course. We're tougher than that. And your Old Man knew that when he slipped it into my last root beer float.

I wasn't proud of the satisfaction that news gave me, but I didn't bother trying to hide it from him.

I spent nearly two months picking that shit out of my system one molecule at a time. For two months, I couldn't take human form without going back into those convulsions. For two months I had to hide so I wouldn't have to defend myself against him.

He was going to make me ask, I realized. The relevant question, the one I wasn't quite sure I wanted him to answer. It was the only way this interview would end.

"What do you want, Robbie?"

I braced for the look, the hungry, scrutinizing one that would have blown his cover as Robbie York the first time he turned it on me if he hadn't had my brain too twisted to believe it was there.

Oh, so many things, he thought into me.

I succeeded in not shuddering, but under the circumstances, the mental effort this took (*don't shudder don't shudder don't shudder*) wasn't much better.

He shrugged and looked away long enough to open a Twinkie, but still I couldn't steal the moment to think.

Sadly, I don't have time for them all. He didn't wait for the space between bites to talk. He didn't need to. *If I don't deliver on my last two targets, like, yesterday, my people are going to decide I'm not up to it and kill me, or shove me back in the dark for good.*

I couldn't help thinking it, in a jumbled undignified rush: *Two targets. The Old Man and me. Your people? Splinters or Slivers? Dad Lying? Not lying? Target. Target. Whose target am I?*

He was listening, I could feel it, but he continued without offering any hints. *Or your Old Man will get me himself if I can't get him first. Either way, I'm finished. So here's what*

I'm thinking, to make the most of short time. You know the Christmas pageant tomorrow?

"The Winter Holiday Showcase?"

Sure, whatever. I'm thinking I'll lock the auditorium and burn it to the ground.

He opened a mini bag of Doritos with a pop and calmly bit into the first chip. Anyone watching without the mental soundtrack would have thought he'd forgotten I was in the room.

Well, probably not actually burn it. All I'll have to do is convince a few of the people inside that it's burning, or full of bees or sarin or something, and they'll take it from there. Maybe they'll start a few real fires. Maybe someone will find that fire axe in the lobby and suddenly notice that his fellow patrons have become brain-eating zombies. It'll be a hell of a grand finale, don't you think?

He took a breath of powdered imitation cheese and sighed.

At least, it would have been. But you'd never let that happen, would you, Mina? Half the town turns out when they get all the schools together like that. All the families, all those children. Backstage packed with defenseless little elementary school cherubs too young for my people to use. That's a lot of guaranteed human fatalities. Enough to bother even a frigid bitch like you.

"Every human fatality bothers me." From a vantage point outside my head, I would have appeared perfectly firm and collected, for what little that was worth.

He chuckled just enough to show off the fresh coating

of neon orange inside his lips. *I know that, Mina. You can play heartless to the rest of the world, but not to me. I know they do. That's why you're going to offer me a better option.*

"I can't give you The Old Man," I said. "I don't know where he is."

Robbie rolled his eyes.

Duh. If you did, I'd know too. He tapped the side of his head, leaving a faint orange smear. *And I already had you lead me to him, remember?*

The image of my birthday card came clearly to mind. I'd known the time and coordinates for two days in advance, more than long enough for him to find them in me.

That should have been the end of it. I wasn't counting on him not having enough of a brain left to pick, but he won't surprise me again.

So The Old Man was immune to him, like he was to the pods. I could feel Robbie's amusement as he observed my bitter urge to tell The Old Man that he wasn't really more careful than the rest of us, just more broken.

What you can *do is meet me in the auditorium tonight.*

That look again.

"So I can help you 'live fast'?" I guessed, adding a smirk to his look. "Or are you just hoping The Old Man will be stupid enough to charge in to rescue me while you have the home court advantage?"

Robbie licked the cheese thoughtfully off his fingers.

Both, he admitted, then snickered behind his hand. *Was I too subtle with the whole I-am-inside-you bit?*

"Alone?" I prompted him, to cut off the memory before he could force it all the way to the surface. "Unarmed?"

He shrugged.

Sure, if you'd prefer to make it a more intimate occasion.

He crumpled up the chip bag and bent the cap off a bottle of cream soda, the expensive kind with real cane sugar that requires a bottle opener. Or a Splinter's adaptable strength and dexterity.

But you know better than to get any lawmen involved anyway, don't you? Anyone who might try to make you skip out on our date? And it's not like I'm going to scrap the only play I've got just because you bring along a few freaks with popguns. In fact, bring them. Bring them all. Bring that freshman you're not taking advantage of, and that cute cheerleader you're not jealous of, and that guy with the hero complex you're not in love with. We'll have a party. And when I'm explaining how I let that one old screwball in the woods get away from me, I'll at least get to explain how I also took out Mina Todd's entire Network in one night. That might actually do the trick. So, shall we say ten? I like a late dinner.

"Ten is fine."

He pulled the backpack away from the door, either giving me permission to leave or daring me to try.

One more thing, he stopped me just as I was about to pass his chair, two lengthening, boneless Splinter fingers twisting easily through three of my belt loops with two muted wooden cracks.

My every muscle itched to execute the quickest possible maneuver to separate myself from him. But I didn't because of the sick, weak, stupid hope that if I did nothing, he might let me leave that room a few seconds sooner.

I gave in and let my knees hit the thin carpet next to his chair when he pulled.

He swallowed a mouthful of soda, then smacked his lips and whispered out loud. "All flirting aside, just so we're clear . . ."

I couldn't help it. I thought about how his tone couldn't possibly reach the bug in the office. I'd spent too long learning not to let such things slip by unconsidered to be able to do the opposite now.

Robbie smiled and continued in my ear and my head at once.

"*I'm going to kill you tonight, Mina,*" he whispered. "*Whether you come alone or with an army, whether I can get both of you at once or not, I'm going to kill you. I wasn't joking about playing my last card here. There's no keeping you around for more leverage later this time. There's no tactical retreat just because a few unauthorized corpses get in the way. I'm going to make you watch me turn everyone who thinks they can stand with you into whimpering, gibbering cowards before they die. Then I'm going to unwrap you as slowly as my very last Kit-Kat.*"

He tightened his grip slightly, and I heard one, two, three stitches of black denim give out along my hip.

"*And I'm going to make you scream for your demented old freak for a few hours, eight or nine tops, and if he shows, he dies too. If he doesn't, my people will either pat me on the back for getting nine out of ten and give me the nice anonymous new body they promised me, or they won't, and I'll at least get to say I went out with a bang. You won't live to find out which.*"

He retracted his fingers.

There it was again, the offer I'd spent my life trying not to hope for.

I could believe him. I could believe that he was strong enough to want me to throw my whole Network at him, strong enough that we wouldn't stand a chance, even all together. I could believe that killing me would rush his people—whichever people they were—to a judgment that would either put him out of the way or give him a new reason to behave. I could believe that there was a chance the others might never have to face him, better than the chance they'd get from having me with them when they did.

It was all as likely to be true as not. A coin toss, as far as I knew, no bet more sensible than the other.

I could let him have me. Just me, without a fight. I could trade away whatever I had left to dread, all the fighting and fearing and feeling there would inevitably be in the months, years, maybe even decades still ahead of me, replaced only by what pain and humiliation this Shard could fit into a single, insignificant night.

I could escape while there was still hope left in the world, believing that I'd done everything in my power to protect it, thinking about all those kids who might yet live out human lives, about my Network that would survive to fight another day because I would not.

I could die without guilt.

Robbie raised an eyebrow at me, the way people do when they're trying to decide if I'm mentally subnormal or not, as if he could only see my blank, staring face instead of every private detail behind it. Only the twitch at the corner of his mouth gave him away.

"Something more I can help you with?" he asked at excessively sweet full volume.

I found my feet, staggered out into the hallway without looking back at him, and stopped to lean against the first stretch of wall, letting its comparative cool soak into my skin.

It took me a few moments to notice Ben and Haley waiting for me along the opposite wall, brazenly in the open, the way other people's friends do for them. They both still looked to be between fits of ecstatic laughter.

Haley gave me a wave, the full, wholehearted kind, and gestured to her phone, as if I didn't know her schedule well enough to realize that guarding Ben through my unexpected delay had kept her late for rehearsal.

"Have you heard?" Ben asked me as Haley cut swiftly through what remained of the afterschool crowd and out of sight.

Vaguely, I recalled the sight of Madison's arrest, concluded that it had apparently been real, unlike Mr. Montresor's grandmother, and noted with silly satisfaction the way Ben assumed I might know already in spite of having been stuck in my counseling session while it happened.

The center workspace of my mind was processing something much bigger, padded and fueled by the shape of the face of my friend.

For the first time since I'd been old enough to give the subject any thought one way or the other, I was under no obligation to live.

And at this most inconvenient of moments, I knew that I wanted to.

Before the moment of greeting could pass, I threw my arms around Ben's shoulders, not caring about the onlookers, hardly caring that Robbie was almost certainly still watching me from the inside, from behind that door.

As my only pretense for the contact, I raised my lips as close to his ear as I could without my toes leaving the floor.

"It happens tonight," I whispered. "Please help me."

24.

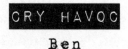

Ben

I was out of breath by the time I got to the school's front entrance. The night was pitch-black and biting cold. There were only a few streetlights around Prospero High School and limited lighting on campus at this time of night. It would conceal us from most onlookers outside of the school, but it might also conceal us from the one person whose attention I wanted. Still, I had to try.

Stopping beneath the HOME OF THE POETS sign, I scrawled a large *T* in the hot pink chalk The Old Man had given me. I had drawn two similar marks on other parts of the school. I knew the odds that he would show up in a timely manner were small at best, but going against Robbie, I knew we needed all the help we could get.

Content that I hadn't been seen, I ran around to the north edge of the school, sneaking under the broken edge of the chain-link fence that we'd found near the construction of the new art building. I slipped quietly through the half-built skeleton of the building to the construction shed we'd found. Courtney and Greg stood smoking nervously as Mina divvied up weapons from her personal supply. Her collection of stun guns, Tasers, and flamethrowers, most homemade, some legitimate, looked pitifully small when spread out on the ground. Knowing what Robbie was capable of, and that he almost certainly had some surprises hidden up his sleeve, I worried that these wouldn't be enough. Haley, Kevin, Aldo, and Julie stood inside the shed, trying to supplement our weapon supply. I knew most of what was in there would be fairly useless, but it was better than nothing.

"Is the perimeter clear?" Mina asked when she saw me come up.

That was my excuse for dropping my cry for help. I didn't like lying to her, but I didn't know how she'd react if I told her I was calling on The Old Man.

"Yeah. This part of town's dead," I said.

"Could you please not say dead?" Courtney asked, nervous.

"Sure," I said. I tried to offer her a grateful smile. She didn't return it.

"No word from our bogeyman?" I asked.

Mina shook her head. "Nothing. Yet. He has to know we're here."

"He's confident," I said.

"Is this the part where you say, 'he's too confident,' Eagle Scout?" Greg asked, a little jittery.

"Maybe," I said. "It could also be a sign that he knows something we don't and that we're in real trouble here."

"You're instilling me with a lot of confidence," Courtney said.

"You don't have to stay," Greg said.

She looked at him coolly. "Yes, I do."

He stared into her eyes for a moment, then broke out in a broad smile. "You're all right," Greg said, dropping his cigarette to the floor and crushing it out.

Kevin and Julie came out, adding a few armfuls of tools to the mix. Aldo followed them, a coil of copper wire around his shoulder and lugging a car battery.

"If he doesn't kill all of us and we still feel like trying to deliver him to the Splinter Council, I think I can contain him with this," Aldo said, trying to hide his irritation. "Did you call your dad?"

"No," Mina said. "Even if he did believe me and decide to come investigate, he'd do everything possible to make me stay out of it. And if Robbie senses I'm not the one coming to meet him, he'd run before Dad could get anywhere near him. This is the only way."

"No it isn't," Aldo said.

"This is the best way," Mina clarified.

"No it isn't," Aldo repeated.

"Are you gonna bitch or are you gonna help us?" Greg said.

"Remember why we're here," Kevin said, defusing the fight before it could start. This was a trap, we all knew that. At the same time, I don't think anyone doubted Robbie's threat. If we didn't stop him that night, he would kill as many people as it took to get to us.

We had to end it.

Mina and Haley traced a crude map of the school in the dirt and ran through our opening moves. We would be entering through the network of steam tunnels and old fifties fallout shelters that connected to every building in school. We would take a tunnel from the science building and come in under the auditorium in the hope that Robbie would be more prepared to greet us at the main entrances. Haley knew the tunnels well from using them as extra changing space in theater. The real Robbie was afraid of the dark, so, hopefully, he hadn't passed on too much knowledge of their layout to his Splinter.

It was a tiny hope, but we would use whatever edge we could get.

I checked my cell phone. The clock read 9:53. We didn't have much time to get this started.

"This won't be easy," Mina said, making her last adjustments to the weapons' distribution.

"Robbie will make your worst fears real and may very well try to turn us against each other. Do not, under any circumstances, split up, and keep an eye on whoever you're with. If they look like they are going to hurt themselves, or anyone else who isn't Robbie York, do what you can to restrain them until the visions pass. He claims to have unlimited range with his mental abilities, but that seems to require more energy and concentration than his close-range effects. He's going to have his physical body somewhere nearby, and it will be vulnerable from the effort. We're going to find it. From what I have seen . . . from what he has threatened, I believe that he has difficulty invading the thoughts of large groups of people. Our numbers will be our greatest advantage," Mina said.

"Or, lacking that, some cold, hard iron," Greg said, cradling a heavy, curved crowbar in his hands.

"Don't let that get you overconfident," I said. "You can hurt Splinters, or at least make them think you've hurt them for a few seconds, but it won't last."

"It lasts long enough to give you the chance to kill them," Greg pointed out.

"Only as a last resort," Mina said quickly. "Remember, we're trying to take him alive."

That thought brought little comfort. Killing a Splinter was hard enough; a Shard would no doubt be even harder.

Trying to capture one alive so we could turn it into the Splinters' authorities? It was probably impossible, and to Aldo's credit, incredibly suicidal.

Still, someone had to stop Robbie.

I grabbed a long-handled, fifteen pound sledgehammer. Testing my grip on the weapon, I tried to reassure myself that we were the right people for the job.

The door to the science building gave way after one sturdy blow from the sledgehammer. It felt weird, destroying school property like this, but given the greater good that we were here to protect, I didn't feel too guilty. The eight of us filed into the long, main hallway that led past more than a dozen classrooms—all decorated for Christmas— and would eventually allow us basement access.

Kevin and I carried the most weight, his backpack

containing the heavy coil of copper wire that Aldo had found, mine holding the car battery. Between my sledge-hammer and Kevin's pickax, and our flamethrowers and Tasers, we were the most heavily armed members of the group. I worried about him. He had as personal an invest-ment in this as Mina did, though unlike Mina, Kevin was a pacifist. He held his ax like he meant to use it. I didn't know if he would.

That worry went for much of this group. I didn't question Mina's fighting ability, and Courtney had proven herself capable. I had no idea how any of the rest of them would fare. They were determined, they looked strong, but when things got bad . . .

Julie had taken the lead, her swift footfalls echoing loudly in the hallway as her heavy boots hit the linoleum. Rounding the corner in the L-shaped hallway, she skidded to a stop, her eyes large and staring.

"So much for the element of surprise, guys," she said.

We hurried to catch up with her. Robbie York stood at the end of the hallway, backlit by the windows behind him. A low, wide-brimmed preacher's hat obscured his face, and he balanced himself jauntily with one hand on a fire ax like some demented cane.

"Hello, boys and girls," he said cheerfully. "I'd really like to thank you all for coming tonight!"

I gripped my sledgehammer tightly and tried to sound brave as I called out, "You know this'll be a lot easier if you come quietly!"

He cocked his head appraisingly, then let loose with a loud, long, braying laugh.

"Did you just say that?" he laughed. "I mean, seriously, did you just tell me to come quietly? Who says that? 'Come quietly!'"

He nearly doubled over from laughter. It felt odd, in the middle of this, to be embarrassed by a serial-killing Splinter laughing at me.

Robbie stood up, straightening his back with a loud, Splintery crack.

"Seriously, though, I'm totally not gonna come quietly. I'd much rather do this," he said, sticking two fingers from his free hand into his mouth and whistling shrilly.

From the open doorway of a classroom near Robbie, we could hear the low growl of several angry animals. I half expected a pack of wolves to come out to meet him.

Instead, we got a small parade of house pets. In one neat line came a border collie, a bulldog, a pit bull, and what appeared to be a rather fat calico cat. The cat had a bell on its collar that jingled and jangled as it slowly walked. It would have been funny had they not all lined up in front of him so obediently, staring at us with almost human intensity.

Cocking his head in the opposite direction, Robbie said, "Kill."

Slowly ambling toward us, the four animals began to expand, limbs snapping with that sound of splintering wood as they grew bigger and more horrific, growing extra eyes, toothy mouths, tentacles, and legs as they saw fit, each reaching at least the size of a pony. The cat nimbly jumped to the ceiling, crawling along it like a spider with its three extra legs.

SHARDS

Breaking away from the group, Mina sprinted down the hallway, dropping to her knees and sliding between the bulldog and the pit bull before any of us could stop her. Smoothly and quickly, she turned around, pulled out her flamethrower and transformed the pit bull into a ball of fire. The beast howled and thrashed. She answered it with more fire.

The cat dropped from the ceiling onto Mina.

That broke us out of our stupor.

I ran for the melee first, swinging my sledgehammer into the cat's now massive ribs. A large, staring eye that had formed in the side burst like a boil as my weapon connected, covering Mina in mossy, green slime as the cat hit the wall, yowling. It lashed out at me, clawing me in the side. I hit it with the hammer again, then in the spine. That kept it down for a moment.

I helped Mina to her feet as the others came to join us, wildly swinging their weapons and trying to join the fray. In the darkened hallway, I could only catch a few, wild images of the attack, illuminated by our wildly bouncing flashlights and the burning remains of the pit bull Splinter.

Greg smashing the collie in the head with a crowbar, only for the head to split into a giant pair of insect-pincers and grab his wrist.

Aldo and Haley wrestling the bulldog off of Kevin.

Courtney howling in pain as the cat locked its jaws around her ankle, then kicking its skull in with her free foot and hobbling away.

Julie and Mina wrestling the collie away from Greg, then Mina setting its fur ablaze with her flamethrower as Julie smashed it repeatedly in the head with a large pair of bolt cutters.

The collie kicked out with one of its legs, catching Julie in the chest. She hit the wall hard and fell to the ground with a heavily bleeding cut on her forehead. I went to her, and she looked up at me, dazed.

I looked around; the science labs had to have first-aid kits. I tried the door nearest to me, found it unlocked. Opening it up, I dragged Julie inside.

The darkened walls were covered with poster board projects demonstrating various principles of physics, with rows of desks looking eerily empty in the darkness. The twin, yard-long prongs of a Jacob's Ladder stood proudly on the teacher's desk. I checked beneath the desk and found the first-aid kit. It was sparse, but it had a couple rolls of gauze that would work.

"You still with me?" I asked her, wrapping her forehead. She looked up at me blearily, but smiled.

"I'm fine, we gotta go help them!" she exclaimed.

"Wait 'til you can see straight before you—"

The door swung open again. Aldo and Courtney spilled in, looking fearfully at the door as they pulled it shut. A heavy, clawed hand broke through the gap, trying to rip the door open.

"Help us, damn it!" Courtney called out to me as she and Aldo pulled at the door handle with all their might. I ran to join them, helping them slam the door shut against the claw, severing three of its fingertips.

The pieces hadn't been on the ground for more than a second when those clawed tips sprouted small, insect legs and began crawling around, searching for us. One by one we were able to crush or corner them, using our stun guns and Tasers to reduce them to small puddles of harmless, raw Splinter.

The sound of claws against the door continued. I felt for the flamethrower clipped to my belt, but it wasn't there. I cursed myself, imagining it getting knocked into the hallway when the cat took a swipe at me.

The door handle jiggled.

"Is there another way out of here?" I asked, looking at the door.

"No," Aldo said.

The handle turned all the way around. The door swung open. The cat, larger and more horrible-looking than before, leaped nimbly inside. It lashed out at us with tentacles and tails, knocking Courtney and Aldo into the row of desks and sending me toppling over the teacher's desk, landing next to Julie. The Jacob's Ladder fell between us with a clang.

I grabbed the edge of the desk and pulled myself up, to see Aldo scrambling our way. The cat had perched itself on a few of the desks, stalking Courtney as she kept low to the floor and crawled away from it. I grabbed the first thing I could find, a stapler from the teacher's desk, and threw it at the Splinter. It turned one of its heads to hiss at me, but continued stalking Courtney.

Frantically, she reached into her pocket and pulled out a canister of mace. She held the can high, spraying the hissing monster directly in the mouth.

The Splinter stumbled away from Courtney, falling

between the desks and thrashing about on the floor as it yowled and spat. Spasming and arching its back grotesquely, the beast vomited gallons of vile, black ooze, and internal organs onto the floor, almost deflating it like a balloon. Courtney was a mess, but she was able to crawl away from the monster to us.

"Think this still works?" Julie asked, toying with the fallen Jacob's Ladder. I looked at the twin, metal prongs of the device and understood what she was getting at.

There was an extension cord with a switch on it in a drawer in the teacher's desk. I gave the cord and the switch to Aldo, plugging the Jacob's Ladder in.

"When I give the word, throw the switch," I said.

"Got it," Aldo said.

"Not a second before," I said.

"Got it," Aldo said.

"Because I'd die," I said.

"I know, now shut up and kill the thing already!" he exclaimed.

Holding the Jacob's Ladder by the prongs like a spear, I ran for the recovering creature Splinter.

I slipped in the puddle of gore after three steps, landing hard on my back (or rather the car battery in my backpack, which felt a thousand times harder than the ground). I looked up, dazed as the cat arched its back, hissing and clicking at me angrily, baring its fangs and pincers. Softly, quietly, it pounced.

Thankfully, Julie was faster than the cat, running to me, picking up the Jacob's Ladder, and stabbing it into the Splinter's chest before it hit the ground, confused. She helped pull me away.

I shouted, "NOW!"

Aldo threw the switch on the extension cord. In a flash, the cat monster went rigid, its fur catching fire as the full electrical arc of the Jacob's Ladder passed through its body. Bright, loud sparks shot from the visible portions of the twin prongs that stuck from the creature's back.

A fluorescent bulb in the ceiling burst. The room filled with putrid smoke as the Splinter was cooked from the inside out. Its flesh melted off in small rivers, puddling on the floor around a rapidly deflating, deteriorating skeleton. As it disintegrated into nothingness, Aldo shut off the switch.

I looked up at Julie. "Thanks."

"Don't mention it," she said, waving a hand in front of her face as she looked at the Splinter's remains.

"Everybody all right?" I asked.

Despite some cuts and bruises, and Splinter gore covering everyone, they were fine.

The hallway outside had fallen silent. I hoped that was a good thing.

Suddenly, the sprinklers overhead cut loose, spraying the room with water.

"Now what?" Courtney said.

"One of the fires probably set it off," I said, making my way for the door. "Hang back a second. I'm going to check on the others."

"I'll come with you," Julie said, getting shakily to her feet.

"I'm good for now, you guys catch your breath," I said. Nobody argued.

I stepped out into the hallway, feet splashing in the heavy puddles. I looked around for anyone, or anything, and found an empty, wet hallway that seemed to stretch on forever.

"Hello?" I called out. No answer.

I turned to face the classroom I'd left behind, and found myself staring at a brick wall. A sick feeling turned my stomach.

Robbie York was in my head.

The science building's hallway had transformed into a dingy back alley, smelling heavily of mildew and decay. The sky above was dark and gray, the rain dark and oily. Crudely spray-painted on the wall opposite me were the words:

FEAR ME

"Subtle, Robbie, real subtle!" I called out.

I thought you'd appreciate this. His voice came from nowhere and everywhere. I had to keep my head together. This was his domain.

I closed my eyes, tried to will it away. *This isn't real. This isn't real. This isn't—*

It may not be real, but who said it had to be? His voice was calm, amused even. I didn't like it.

I started walking down the alley, trying to find a way out. I didn't think I'd find one, but I hoped that someone would see what was happening and stop me.

"I'm not afraid of you," I said.

Give it time.

"What do you want?" I asked.

The same thing you want. To live up here. To experience—

I interrupted him. "I've heard this speech before. 'I'm a poor Splinter who comes from a world without feeling.' It didn't save Splinter-Haley and it's not going to save you."

Fair enough. Let's play this your way, then. All the amusement had left his voice. Now it was pure threat.

The brick wall in front of me began to contort and split open with glowing, sickly-yellow light spewing forth from its new openings. Soon I could see that the wall had become a ghastly perversion of Robbie's face, smiling at me as rancid-smelling curls of smoke came from his mouth.

I tried to run away. The smoke lashed around me like tentacles, lifting me from the ground and drawing me into the monstrous mouth.

I was set on my feet in a world of madness and despair. Towering pillars of rock lined with eyes and teeth, skeletons and people tied to them with chains. The thick smell of sulfur and brimstone filling the air. Screams surrounded me, and everything was hot, so hot.

Hell.

"I know," I responded.

And it doesn't get any reaction from a God-fearing boy like you?

"No," I tried to lie.

He chuckled. *See, this is why I love humans. So imaginative. There is so much to fear in your own world, so much death and vileness that the very act of living should scare you to death. And what do you people really fear? This!*

A pillar of fire erupted next to me. I turned to it,

distracted. Before I could react, Robbie was standing next to me, knocking me to the ground and disappearing.

You fear the unknown. You fear made up bogeymen because they make it easier for you to live in a world with so much to fear.

He appeared before me in a wisp of smoke.

"Like this boy. A strapping young lad, in the prime of his life."

He darted for me, quickly punching me in the head and the stomach, easily wrenching the hammer from my hands. I punched him and flung him to the ground. He looked up at me, laughing.

"Afraid of the dark! Pitiful, right?"

He jumped up at me, knocking me down. I punched him in the back and stomach with everything I had.

And this! He was back in my head. *This! So many peo-ple fear death, not because it means a cessation of life, but because they fear that this is what they have waiting for them on the other side! Is this why you fight me, Ben? Because you fear you're going here?*

"No!" I said, defiantly, kicking him in the ribs and knocking him to the ground. He looked up at me, smil-ing wickedly.

"Do you fear death because you think you'll find your father in a place like this?"

A fire had been building in me ever since he'd gotten into my head. I thought I could control it. I thought I could keep cool for the sake of the group. As soon as he mentioned my father, that fire exploded within me. I was no longer in control of myself. It felt *good.*

I jumped on him, punching him in the face repeatedly as he laughed, imagining Patrick, Madison, Mina's dad beneath me. He wouldn't stop laughing; if anything he got louder. I had to shut him up. I wrapped my hands around his neck, pressing my thumbs into his throat with all my might. Despite his thrashing and his fighting to get free from me, Robbie York grinned up at me the entire time. I smashed his head into the ground, trying to make it go away.

"STOP SMILING, DAMN IT!" I yelled.

Hands grabbed me by the back, wrenching me free from Robbie. Someone I could not see clocked me in the head, hard. The world melted away. I was in some dark, concrete tunnel. Kevin was grabbing me by the arms, looking at me fearfully.

"Stop fighting me, brother!" he said. "You're all right, you're okay!"

I looked down where Robbie should have been and only saw Mina Todd, crawling on all fours, wheezing for breath. A spatter of blood hit the ground where she coughed. She looked up at me, eyes strained and red, fresh bruises forming around her throat. Haley tried to help her to her feet, but she was incredibly unsteady. What happened hit me like a ton of bricks.

"Oh God."

"It's all right," she choked hoarsely.

"Mina, I—"

"It was Robbie!" she choked again.

"I'm so sor—"

"Save it for him," she said, angrily. I had hurt her. Badly.

Beaten her and choked her nearly to death. Words my dad had told me long ago echoed in my mind. *A man who takes out his anger on a woman is a poor excuse for a man.* Seeing her, seeing what I'd done, I could barely hold it together.

"This is his fault, not yours," she said.

"I nearly killed you," I said.

"I'm sure that was the idea," Mina said. "I'll be fine."

"Will you?" I asked.

She smiled up at me. Even in her bruised, bloodied state, she still managed to pull off most of that radiant smile.

A wave of relief stronger than any I'd felt before hit me. Before I knew what I was doing I grabbed Mina and pulled her into a powerful hug. She responded slowly and awkwardly, clearly pained and even more uncomfortable with the action in a dark, Splinter-filled school than a crowded, human-and-Splinter-filled one, but soon wrapped her arms around me in kind.

"We should get moving soon," Haley said. Mina and I parted. I came to my senses, finally realizing where we were.

"Are we . . . ?"

"We're under the school," Haley confirmed.

I looked further down the tunnel, caught sight of Aldo, Greg, Julie, and Courtney with us.

"When we were dealing with the other Splinters, you broke off and followed Robbie down here. Mina followed you. We didn't know he had you," Kevin confirmed.

Almost as a peace offering, he reached down and handed me the sledgehammer I'd dropped. I could have sworn that I'd dropped it miles away. I took it, gratefully.

"Which way did he go?" I asked.

Haley pointed down the sloping path of the corridor. I nodded. We pursued him.

We were tired, battered, bloodied, and soaking wet, but we did not stop. If anything, I could swear that his siccing the creature Splinters upon us and forcing me to attack Mina had made us a more determined, more dangerous group. I knew then that he'd made a terrible mistake in telling Mina to bring us all here.

Haley led us to the ladder that went up into the auditorium. She led the way, and one at a time we followed. I was last, helping Mina keep her footing.

The trapdoor above the ladder opened up on the main stage. We stood around in darkness, wondering just what kind of trap he had set for us.

Then the main lights above the stage lit up, blinding us. Somewhere in the darkness, Robbie York laughed at us. "AND . . . SCENE!"

25.

Mina

It was just light, but for those first few seconds, it might as well have been acid thrown in our faces. I turned a small circle, willing my eyes to adjust and show me my surroundings, which direction the next attack would come from, but nothing moved in the opaque brightness. Nothing but a little ball of fluff at shoe height.

It hopped into sight, a rabbit, no bigger than my foot, fluffy and white and—I couldn't help noticing—uncommonly cute, wearing a tiny Santa hat.

Knowing the Shard-Robbie's sense of humor, I had to fight back a wild rush of dread at the sight of it.

I feel nothing.

I'd been saying this to myself a lot since Robbie's invitation. It wasn't quite like grief armor, too stretched and general to be as strong, but it was something.

I feel nothing.

"Don't touch it," I warned the others when the rabbit hopped past me. "It's either a Splinter or an illusion, and either way—"

Julie's bleary eyes found the rabbit, and she leapt onto Greg's back with a bloodcurdling scream.

"What is it?" I asked.

"I'm fine! It's nothing! I'm fine!" she insisted breathlessly into Greg's shoulder, her arms and legs still clutching at his neck and waist. "Just . . . just get it away!"

"You're scared of bunnies?" Aldo asked her.

"It's not funny!" Greg snapped at him hoarsely, trying to get a secure grip on Julie and shift her arms away from his windpipe. When he found his balance, he kicked the rabbit in Aldo's direction. It made a pitiful chirping sound of fright and scampered into the darkness of the wings. "It's called an irrational f—" The floor behind me exploded with a plume of green smoke.

I'd turned half a step when something in the cloud hit me hard in the side, knocking me off the stage.

"Mina?" Ben called out, staring at the place where I'd just been standing as if it were empty, as if the fire-faced Halloween gunslinger were not stepping out of the smoke cloud to stare down at me, lasso poised at his side. "Mina!"

"Ben!" I shouted back.

The gunslinger twirled the lasso once before throwing it at me where I'd landed, sprawled on the hardwood between the stage and the first row. I rolled, and if it had been an ordinary circle of lifeless rope, it would have missed me. It corrected in midflight, stretching to wrap around my upper torso and the back of the nearest uncomfortable wooden stadium chair, then cinched tight in one rough instant, forcing me to sit in it. The trailing end twisted just as easily around my arms, pinning them to the armrests, crushing the taser out of my right hand.

"Ben!"

"They can't hear you," the gunslinger told me in Robbie's undisguised voice. With a snap of his fingers, he was in the seat next to me, one arm stretched along the back of mine. A gesture of the other hand removed the fire to show Robbie's face.

"I'm going to give you one chance, Mina," he said as if gently reprimanding a misbehaving child. "One chance to die with your eyelids attached. So be a good, attentive audience."

He gestured the fire back on, then reached up like an eccentric conductor and pulled down on thin air. The lights dimmed with his movements to a moody, graveyard scene pitch, the temperature dropping ten degrees to match, the remaining, greenish aura glinting off the ornaments in the Christmas garlands draped over the stage and aisles.

"Showtime," he whispered, and, with another thoroughly unnecessary snap of his fingers, vanished.

I pulled against the lasso he'd left behind, and it held fast, sticky and rubbery. Splinter matter. Part of him.

I feel nothing.

"Mina!"

It was Aldo calling out through the dark this time, and I tried calling his name back, not expecting him to hear it through Robbie's mind blocks. I was already working on shuffling my bag toward my left hand with my knees, to see if I could get a knife out of it. Robbie might pick the idea right out of my head and stop me, but that didn't mean I had to make things easier for him than they needed to be.

"She's here somewhere." That was Haley, looking soothingly from Ben to Aldo and back again. "He's the one we need to find. We stop him, everything else will start making sense again."

Greg gave this levelheaded advice its least levelheaded interpretation, shouting wildly into the darkened audience, "You hear that, Robbie? You want a fight? Get out here, and we'll give you one!" He set Julie on her feet behind him on the currently rabbit-free stage, ignoring almost all of his natural blind spots. I could hear them before I could see them—a low, almost imperceptible, rustling hum of tiny moving legs, too small to make a sound alone, too many to be silent together. Then the tidal wave of spiders broke over me on its way to the stage, coating every surface with a double-thick layer of pincers and writhing feet.

I feel nothing I feel nothing I feel nothing.

They wriggled over my skin, and under, and over again, with a sting like a cactus spine each time one broke through. Something particularly hairy and about the size of a quarter crawled in through my right cheek, over my tongue, and out through my left, while something smaller and startlingly strong tried to fold itself into my left ear canal.

I feel nothing I feel nothing.

Greg did his best. He stood in front of Julie, breathing in increasingly jagged gasps, until the first spiders brushed his shoes. That's when his legs gave out. Julie tried to catch him, but she was still shaking herself, and they both toppled into flood.

"Sweetie, it's okay," she cooed desperately over his screams, spitting out what spiders got in the way of her tongue. "It's okay, just let it pass."

Ben and Kevin hurried to help Julie hold him still, frantically brushing more spiders off themselves as they went.

There was another stage-like explosion, and the head of the gunslinger appeared stage right, magnified to a hundred times its size. Robbie's voice boomed louder than the theater's amplifier.

Ladies and gentlemen of Mina Todd's Resistance Network. Your fearless leader has led you right through the gates of your own personal hell. I am the Bogeyman! I am Fear! And you cannot fight me!

Greg struck out at the image, which dissolved into smoke. He thrashed out of Julie's arms, and then bolted for the edge of the stage, already scratching a bloody gash in one of his arms as he went. Julie grabbed for him and missed, but Courtney was closer to the edge and pushed him back with a firm hand on each shoulder.

"We stay together!" she said. "That's the whole point!"

It looked like Courtney and Julie might have held him, if Courtney had not at that moment cried out and clapped a hand to her stomach, ignoring the spiders she crushed into her own shirt and palm.

"No!" she shrieked. "No, not yet! I'm not ready!"

Courtney's flat stomach ballooned over the course of ten seconds to the distinct shape of advanced pregnancy, and she doubled over with an agonized cry.

"It's not real," Ben reminded her. "Think about it. It can't be real."

But Courtney was beyond consolation.

"I can't do this! I haven't lived my life yet!" Another obvious wave of pain shot through her body, and she collapsed against the nearest edge of the backdrop, nails raking down it for support, blood stains appearing under the layer of spiders on her pressed grey slacks.

I'd worked my left hand under the flap of my bag. There had to be a knife just inches from my fingertips.

Greg stole his opportunity and ran into the wings, still digging at himself, Julie right behind. There were two loud puffs of stage smoke for emphasis when they left sight of the others, and a third when Courtney crawled somewhere behind the curtains. From the way Ben, Kevin, and Aldo were squinting after them, I knew Robbie hadn't let them see exactly where the others had taken cover.

Only Haley had barely moved since the beginning of the spider onslaught. She was shaking violently from head to toe, but was otherwise doing nothing to remove them from herself, and her eyes had not stopped scanning the dark on all sides, searching for a hint of something real. I could just read the words her lips kept forming whenever I could shake the spiders from my eyes.

"Not real and not crazy, not real and not crazy."

If we got out of this, I was going to buy her the biggest malt she could drink.

When we got out of this.

My fingers finally brushed the handle of a pocketknife, small but adequate, and fumbled to pry out the blade.

Hale-y, Robbie sang. *Is this the first time you've heard voices in your head? If you insist on living, it won't be the last. Mina's told you, hasn't she? What happens to people who escape? What happens to people who resist too long?*

"Not real and not crazy," she muttered louder.

A Splinter tendril shot out of the stage with a *crack* and wrapped around her leg. She blasted it with her flame-thrower and jumped backward, squarely onto the stage's trapdoor, which gave way under her, a squirming tangle of purple tentacles dragging her into the cramped maze beneath the stage with another puff of smoke. The spiders poured into the opening after her like floodwater until they piled level with the stage, and it was hardly possible to tell that there had been a door at all. Ben, Aldo, and Kevin were shoveling barehanded through the itching, burrowing, biting black swarm where she had disappeared when another snap of fingers and flash of light removed it, all of it, every spider gone, as if they had never been, leaving the stage impermeable and intact.

In the spiders' place, Shaun Brundle stood downstage center. For a moment I hoped that this was it, this was my turn, that Robbie's attention was mine, away from the others. The blade came free. All I had to do was work it carefully between the Splinter rope and my wrist and pull, and as soon as Robbie made the slightest error, gave me the vaguest hint of where he was, I'd drive the blade clean through his brain and have him wrapped in copper wiring before he could re-form a working cerebellum.

But of course (*guess who I'm saving for last*), this one wasn't for me.

Shaun winked at me before turning to face his brother.

Kevin kept staring at the polished wooden surface where Haley had disappeared and wouldn't look at him.

"Give it up, Robbie," he said blankly. "I dealt with that. I mourned. I'm over it."

"Yeah, I know," said Shaun, beginning a slow circle around where Kevin stood. Ben tried to block his path, but Shaun walked right through him.

A ghost.

"I know exactly how fast you got over me. I know how you *mourned*. You never fought for me when I was alive. Why would you after I was dead?"

"I'm not sorry I haven't spent my life punching out my problems, *Robbie*," Kevin said, still not looking at the circling Shaun illusion. "It wouldn't have solved anything."

"You never wanted to solve problems for me," said Shaun. "I was your problem. Your embarrassing, immature, hotheaded little brother. The one who actually did things you were afraid to take a chance on. And you were jealous of what it got me. How long did it take? How long had my life been over before you started thinking about stealing it?"

I feel nothing I feel nothing.

"It wasn't like that!" Kevin broke and looked up. Shaun looked ready to punch him. "There was nothing between us! She was there! She was hurting too! She understood! That's all it was!"

"Sure." Shaun rolled his eyes.

"Nothing happened!" Kevin shouted and elbowed Ben away hard when he tried to restrain him.

"I don't care!" Shaun shouted back. "I don't care that you

never had the guts to make anything happen! Even when you found your own girl, she had to ask you, didn't she? And what was it she left you for? For wanting to run away!"

"College isn't running away!"

Shaun ignored him. "Of course nothing happened! Nothing ever happens for you! The point is that you wanted it to!"

The metal was against my skin, under the rubbery coil, digging in. With all the strength in my wrist, I pulled, and the Splinter lasso broke like a giant, overwrought rubber band, snapping hard against my skin as it pulled away, leaving me free.

This happened in the same second something invisible and very heavy knocked Aldo backward off his feet.

The same second that Ben turned to look at him, and Shaun and Kevin both vanished mid-insult in another puff of smoke behind his back.

Just two left.

No, just two left that I could see. Fresh flamethrower in hand, I hoisted myself back onto the stage.

Aldo was crouching in a defensive position. Ben was kneeling next to him, shaking his unresponsive shoulder.

"Stop, please stop, I can explain!" Aldo begged the empty air in front of him. I didn't know if he was seeing his mother or his father or both, or why Robbie had decided not to let Ben and me see them, too, but even if I had to shake him a lot harder than Ben was, I would make the illusion leave him alone, the way he had done for me.

"Wait!" he whimpered, arms raised to protect his face.

I tried to hold his stiff hands, but they wouldn't hold mine back. "It's me," I said. "It's okay, it's just me."

"It's not what you think! Please, Mina, don't do this, you don't understand!"

An invisible force that had nothing to do with Robbie knocked the air out of my lungs. "Aldo?" I whispered. "What don't I understand?"

Robbie's laughter filled the auditorium.

Now, if THAT one isn't a heartbreaker!

I could feel his eyes on me, from wherever he was. He was watching and laughing and—I was suddenly sure—delighted that I'd cut myself free on schedule, at exactly the right moment to see the fear in Aldo's face close up. He'd let me go. He'd thinned my forces, and he'd *let* me go.

What do you say, Aldo? She's right here. Should I tell her? Should I tell her what's had you so worried all these years?

"No!" Aldo screamed, crawling backward away from me. "Please! I'll do anything!"

"Mina?" Ben called out, towering protectively over Aldo, searching the darkness at the words "she's right here." "Mina! Where are you?"

"I'm here!"

I knew it would happen, the moment I looked at him, and he looked through me. Before either of us looked back, there was another puff of smoke, and Aldo was gone.

"Mina!" Ben called out more desperately, alone on the empty stage. "Haley! Kevin! Anybody!"

I tried calling back. I tried shaking him, slamming the underside of my fist against his chest until it should have made him gasp for breath, but he was utterly numb to me.

"Mina!" Ben tried again.

She won't be there for you, Robbie's voice answered. *She won't be there at the end. Not the way you were for your father. She's too smart to volunteer for what you and your mother went through.*

For the first time since I'd stopped coughing up blood, I saw Ben's control break. Not just a momentary, reflexive falter, but a shattering. His knees shook and then refused to carry his weight. In elapsed time, quicker than Courtney's pregnancy, I watched him wasting away, staring with horror down at his own limbs as his tough, powerful layer of muscle dissolved, leaving sickly, quivering skin and bones.

She won't care. She can't care about losing people. It happens too often. She doesn't get attached. She doesn't trust anything outside her own body. But you know that's the last thing you should trust, don't you?

Ben ran a nervous hand through that impractical, distracting, and yet so fascinating heartthrob hair, the way I'd seen him do countless times. This time it came away in his hands in thick, sprinkler-wet clumps.

You wake up fine in the morning, and a routine checkup later, you find out you've got nothing left but a few miserable months, and then it's over. Every hope, every plan, everything gone. No reason, no point, no noble cause.

Both Ben's hands went to his newly skinny chest as he drew a wet, rattling breath.

But you don't get the small last comfort of dying in a loving partner's arms. Not the way he did. There'll never be time to find one. No normal, innocent girl wanted the wanderer's son, and they certainly won't want the Splinter hunter. And she won't be there.

"I AM HERE!"

My voice would have reached every seat in the house, even to Alexei's satisfaction, but it couldn't reach Ben. I knelt next to him and pulled him into my lap, trying to stop the shaking.

"I won't look away, not this time," I said, to Ben, or Robbie, or myself, I wasn't sure.

I didn't. For a minute and forty-seven seconds, I looked at him, without even glancing to check behind me.

In the end, the puff of smoke came to spirit him away in an ordinary, unavoidable blink.

Alone at last.

Robbie laughed, and I shot a burst of flame over my left shoulder, just in case he was standing there. He wasn't.

I forced my legs to straighten and carry me away from where Ben had vanished, starting a slow circuit of the stage. Flamethrower poised, ready. Focused (*I feel nothing*) on the creak of the floorboards, the rustle of the curtains, my finger on the trigger, nothing else. There would be an error, a clue. There would be an opening, and I would use it to whatever advantage there was left to have. That was all.

That's right, said Robbie's voice. I circled a little faster, more deliberately, trying to detect any change in his volume with the change in our proximity. *Now you're in your element, aren't you? Don't pretend you didn't always think it would be easier this way. No one else left to worry about.*

"So where is it?" I projected into the auditorium's broad

space, hoping to keep him talking, tiring, fluctuating. "The grand finale? What's it going to be? What's my deep, secret nightmare?"

Don't you know yet?

My foot brushed something alive, and I hurried to make out the shape of it before Robbie could shore up his block on my senses.

Ben. I reached down to touch him, half expecting him to vanish on contact and become undetectable again, but wherever my fingers confirmed his presence, he only came into sharper focus, like brushing dust off a photograph. The illusion of illness was gone, and I could see him as he was, strong and healthy-looking in all ways except for the fact that he wasn't moving. His hands were warm, a pulse easily detectable in his wrists, but there was no sign of breath.

I remembered the illusion of being strangled, the way my diaphragm had refused to draw breath even with nothing real in the way, and I slapped him gently across the face to cut through the imaginary fluid in his lungs. Nothing happened. I slapped him harder, hard enough to make his head snap back off the wooden stage. Nothing.

I knew my first aid books, knew the obvious and urgent next step. I tucked the flamethrower into my bag so I could put a hand each on his nose and chin, tipped his airway open, and (*I feel nothing*) sealed my mouth over his.

Stupid. The stupid act of a friend, and one I knew perfectly well I'd repeat in the unlikely event that I ever got another chance.

That's when the illusion around him did in fact break, and he stopped being Ben.

Robbie sank his teeth into my lower lip and flipped me onto my back like a rag doll, if a rag doll could have a fresh concussion to aggravate by hitting the ground too fast. The side seams of the costume he was wearing, the Ghost of Christmas Future's black and red robe, split open. Two Splintery, fleshy wings stretched down from him to the stage on either side of me, one of them cutting neatly through the strap of my bag and flicking it out of reach. The contents scattered out in front of it, the way the Splinter-Shaun had fatally forgotten to do in my most often raided memory. Two extra wing prongs at his shoulders grew claws and pinned my empty, useless hands.

Robbie pulled back from my face just enough to look at me.

I AM your nightmare, Mina. Someone you can't hold at arm's length. Someone you can't keep out.

The wings started to seal themselves over me, crushingly tight, an inch at a time, anchoring themselves into the stage with the force of an industrial staple gun, so close to my skin that each anchor caught the edge of my clothes, sending frays and ladders through the fabric. I almost expected him to transform enough to start doing the same along the inner seams of my jeans and immobilize me completely, but the half of him occupying the space between my legs remained a mocking imitation of human anatomy.

A small, defeatist fragment of my mind flicked to Ben, where his hallucination might really have taken him, what would happen to him without me in this town where I'd trapped him, if he lived through the night? Then to Aldo, and then, of all places, to Dad—not my real father but my Splinter dad—suddenly painfully curious whether he would laugh or cry if he could see this.

Oh, he'd fly off the handle pretty bad, Robbie answered me. *And the others would back him up. They just love to nitpick the rules for people like me, for the special ones, to make sure they've got us in line.*

So the plan would have worked. Would work, if I could just find any advantage. If I could just move.

But the Queen understands what it's like, he told me.

"Queen?" I repeated, searching my aching head for a place where the word fit and finding none.

The rule followers did the same to her, Robbie thought fervently. *So she made me a better offer. Just add you to my list, and I get a body to keep after the job, courtesy of the revolution. Just between us, I think she's overpaying me. I knew the moment she pointed you out that I'd have done it for free.*

"Too tired to do it from across the room?" I stalled aimlessly. "Isn't that the trick they— she hired you for?"

He put one hand to the side of my face, slowly eased my glasses off, and set them aside on the floor.

Oh, I wouldn't miss this. You'd never have met anyone who wants you for your mind the way I do, Mina. I've broken a lot of them. They're like playing connect the dots in a child's coloring book. Yours is like quantum physics microetched into the facets of a perfect volcanic geode. When I finish with you, I'm going to find out what a brain like that feels like crushed between my fingers.

There was another ripping sound of fabric somewhere

between us, and I decided that, if nothing else, I would ruin one small detail of his plan as he'd so vividly explained it to me.

I would not scream.

I stared over his shoulder at the out-of-focus ropes and pulleys overhanging the stage and (*I feel nothing I feel nothing I feel nothing*) waited for what came next.

What did come next was a jolt of electricity so sudden and intense that I had the brief, irrational impression of having been struck by lightning.

No, of course it had to be something Robbie was doing to me. But that wasn't right either. I could feel him twitching too, and the theater around us flickered with his convulsions—movement, *people*, flicking in and out of existence. I didn't understand until Robbie reached back and pulled the cattle prod out from between his shoulders, where it had lodged like a harpoon, and a real voice echoed down from the catwalk.

"Lying down on the job, Robin?"

Mad, instinctive relief flooded my system, and I tried to scramble backward. I got less than a foot before Robbie regained enough shape to secure me again, and all hints of other company vanished. Robbie squinted up toward the catwalk where The Old Man was hiding and threw a hand out in the direction his voice had come from.

It sprouted batwings and detached from his wrist, flapping off in search while a new one grew in its place.

Reality set in. The Old Man was there, the way Robbie had wanted, so either he was going to die because of me, or I was going to live because of him. After the way our last meeting up in the hills had gone, neither option had the potential to be pleasant. And so far, I still couldn't move.

I was just able to make out the click of an electric dart through my muffled ears before it struck with another paralyzing, agonizing shock.

(I feel nothing I feel nothing)

"Stop doing that!" I shouted at the ceiling.

"You're welcome!" The Old Man shouted back through another flicker in Robbie's concentration. This one was longer and clearer. As well as The Old Man shifting positions to stay out of sight, I could hear multiple sets of footsteps and make out the shape closest to me.

Ben.

Ben was alive, along with at least a few others. He was on his feet, looking for me, the way I'd been looking for him, but he didn't find me in the flicker.

"A little help?!" I called out.

There was no answer. Ben was twelve feet away and couldn't hear me. The Old Man was thirty feet above and wouldn't come any closer. My hearing kept fading in and out. The Old Man was moving around, trying to stay ahead of Robbie's multiplying drones, shouting down at me, getting progressively more annoyed.

"Get *up*, Robin! W . . . the f . . . think you're doing? Get up bef . . . someone starts to think . . . enjoying yourself!"

"I'm trying!" I snapped.

"You want h . . . think you're f . . . slow? You try one way, a . . . doesn't work, what do y . . . Little Girl?"

Try a different way.

Absolutely no alternatives to kicking and battering at the unbreaking Splinter layer around me presented themselves.

"Such as?"

The Old Man didn't stop to help analyze my options.

"You gonna g . . . up and fight b . . .? Or y . . . take this lying on your back and m . . . your mother proud? Got j . . . one left."

"Please don't," I said pointlessly.

I heard the click of the dart and tried not to moan.

I feel n—

"I hate you!"

The forbidden word surged out of me when the electrical current released my seizing jaw again, dragging along a rush of the white-hot, churning, uncontrollable killing feeling that came with it.

I felt Robbie recoil slightly on top of me, not from the electricity or from the hate itself, but from the sudden, total absence of fear.

"Hate m . . . all you w . . . just get it done!"

Hate is worse than fear, more dangerous. It killed Shaun, and it let the Splinter-Haley get a pod around me. That's why I don't feel it, don't give it its real name, don't let it command my life the way The Old Man does. But that's the one advantage it has. It displaces fear. I simply can't feel both at once.

And The Old Man was right about one thing. Feeling fear and nothingness wasn't working.

So I let it in.

"I hate you *both*."

Robbie was stunned enough to allow me to wriggle one

hand free, and I reached up to claw his face, grasp for any possible way to hurt him.

I found it. I felt it, not in his body language or the timbre of his projected voice, but through his skin.

I could feel what he meant for me to feel, his glee and anticipation, the way I could from across the room, but in the places where the physical contact amplified it, the places where even an ordinary Splinter could push thoughts across, I discovered that I could push back. Not only push, but reach in and pull.

"You're scared, Robbie!" I read him out loud.

It had never occurred to me to try to heighten any kind of contact with a Splinter, but when he jerked his upper body away from me so hard that it freed my other hand, I grabbed him by both ears and dug into him, skin and mind, as deep as I could reach.

"You're more afraid than anyone else in this room!" Excess hate spilled out of me in a sound that was a lot like laughter, but carried none of the same relief. "They're alive, aren't they? Every one of them!"

The laughter came harder, more jagged and painful. Nothing about this was funny, not remotely, but with every vocal exhalation, every sharp little "ha," I could feel Robbie's pompous, bombastic ego crumbling like dried mud in my hands.

And it felt good.

"Of course they are! If anything real had happened to them, you'd never have let me miss it! You wanted so badly to make them kill themselves in front of me. You just weren't up to it!" My hands found more stinging words and I grabbed them eagerly. "You knew you were too weak! So you locked them all in their nightmares, deep enough to keep them apart, and you went right for me, right for the bare minimum victory you needed out of tonight, and you can't even do that right! You're too terrified that someone's going to wake up and realize they're not alone!"

Robbie's concentration flickered, and Ben saw me. He met my eyes and said my name, and behind him I could see enough shapes to account for everyone else stumbling closer. Then he lost track of me again, confused.

I grabbed for more of Robbie's mind, barely listening to the words that continued to spill out of my mouth. They came from him, not me, the very last things he wanted to hear, pre-constructed and waiting for me to take them and give them sound.

"What happened to unwrapping me like a Kit-Kat?" I snarled into his ear, which fell off in my hand, allowing the rest of him to pull further away. The batwings of his lower half still caged me carefully, as if I were a venomous insect, avoiding as much of my newly bared skin as possible, pressing down harder on what clothing was left.

"You're not afraid to touch me, are you, Bogeyman?" I couldn't catch my breath. The laughter was too strong. "What happened to eight or nine hours? What happened to 'if he shows, he dies too'? You got your best case scenario! You got your targets, your senile Old Man and his Little Girl sidekick, and now you're too tired? Too scared? Let's see what else you're hiding in there!"

I grabbed for his head again, and he pulled back further, kneeling almost straight up, a look of pure terror on his face. It only made me laugh harder.

I splayed myself flat on the stage, reveling in the free space he'd put between our upper torsos, more than an arm's length, and in the fear pulsing out of him and in through the holes in my jeans where he was still gripping me.

"You want me, Robbie? I'm right here! Time's running out! What are you going to do with me?"

The illusions died, all of them, all at once, leaving my eyes and ears perfectly clear to take in the welcome presence of my entire Network standing around us.

Robbie's hands were clasped together over my head, shaking with panic, gathering matter from the rest of him, forming into an executioner's ax blade, raising higher, ready to finish me as quickly as possible.

The urge to laugh died too, no longer needed.

"Get him," I said.

And they did.

Ben's sledgehammer caught him just above the left ear, knocking him clean off of me and crushing his skull like an egg on the floor. The rest of my Network was on top of him like a pack of feral dogs before the puddle of blood and brain could begin to reclaim its shape.

"Aldo, wires!" Ben called, wrenching Robbie's temporarily lifeless arms behind his back, but Aldo was already ahead of him, coiling the copper wiring of the makeshift containment field around Robbie's legs, weaving between Courtney and Kevin's restraining hands.

"Give me the switch!" I shouted at Aldo the moment the coil was finished, when Robbie's re-formed eyes started to blink open.

The killing feeling (*hate*) had built to a pounding, feverish pitch during the endless sixteen seconds it had taken Robbie to regain the ability to feel pain.

Aldo passed me the switch to the contraption, and finally, I turned it on.

Robbie's scream and convulsion into a series of unnatural shapes was a relief akin to cutting into a swollen blister.

I let up for a moment to give him shape again, and Ben knelt down next to him.

"Like I said, you might want to come quietly," he advised, pulling out a clean, new burner cell, and holding it next to Robbie's face. "First, we're going to need you to call your friends to set up an emergency meet—"

I turned the switch back on.

"Uh, Mina?" Ben looked up at me. I could sense my Network's looks of triumph shifting to wariness of me, but I had no room to care. I was too busy watching Robbie twitch.

"Heads up, kiddos!" The Old Man's voice called from the catwalk above.

Most of my Network jumped away from Robbie fast enough to avoid the worst of the shower of gasoline that poured down on him. Ben was soaked jumping over him to force the switch off and out of my hands before the stream could hit the live circuit.

"Now there's the Robin I know!" The Old Man slid down one of the catwalk ladders like a fireman's pole and was at my shoulder before I could calculate the right move to retrieve the switch.

Easily, as if we'd done something like this only yesterday, The Old Man slipped a dry, reassuring kitchen match into my right hand, and with a practiced flick of my thumbnail, I lit it.

Ben didn't run from me, not the way a sensible gasoline-soaked person would have.

"Get out of the way, Benji," The Old Man snapped at him. "Take a look at your woman and tell me that monster doesn't deserve to die."

Ben seemed to be having a difficult time with the looking-at-me part. It took a few seconds for my pounding brain to consider the way my shredded clothes must have been hanging off of me. But he held The Old Man's gaze just fine.

"Of course he does!" Ben shouted. "But there are more important things than what he deserves! If we kill him, the Slivers win, and we all die! If you gave a damn about Prospero or Mina, you'd care about that!"

"You want to pretend their treaties mean anything?" The Old Man laughed grimly, reopening the matchbook. "Fine, I'll do it if that makes you feel better."

"We need him alive!" Ben insisted, still standing fast between Robbie and The Old Man and me. "If it looks like Sam's going to blow us off and let him keep walking around after this, I swear, I'll kill him myself. But right now he's our only shot at avoiding a losing, two-front war. Right, Mina?"

I couldn't answer questions. I couldn't think about anything other than how to get closer to Robbie to sate the murderous throbbing in my head and chest.

I stared at the floor, at the puddle of gasoline spreading from Robbie's twitching form across the perfectly flat stage, the little ripples that shuddered across it from under Ben's still dripping shirt, where the flammable coating connected them.

Where the flammable coating connected them.

The instant that detail clicked into place, the fear returned. Sane, beautiful, *rational* fear of losing my ally, my friend, in a sudden, unstoppable inferno.

I blew out the match in my suddenly shaking fingers.

"Right," I agreed.

The Old Man went for another match, but I knocked the book out of his hand and into the puddle.

"Don't follow us," I warned him, then picked up my glasses, wiped them off, and looked back at my Network. They all looked a great deal more than shell-shocked, but their triumph was returning. Except . . .

"Where's Haley?" I asked.

Haley tapped me on the shoulder from behind and handed me a long piece of light fabric. Scrooge's nightshirt.

"For the walk," she explained.

"Thanks." I pulled it over my tattered clothes and gathered the things from my bag, while she cleared a bunch of Poet mascot masks out of one of the old shopping carts the stage crew used for moving props, and helped Ben and Kevin hoist Robbie into it, wires and all. Robbie made the call to the Council with all his stolen theatrical talent, and we left The Old Man in the empty auditorium, looking both furious and crestfallen. I didn't glance back to acknowledge his shouted prediction that we'd regret this.

"Mina," Aldo began tentatively as we both walked at the front of the cart into the night air, the rest of my Network behind us. The switch for the wires sat safely in his hands. "Just in case you were wondering, what I said, I wasn't in my right mind. I mean, obviously, I wasn't in—"

"I know I'm not always the most understanding friend," I stopped him. "I'm sorry."

He still looked painfully guilty, and I tried to think of another way to tell him that there was nothing I could imagine he was capable of doing that would ever make me turn on him.

I couldn't quite form the words. It had been a particularly difficult night. Assuming Robbie and I were both right about how Dad would respond to our delivery, I was going to have a lot of better nights ahead to find how to say it just right, to say a lot of things just right.

"The envelopes I gave you?" I reminded Aldo, and he nodded. "Burn them for me. I'd rather tell people myself, when I'm ready."

Aldo gave me a weak smile and nodded again.

26.

LEVERAGE

Ben

We could see lights on in the back room of Foxfire Collectibles through the glass front door. The Splinter Council. There were no guards out front, maybe because they didn't want to draw any negative attention, maybe because they were arrogant enough to believe nothing like this could happen. Either way, we were going to give them a rude awakening.

"Are you guys ready?" I asked.

They all nodded. Sitting in the shopping cart, wrapped in copper wiring tied to the car battery, the Splinter pretending to be Robbie York made a noise of dissent through his gag.

"Do you all remember your lines?" Haley asked.

"Are the lines really necessary?" Courtney asked.

"Of course they are," Mina said. "They prove we now offer a unified front against them."

"And they sound pretty creepy," Julie confirmed.

"So, are we ready?" I asked again.

I looked to the group, catching their nods and their

nervous, but hopeful, faces. Before tonight we were just a group of scattered individuals with a goal. Whether we liked it or not, defeating Robbie York put us all in this battle for the long haul. Mina smiled at me hopefully. That was all I needed.

I pulled the cheap, plastic Prospero Poets mask over my face. The others followed suit; Mina, Aldo, Julie, and Courtney favoring tragedy, while Greg, Haley, Kevin, and myself wore comedy. The masks didn't do much for ano-nymity, their big, open mouths showing off most of the bottom halves of our faces (like the Splinters didn't know who we were anyway), but like Mina said, they did show we were united.

Besides, it felt good to be the ones wearing false faces for once.

The glass door gave way with a shattering roar when I swung the sledgehammer through it. Mina and Aldo darted through with flamethrowers held high, unlocking and opening what was left of the doorframe to let us through, Kevin and Greg holding up the rear as they pushed the cart with Robbie in it.

A thin, middle-aged man with a moustache wearing a postman's uniform ran out of the backroom to meet us, one of his hands transformed into a deadly-looking claw.

"BACK OFF, HERMES!" Mina roared. "Slowly."

"Mina, this is highly un—"

Mina cut him off, motioning to the backroom with her unlit flamethrower. "I want to speak to my father."

I could see he wanted to argue, but a couple flame-throwers aimed threateningly are usually pretty good at shutting people up. The unlit Molotov cocktails that Haley and Courtney had were icing on the cake.

"Crazy bitch," Hermes muttered, shaking his head as he walked into the backroom. We followed closely. He let off a long call of chittering pops, presumably warning those inside of what was happening. Mina ran up behind him, clocking him on the back of the head with her flame-thrower. He fell to the floor of the backroom in a heap.

"Was that necessary?" I asked.

"No," Mina said. I couldn't help smiling.

There were fourteen of them gathered around a large gaming table in the backroom of Foxfire Collectibles. Most of them had transformed into those anonymous, gray faces with the bulging black eyes by the time we got back there, trying to hide their identities. There were enough familiar faces hiding in the crowd who hadn't had the time to change; my math teacher, Ms. Velasquez, Alexei Smith, Mina's dad, even Madison Holland standing off to the side looking terribly put upon.

Hermes stepped around the table, getting behind Alexei and Mr. Todd.

"They—" he began, cut off when Mr. Todd put a hand on top of his claw. Some brief communication must have passed between them because Hermes quickly backed off.

"I understand," he said, stepping aside.

"Hello, Mina, Ben," Mr. Todd said, nodding at us. "Robbie."

"Hey," Robbie said weakly from the shopping cart.

"I'm guessing we have you two and your friends to thank for calling this meeting tonight?" Mr. Todd said.

Mina looked to Haley. "Now?"

"It's your show," Haley said, comfortingly.

Mina took a deep breath. It was fascinating, seeing this girl who could unhesitatingly fight off inhuman monsters with whatever she could get her hands on suffering from stage fright, but we had worked out this routine on the walk over as a way to 'shock and awe' the Splinters. I knew she wouldn't disappoint.

"Ladies and gentlemen of the Splinter Council, we come here tonight with a message for you," Mina started.

"You have failed," I said, tightening my grip on the sledgehammer.

"You sent a warrior out into the world to kill the hunters of Prospero," Courtney said.

"And we bring him before you in chains. Well, exposed copper wire and a car battery to be precise, but you know what I mean; for you guys it might as well be the same thing," Aldo said.

Mina shot him a glare for breaking from the script. Aldo sheepishly said, "Sorry."

"You thought that you could destroy resistance in this town with one stupid, desperate act," Greg said.

"But you were wrong!" Julie said perkily. "As long as you folks call this town home, we'll be here to stop ya!"

"We will fight you with our every last breath, and we will never give up," Kevin said.

"And if you even think about infiltrating us, or driving a wedge between us, we will destroy you," Haley said. I could see a wicked grin forming underneath her mask as she quickly left the script. "Just like we destroyed Madison."

This was new to me. I looked to Haley for confirmation, but she was too busy blowing Madison a taunting kiss. Madison snarled bestially, lunging around the table for Haley.

"YOU BITCH! WE MADE A DEAL!" Madison shrieked as her arms and legs contorted into violent, vicious-looking weapons. Three members of the Council grabbed her, trying to hold her back.

Haley lit a lighter beneath the wick of her Molotov cocktail and threatened, "Just give me one reason. One good reason to burn this place down and, so help me, I will."

Mr. Todd got up from the table calmly, and placed a hand on the back of Madison's head. Briefly I could see his fingers disappearing into her skull with an unsettling crackling and snapping sound. She calmed down, going almost limp as her limbs transformed back to normal.

"Now, I don't think any of us want to end this night in a burn unit," Mr. Todd said, then looking at Madison threateningly, "Do we?"

She shook her head, fearful. "No, sir."

"Good," Mr. Todd said. "It seems like my daughter—"

"I'm not your daughter," Mina spat.

"Okay . . . it seems like Mina and her friends have gone through a lot of trouble to meet with us tonight, and as they're the ones with the torches and pitchforks, I think we're all better off letting them have their say instead of doing anything we'll regret," he said firmly. He tried to sound unconcerned, but by the way he addressed that more to his people than ours, I could tell we'd gotten his attention.

"If you think we're your biggest problem, you're wrong," Greg continued.

"Last summer, a rogue group of Splinters, whose members included Billy Crane and the Splinter–Haley Perkins, tried to incite a war between your people and ours," Kevin said.

"They're still here. They tried to kidnap me, and they have almost certainly taken more people in this town from under your noses," Courtney said.

"A revolution is forming. They wanna upset the apple-cart. They wanna take us over, not like you guys," Julie said. "Not that we're callin' you good guys or anything."

"But, as much as we don't like it, at the moment we'd prefer the devil we know to the devil we don't. So tonight we come bearing a gift," Aldo said.

Haley slapped the side of the cart theatrically. "Robbie York, ladies and gentlemen! He sings, he dances, he acts! He's also a skilled psychic serial killer who has really been trying, and failing, to kill Mina over the past few months!"

"He also talks too much," I said. "Tonight, when he was trying to kill us all, he admitted to us that he was working with the Slivers—"

"Slivers?" someone on the Council asked.

I rolled my eyes. "The rogue Splinters? The bad guys worse than you? It's a creepy sounding name and we got the flamethrowers. Will you let me finish?"

"Of course," Alexei said.

I continued. "He admitted that he was working with the Slivers against not only us, but you too, because the Slivers are more willing to give him and his kind a better deal in the coming revolution."

"Bullshit!" Robbie cried out from the cart, frantic. "Alexei, Sammy, guys . . . they're trying to turn you against me!"

Mr. Todd and the others at the table looked skeptical at my claim. I tried to sound casual when I said, "If you don't believe me, read his mind. You can do that, can't you?"

Alexei raised an eyebrow, curious. "Well, Robert, if you're telling the truth . . ."

"Alexei, you know me!" Robbie pleaded. "Sam! Who was it who smacked down those new kids who accused you of going too human on us? They laughed when you said 'hands off my daughter,' but I respected that! Would I ever—"

In a flash, Alexei was over the table, then behind us, slowly thrusting his fingers into Robbie's skull as he pled and screamed his innocence, and finally gave way to an inhuman roar of anguish. Soon enough, Alexei pulled his fingers free. His face looked shaken and unsteady.

"These children, they speak the truth," he said. "You really made a mess of that school. A very naughty boy you are."

Alexei pushed the cart past us into the middle of the room, and we let him pass without trouble. Robbie was practically sobbing as he took in the angry glares and whispers from the Splinter Council.

Finally, Mr. Todd looked to Mina, lingering for a moment to take in what could be seen of her bruises and hastily covered, ruined clothes. "Thank you, all of you, for this service. You are free to go. You have my every assurance that none of you will be harmed for your involvement in what happened tonight."

Greg laughed sarcastically. I don't think any of us really believed it.

"I have something else to say," Mina said.

"By all means," Mr. Todd replied.

"What happened here changes nothing. I will still dedicate my every waking moment to stopping what you monsters are doing. However, due to the greater threat that the Slivers pose, I am going to dedicate my energies toward eliminating them. So long as you do not get in my way while I am doing this, I will not focus on interfering with your . . . less malevolent, if still sinister activities. Do I make myself clear?"

Mr. Todd sighed, pushing his glasses up the bridge of his nose. "You know I'm not a fan of your meddling, Mina. I know the answer to this question already, but on the off-chance this is the one time you'd answer differently, is there anything I can say to talk you out of this?"

"No," Mina said unhesitatingly.

"It was worth asking," Mr. Todd said, sighing again. "Well, I'd rather have you helping us than against us."

I could see Mina narrow her eyes behind the mask. "I am not helping you. I am doing this because they are a greater threat to mankind. Once their threat has been extinguished, we're back to business as usual. Do I make myself clear?"

Mr. Todd smiled when he got up from his seat. "Let the games begin! Now, if I could kindly ask you all to leave right now, we're going to have to have a conversation with

Mr. York here. Don't worry, the old human model will be back in school after Winter Break, but if you want to sleep a wink tonight, I highly recommend leaving this room in the next two minutes."

As if for emphasis, Alexei tipped the cart holding Robbie onto the floor. Robbie screamed and fought, transforming to try and get out of the coil of wire, but three council members were quickly on him, pinning him down.

Mr. Todd was good to his word. No one stopped us from leaving the store, the sounds of Robbie's screams and tearing flesh following us as we went.

I was glad that The Soda Fountain of Youth was open late on Fridays. Assuming we lived through the night, the plan had been to meet up there afterward to lick our wounds and celebrate. Since we were about as wounded and tired as we'd expected to be, their open doors and cheap Christmas decorations called to us like the promised land.

Our waitress looked at us oddly as she served our burgers and malts. I didn't blame her. We were loud, laughing and sharing stories, bloodied and bruised and covered in the slimy, dusty castoff of dissolving Splinter (and, in my case, gasoline). She'd asked us when we first came in if we were all right. Aldo joked that we had come back from a fight club.

This got her to keep a respectful distance from our table.

"We need a name," Greg said, toying with the miniature Christmas tree in the middle of our table.

"A name?" Kevin asked.

"Yeah, if we're gonna be a team of badass Splinter

hunters, we need something to call ourselves. Something to strike fear into the hearts of any inter-dimensional asshole we come across," Greg continued.

"Something more cohesive than 'The Network' might be appropriate," Mina agreed. "If we're planning to work in closer contact with each other."

"The Resistance?" Courtney suggested. "It's classic. It will never go out of style."

"Clichéd," Greg said, shaking his head.

"The Poets?" Haley said as she tapped one of the masks set down on the table.

"It's not exactly fear-inspirin', Hales," Julie said.

"No . . . but can we keep the masks?" Haley asked, smiling. "They really seemed to add something, I think."

"I don't see why not," Mina said.

"The Carpenters? You know, for taking out Splinters?" I suggested, stealing a glance at the large Christmas tree over by the jukebox, making sure the present I'd stashed beneath it earlier this afternoon was still there. It was.

"Sounds more like a seventies folk band than a group of battle-hardened monster-hunters," Greg said.

"Yeah, and they tend to be pretty litigious," Julie added.

"John Carpenter's *Breakfast Club?*" Aldo joked.

"'The Network' is starting to sound a lot better," I said. "Maybe keep it for now? We'll know it means something new, and it's nice and generic, not bad for anonymity in public."

Greg laughed. "Anonymity, after what we just did?"

"Yeah, we did just pull something major there. What's going to happen to us after that?" Aldo asked.

"Probably what Dad said would happen," Mina said, begrudgingly. "When he said that we would be safe, he meant it. We'd be dead if he didn't. Though it's probably only because we'll be useful bait to draw out the Slivers."

"And what are we going to do about them?" Aldo asked.

"After what we did tonight, they're gonna come after us," I said. "We've interfered with their plans twice already. They're gonna be pissed. They can't just come after us on the street like they did with Courtney. The mainstream Splinters are going to be watching us like hawks, and if they see a Sliver make a move, they'll try to intercept them."

"So we'll be watched more than usual? Lovely," Greg said.

"At least we get to fight some Splinters again," Mina said, smiling. "Besides, I fully intend to keep a completely open line of communication this time. We can have meetings whenever they are practical, daily texts, and of course a regularly updated Need-to-Know Newsletter."

She looked to me, so proud, so happy with the thought of sharing information with the entire team. This was a new Mina Todd, one who was starting to understand how to play well with others.

I liked it.

"On that happy note, anyone else feel like dancin'?" Julie said as she sidled over to the jukebox, popped in a quarter and cued up some eighties dance music. She held out a hand, and Greg was more than happy to take it. It looked a little absurd, after all we had been through tonight, to be dancing in the middle of a diner decked out with Christmas decorations and UFO memorabilia, but a little release felt warranted.

They weren't the only ones. Aldo and Kevin (well, mostly Aldo) were talking animatedly about the fight against the Splinter-beasts while Courtney pulled Mina aside and said she had an idea she wanted to talk about. That left the person I wanted to talk to most all alone.

Perfect.

"Dance with me?" I asked Haley.

She smiled up at me, almost sheepishly, but joined me in the small space in front of the jukebox that would have to act as a dance floor. She seemed uncertain about how she wanted to dance with me; the song was neither fast nor slow (though, the way Greg and Julie were careening around the dance floor, you'd think it was the fastest song man had ever written). Eventually we settled on a close, casual posture, more or less holding each other up against the exhaustion that threatened to pull us down at a moment's notice.

"You're not bad," she said.

"At dancing?" I said.

"Yeah," she said, holding back a nervous smile.

"Thanks. Mom always wanted to make sure I knew how to dance well enough, just in case," I said.

"Just in case what?" she asked.

I gave her a playful twirl, getting her to giggle. "In case I ever needed to butter up a girl for interrogation."

She rolled her eyes. "Oh, that?"

"Yeah, that," I said. "Just what the hell did you do to Madison?"

"It was supposed to be your Christmas present, but what can I say, when we got all our ducks in a row, I got a little excited and kinda-maybe threw the switch a little early," she said.

I looked at her, skeptical. She continued. "Remember when Greg was explaining dead agenting? Attacking your attackers? It got me thinking. So I got Greg, Julie, and Aldo together, and we worked out a plan. Greg got some of his . . . associates, to provide enough resources to make Madison appear to be a low-level drug dealer. Aldo got into her computer and cell phone to make it look like she had a side-business selling pictures of underage girls in the locker room. And Julie and me, well, we just started dropping a few rumors and let them linger and grow. Then I confronted Madison and told her that if she didn't tell Patrick and some other influential kids in school that nothing had happened between you and her that I would go to the police and the principal with proof of her criminal enterprises."

"And she didn't?" I asked.

Haley smiled sweetly, shaking her head. "No, she played her part well. She told all the right people that you had rejected her advances and she was humiliated, and she wanted to make you look bad, and that she would never make up a lie about you again. It was fun, watching her embarrass herself in front of these people, standing by her as the supportive friend. Once she started getting torn apart by the court of public opinion, I gave the cops and the principal her information."

That was cold. I liked Haley, and I considered her one of my best friends here. I didn't know she was capable of something like this. Part of me was impressed. An even bigger part of me was scared for her.

"You shouldn't have done that," I said.

"Maybe not, but I did. And you know what? It worked," she said.

"You got rid of Madison, sure, but have you thought about what the Splinters are gonna do to you for this?" I said.

She rolled her eyes. "Like they haven't already destroyed my life?"

"You know what I mean," I said.

"Yes, I do, and maybe you're right, but my time in their Warehouse has given me some perspective on the Splinters that you don't have. They like their lives here and they're terrified of them falling apart. After what we did to Madison, they will fear us, and they will think twice about messing with us again. Whether you believe it or not, Ben, what I did was not only right, but necessary," Haley said.

I could see the logic of every word she said, and I was glad to see that my reputation had been salvaged. It didn't make me feel any better about what she had done. I had built up this image of her as someone who wouldn't sink into the darkness that Prospero welcomed.

"Maybe you're right," I said. "Just promise me you'll always remember what it's like to be human?"

She smiled, standing up on her toes to kiss me on my right cheek, the one that didn't smell of gasoline. "For you, Ben Pastor, I promise."

Unconsciously, I looked across the room to see if Mina had seen that. I breathed a sigh of relief when I saw her engrossed in conversation with Courtney. I knew I shouldn't have been nervous, that there was nothing going on with either Haley or Mina, but I couldn't keep my heart from pounding when I thought Mina might have caught Haley kissing me.

After the song, Courtney and Kevin both offered rides to whoever needed them, and Haley, Aldo, Greg, and Julie gladly took them. Seeing Mina hanging back, I excused myself, saying I'd walk her home. We all exchanged our handshakes and hugs as we separated.

It felt bittersweet to see them leave. We'd just signed on for the coming war against the Slivers, and there was a good chance we might not all live to see the end of it. Right then we were alive, and we were human, and it felt good to pretend that everything would stay that way forever.

I walked to the Christmas tree by the jukebox and pulled free the present I had stashed beneath it. I joined Mina by the table where she'd first explained Splinters to me, a miniature Santa hat on the head of the stuffed jackalope off to the side. She stood looking up at a large sprig of mistletoe that hung from the ceiling above the table.

"I've never understood the mistletoe tradition. Mistletoe is poisonous if ingested. You might as well be kissing beneath a bottle of cyanide," she said idly.

I looked up at the white berries above us. "I'm sure it has some ancient pagan origin that I'm too tired to pretend to know anything about right now. Do you have a problem with the Christmas tradition of gift-giving?"

"No," Mina said.

"Good," I said, handing her the wrapped parcel. "Then

merry Christmas. And happy birthday, for that matter. Since you didn't tell me about that, this'll have to count for both."

She smiled faintly. "I didn't get you anything."

I shrugged it off. "There're still some shopping days left before Christmas. I'm sure you'll think of something."

Mina tore off the paper to reveal the new bag I had gotten her (with Haley's help). It wasn't quite as big as her old one, but it also wasn't being held together by a series of patches, a wish, and a prayer.

"Thank you, Ben," she said.

"Merry Christmas," I repeated.

She smiled, emptying the contents of her old bag onto the table and putting them in the new one. I didn't want to break up this sweet moment, but there was something I had to get off my chest.

"Did you know what Haley did to Madison?"

"Not in advance. I overheard you talking," she said. "It makes sense, really, why she did it, and that she didn't tell us, because we would have probably tried to stop her."

"You heard us all the way over there?" I said, nervous again.

"I have good hearing," she said. Then it was her turn to look nervous. "You know, maybe you should ask her out sometime. I believe she is interested in you, and you two would make a very compatible couple."

I don't think Mina could have said anything more surprising to me at that moment, shy of admitting she was a Splinter. I struggled for an answer, trying to find something nice to say. The longer I struggled, the more I could see the pain growing on her face.

"I don't think I can do that," I said.

"Why not?" Mina asked.

Honest or safe. Take your pick.

"I don't think I'm ready for a relationship right now, not with all of this going on. Let's defeat the Slivers first, then we'll talk about my love life," I said, trying to make a joke out of it. *Safe it is.*

This got a smile out of her. "Fair enough."

"So what were you and Courtney talking about?" I asked, trying desperately to change the subject.

"She was asking if the two of us would like to be on the school newspaper," Mina said.

"Really?" I asked.

She nodded. "Yes. She said that there were a couple of openings, and that it would give us a perfect excuse to walk around the school carrying notebooks and surveillance equipment. Since there is so much Splinter, and possible Sliver, activity going on at school, you must admit it is a tempting offer."

It was. It was also an extracurricular activity I had never once considered. Writing had never been one of my strong suits, but if it would further our research and investigation, I would learn.

"It is," I said.

Mina sighed. "It will also give us an opportunity to keep an eye on Courtney."

This took me off guard. "What?"

"I still believe there is a good chance that she is a Splinter. Maybe even a Sliver," Mina said.

"Mina, stop."

She kept going. "Think about how easily she has ingratiated herself to our group, the way she always wants all the information we have, how easily we fought off the Splinters who tried to take her, how—"

"Mina, stop this," I said, firmly.

"Why? This is potentially a serious problem!" she said.

"It may be. It may also be the fact that Courtney's a tough woman and an even tougher reporter," I said. This next part would be harder to say. It had been building in me for a long time, and though I wasn't sure I'd ever get the words right, they needed to be said.

"Seeing Splinters everywhere has been a fantastic survival mechanism for you, and I'm glad it's gotten you this far in life, but survival will only get you so far. If all you're doing is surviving, you're going to turn out like The Old Man."

This statement hit her hard, almost as if she'd been punched in the stomach. I didn't want to hurt her again, not after what I had done tonight, but this was necessary.

"I'm not saying we give up the fight because I know we can't. I am saying that you need to live from time to time. Otherwise, what are you surviving for?" I said.

She cast her eyes down to the floor. "I haven't lived for a long time. I don't know if I still can."

I wrapped an arm around her shoulders and smiled, trying to sound cheerful. "Hey, there's still time. With both of us working on it, I'll bet you can learn."

SHARDS

Mina looked up at me, almost teary, her smile grateful. "You promise?"

I cast my eyes upward, toward the mistletoe. "Cross my heart and hope to die."

She poked me in the ribs. Hard.

"Okay, maybe that was a poor choice of words."

Acknowledgments

As is likely to become a trend in our published works, we'd first like to thank our lovely and always awesome agent, Jennifer Mishler, for everything she has done, will do, and is likely currently doing for us at the moment you are reading this. Thank you for helping us sculpt and transform *The Prospero Chronicles* into what has made it to the page this day.

Thank you to everyone at Jolly Fish Press for all the work you do in helping us make this a coherent manuscript, putting it literally on pages (and e-readers as it may be) and doing everything you can to get us out in the world.

Matt would like to thank Scott Carter, his ever-patient and infinitely strong father, for giving him his sense of humor and appreciation for strong storytelling, and his best-friend-he's-not-married-to Boris Palencia for helping him gain a new understanding for friendship and brotherhood (as comes up in this book a bit).

Fiona would like to thank her parents and sister for all their support and enthusiasm, as always with a special mention for her dad, Denis Titchenell, for being her first and best English teacher.

Thanks to all the wonderful readers, bloggers and authors who frequent our blogs and pages.

And of course, thank you everyone who's ever produced a work of art we've come into contact with, because you've all shaped our work in some way or other. Even the bad ones we enjoy for all the wrong reasons.

MATT CARTER is an author of horror, sci-fi, and young adult fiction, co-authoring the first book in *The Prospero Chronicles: Splinters*. He earned his degree in History from Cal State University Los Angeles, and lives in the usually sunny town of San Gabriel, California with his wife, best friend and awesome co-writer, F.J.R. Titchenell. *Shards* is his second published novel.

F.J.R. TITCHENELL is an author of young adult, sci-fi, and horror fiction, including *Confessions of the Very First Zombie Slayer (That I Know Of)* and co-authoring *The Prospero Chronicles: Splinters*. She graduated from Cal State University Los Angeles with a B.A. in English in 2009 at the age of twenty. She currently lives in San Gabriel, California, with her husband, coauthor and amazing partner in all things, Matt Carter, and their pet king snake, Mica.